Kaisa

A Novel of
Michigan's Copper Mining &
Oil and Gas Exploration Industries:
Calumet; Holland; Mt. Pleasant;
Mackinac Island,
and
Jekyll Island, Georgia.

By Jack R. Westbrook
ORSB Publishing Mt. Pleasant MI

PROLOGUE

Faith Chapel
Jekyll Island, Georgia – April, 2002

"I still think it's damn silly to have all these cathedral doo-dads in just a wood cabin." Kaisa, of Holland Michigan and Jekyll Island, Georgia, said to herself in the front row of the Faith Chapel of Jekyll Island's Historic District. "I've got more money than most of those Jekyll Island Club millionaires had when this was their island but I'll be damned if I'd have gussied up a praying place this way."

She glanced around the chapel where she sat quietly alongside her husband Deiderick. They were oblivious to the coming and going of tourists demonstrating varying degrees of reverence for the sanctity of a historic house of worship. Some whispered, some spoke aloud, against a background of "shushing" by the volunteer docent stationed near the back door. Kaisa wondered if she had made her observations aloud and decided she probably had not, telling herself again that she was going to have to keep her thoughts more closely in check. Whether it was her eighty-seven years or the strain of the past few weeks catching up with her, lately the time span between thought and speech was a lot shorter … and she was saying "damn" a lot more.

A trim woman whose natural platinum blonde hair had slipped over to silver without much notice, Kaisa still bore the open-faced creamy complexion of her Finnish-Dutch heritage. Just a touch of ruddiness in the cheeks served as an ancestral beauty mark over a figure which had not changed significantly from her teen years. Her curiosity,

In an alcove up the mountainside from the Delaware copper mineshaft opening near the tip of Michigan's Keweenaw Peninsula, young Kaisa Koistenin and Eino Heinonen chatted about their respective summers.

Eino talked mostly about his summer job on the timber crew, cutting trees used for timbers in the mine. Kiasa spoke of the theaters, stores, and libraries she visited with her grandmother in Holland, Michigan, then spoke of the exciting bit of history she had witnessed.

"We went to the Women's Literary Club where I heard a speech about how the Literary Club should spearhead a movement to urge Holland residents to grow tulips and organize a festival to celebrate the flowers symbolizing their Dutch heritage. Eino, it looks like they are going to do it. Grandmother told me next year they are having their first Tulip Festival in Holland."

"I thought you hated being shuffled back and forth."

"I do, but this was something really big and I, a little copper town girl will be part of it. I miss downstate, but when I'm there and things slow down, I also miss it up here in the Upper Peninsula."

"And do you miss me too?" Eino asked, sidling closer to her.

"Of course I do," Kaisa replied. "We share thoughts and we share laughs …."

"And I'd like to share more." Eino said breathlessly as he wrapped his arms around her, kissing her. Shocked at first, Kaisa felt his lips on hers and warmth she'd never known began creeping through her body. She kissed back.

Suddenly they parted just as a shadow blocked out the sun and she heard

"Come quick Miss Kaisa. Th-h-h-h-h-here's been an accident."

JACK R. WESTBROOK

Copyright 2013 by Jack R. Westbrook
ISBN: 10- 09484036121
Library of Congress - 2001012345
ISBN 13/EAN 13 9780984036127

Published by ORSB Publishing
POB 16 Mount Pleasant, Michigan, 48804-0016
989-773-5741

Dedicated to all those people who patiently listened to me spout plot scenarios during the eleven years this story bounced around in my head ..... especially to Mary Lou, my proofreader, researcher, organizer and wife, who has suffered my ramblings most and longest. Also dedicated to those who work below the ground in mining and above the ground in drilling to satisfy our metal and petroleum energy needs.

slightly skewed view of the world, quick intellect and quicker tongue came from her mother. Combined with the eidetic memory, stubborn single-mindedness of purpose and dogged determination of goal inherited from her father, Kaisa had always "been a handful."

Gothic gargoyles probably better suited to a soaring European cathedral spire than an April sun-drenched simple wooden structure on a Georgia barrier island adorned the cypress shingle-sided chapel where she sat. Like many overdone elements in this late 19th and early 20th Century winter retreat for the American moneyed, the architectural incongruities said "this is the way we want it and we're paying for it so do it."

Faith Chapel on Jekyll Island was inspired by the design of colonial meetinghouses, echoing with eloquence about life and death, delivered by the eras most prominent of clergy for the benefit of the world's wealthiest families.

Completed for the Club's 1904 season, the Faith Chapel, located not far from the elegant Jekyll Island Club Hotel in historic District of Jekyll Island, Georgia, had served as a worship site for ninety-eight years. At the east end, behind the worship area of the chapel, the Louis Comfort Tiffany-designed stained glass window - *David Sings unto the Lord* – glowed triumphantly in the afternoon sunlight.

In the front row, Kaisa returned her attentions to the low wooden cabinet behind the railing at the front of the chapel, under another magnificent stained glass window – *Adoration of the Christ Child* – recently restored by artists from Shadetree Studios of Petoskey in her home state of Michigan.

Oh well, she thought, even if somebody did hear me they would just chalk it up to the crankiness of an old lady, not knowing I have felt this way since I first saw the place in 1935.

I have to admit that it is a startling effect and is one of the few things about the Jekyll Island Club Cottage Colony historical area that has not changed in almost a hundred years. Silently she mouthed the comforting words of The Lord's Prayer in Dutch, her third language, as her thoughts transported her back along the path that brought Deiderick to her at this spot sixty years before.

"*Onze Vader, die in de hemel* ....Our Father, who art in heaven"

Part I:
KATRINA
&
ERIK

1

Red Jacket, Keweenaw Peninsula, Michigan – June 10, 1913 - noon

"Excuse me. My name is Katrina Golder from Holland, Michigan. I have some questions."

Erik Koistinen, third-generation Finnish Michigan Upper Peninsula copper mineworker, stood in front of Italian Hall at the corner of Seventh and Elm streets in Red Jacket, Michigan. He was handing out printed flyers inviting potential supporters of a miner's strike to a social that evening. The strike could change the destiny of his friends and fellows. He was so intent on the task he had missed the approach of the woman who would change his life forever.

A flash of light blue moved into his peripheral vision as the striking blonde young woman looked at him expectantly. He had seen a few pretty people in his life but this was the first woman he could truly describe as beautiful. She was dressed in a fashion not seen in Red Jacket normally except on members of the Calumet & Hecla Mining Company management and almost never in this workingman's section of the mining town. Having her so near, he suddenly understood the term "breathtaking." Her long blonde hair was styled with a single braid cascading over her left shoulder, giving her the look of a svelte fashionable

KAISA

Dutch milkmaid

"Are you dumb?" the vision asked impatiently.

"Not many people think so up here or down in the shafts," Erik replied testily. "Are you lost, Miss?"

"Excuse me. I didn't mean that kind of dumb. I just wondered if you could speak, since you were taking so long to answer." She said. "I'm not lost. My father is here on business. He has meetings this afternoon. I got tired of lounging around the Michigan Hotel. Even though your two department stores, Vertin's and Rupp's, are nice, I am just not in the mood for shopping on such a beautiful day. I visited your St. Joseph's church to say a prayer for Poppa's success in the face of all this strike talk and decided to go for a walk.

"Your town is much more sophisticated than I expected. But all day I've heard worried talk about a miner's strike. Since you are handing out flyers about it, I thought you could answer some questions for me."

"How is that any concern of yours" Erik asked suspiciously. She was obviously a company spy.

"Look, mister," Katrina sparked "I resent your tone. You must be one of those who think women my age should be content to sit around waiting to be swept off our feet by somebody like you. Then we should be happy with a nice place to live, breeding heirs for you while thinking about nothing more complex than whether the napkins clash with the drapes between babies while you men folk make all the big decisions. I'm here to tell you that I am a teacher, a first year one at that, who is interested in the way the whole world works. You seem to be the one who can tell me about the miner's side of all this strike talk I've heard ever since we got here. But if you can't tell me, tell me who can. Then I'll be on my way."

"Whoa…..whoa…whoa, lady, hold your horses. You may think you are talking to some bohunk just fresh above-ground who can't see farther than the end of his pickaxe or think beyond where to swing it next. Let me tell _you_. I have been beyond Red Jacket and I am back here by choice. For three generations the men of my family have worked Upper Peninsula copper mines and my mother has been a school-teacher for many years, so I've probably read more books than you have. Our library has several thousand books. Red Jacket is the central village for several surrounding communities within walking distance so the area has a population of over 30,000 people, I dare say that's more than wherever you are from."

"You are right." The girl admitted grudgingly, with a tinge of blush on her face. "We have only about 12,000 people in our Holland, even counting nearby Zeeland."

"Then don't start rawing on me because you're stuck out here among the savages while daddy does the big boy stuff. Just what does he do, anyway?"

"Poppa is the largest wholesale grocer in Michigan. He is here meeting with your local merchants to get their orders for what they think they will need for next winter. He comes here twice a year: once for them to place their orders directly, then to supervise delivery of their orders in September. I came with him this trip because the school where I teach in Holland, Michigan, has just finished the school year season. I thought it would be a pleasant outing. It was until a few minutes ago."

"Look, I'm sorry." Erik apologized, now satisfied she was not an agent of Calumet and Hecla. "We got off on the wrong foot here so let's start all over again ….. Hello, I'm Erik Koistinen. I already know your name."

"Apology accepted" Katrina replied, her deep blue

eyes quickly changing from frosty to sparkly warm. "I guess I was a little quick on the trigger too. As you can probably tell, I get a little feisty when I think I'm being dismissed as a lightweight."

"Amen to that" Erik laughed. "Hey, it's almost lunchtime. Let's go down the street to Curto's. I'll buy you a pasty while I answer your questions. I guess the cause can spare me a few minutes to preach at a different altar to a new audience."

"What is a pasty?"

"Let's just call it your introduction to the tastes of Upper Peninsula mining country. Let's go."

Mario Curto's Saloon, built in 1895, boasted a stained-glass canopy over the bar. By 1900, the saloon was one of forty-eight bars in Red Jacket and by 1908 there were seventy-eight such establishments in the community. Recognizing a need to distinguish his place from his seventy-seven competitors, Curto expanded the scope of his potential clientele by separating his barroom from an annexed restaurant. While the main emphasis of the popular eatery was on northern Italian cuisine, the menu included a number of local dishes, including the miner's favorite, the pasty.

Pasties, large thick pastry shells filled with meat and vegetables, dated from ancient times in northern Europe but in the United States were primarily associated with Cornwall, the westernmost county of Great Britain. Cornish miners favored the hand-sized crescent-shaped portable meals. They traveled well, stayed warm for a long time, did not need tableware and reheated easily in the mine by warming on a shovel over a candle or miner's lamp. The restaurant-style pasty, lavished with gravy, consisted of a higher grade and wider selection of meat as well as a greater variety of vegetables and spices than the workingman's version.

Erik and Katrina found a table in a quiet corner of the crowded restaurant. Both ordered beef pasties with potatoes, celery, carrots and the ubiquitous rutabaga, one of the few vegetables easily locally grown. They were served faster than they expected. The lunch hour crowd was rapidly clearing while the pair exchanged personal information.

"I am an only child," Katrina said "and I was born in Holland, Michigan, twenty years ago. I think Poppa wanted a boy so that there would be a second generation of Golders to carry on the wholesale grocery business but it will not be. My mother had a very difficult time with my birth. She was told she could have no more children.

"We live very close to downtown. Soon we will have a new post office building just across the Centennial Park from where we live. After completing high school, I took the teacher course at Central Michigan Normal School at Mt. Pleasant two years ago and had my first year of teaching at Maple Grove School this last year. Poppa thought I should go to Hope College in Holland, right across the street from where we live. It is more of a liberal arts Christian school that seems to be more about training clergy and I wanted to teach, so I guess I disappointed him again, along with not being married yet.

"What about you?"

"Not much to tell." Erik said. "I'm strictly a hometown Red Jacket boy. I...."

"Before you go any further," Katrina interrupted. "why the strange town name?"

"Red Jacket was incorporated as a town in 1867." Erik replied. "The settlement came into being because of the copper mining in the area. Since Alexander Agassiz, president of Calumet and Hecla Mining Company, did not want stores or houses on company property, mineworkers settled

nearby and so did the stores to serve them. Red Jacket became the center of commerce for people in the surrounding
areas of Allouez Anmeek, Blue Jacket, Calumet, Hecla,
Larium, Osceola, Ray-baultown, Red Jacket Shaft, Tama-
rack and Yellow Jacket.

"The town was named for a Seneca tribe Indian chief
who was *Otetiani* when he was young and *Sagoyewatatha*,
translated as 'he who keeps them awake' in his later years.
Known as a great orator, he lived from 1750 until 1830. He
was Chief of the Wolf Clan of the Seneca. He negotiated for
the rights of his people with both the Americans and the
British, became known as Red Jacket for an embroidered
jacket the British gave him for his services during the war.

"After the Americans won their freedom and became
a nation, Red Jacket spoke with both George Washington
and John Adams in the presidential home in the temporary
national capital, Philadelphia. In 1805, Red Jacket addressed
the United States Senate with a speech called *'Religion for
the White Man and the Red.'* In his later years, he lived in
Buffalo, New York. When he died, his remains were placed
first in an Indian cemetery, then moved to Forest Lawn
Cemetery, at Buffalo, where his monument now stands.
Chief Red Jacket is my longtime all-time hero. Imagine being such a great negotiator that both sides of an issue would
honor you for your oratory skills. I've read his speech to the
Senate many times."

"Well that certainly answers my question. You must
have swallowed a history book."

"My mother always encouraged all of us six boys to
read. As I said before, she still teaches school at Franklin
School just across the street there. Since I was the youngest,
I'm twenty-four, she had more time to spend with my education than when everybody was home. She thinks it is very

important to know where you came from, to be proud of your heritage, especially when you belong to one of only three Finnish families who attend St. Joseph's Catholic Church. I think Mom's right. You need a clear vision of who you are. Some say we should not be Catholics at all. We are Finnish and should be Lutherans according to them. My mother and father were raised Catholics, as were their parents, so Catholicism is more or less a family tradition. "

"So I guess I picked the right person to complete my education about mining and this strike business." Katrina said, smiling. She had never met someone quite like this history spouting man. Usually people who talked like him were old, monotoned and boring. Erik seemed to bring history to life however, as though the people he spoke of were joining them at the table.

"I'll do my best." Erik replied, beginning his narrative.

"For centuries before Europeans, American Indians dug for and processed copper on the Keweenaw Peninsula of Michigan's Upper Peninsula." Erik told her. "The copper, a geological residue of the volcanic forces forming Lake Superior, caused the United States' first mineral rush in 1842. Michigan's first State Geologist Douglass Houghton mentioned its presence in his report on his 1840 geological and geographical survey of the Upper Peninsula with Henry Rowe Schoolcraft.

"The U.P., as it is known to native Michiganians, or Michiganders to those not finicky, was awarded to Michigan by the United States Congress as a 'booby prize' in exchange for the Toledo Strip, an area that was subject of a three-year war so ridiculous that Congress made ending the dispute a condition of Michigan statehood in 1837. Most citizens of the new state were not happy to have possession of a big slab of land accessible from the Michigan mitten only by crossing the waters of the Straits of Mackinaw.

"The Houghton survey was launched primarily to appease those Michi-Citizen's who still had big eyes for possessing the Toledo Strip. The 'strip' commands the mouth of the Maumee River at Lake Erie, thus controlling a lot of shipping. Michiganders wanted this, rather than a big hunk of seemingly worthless wilderness carved out of the Wisconsin Territory, peopled by folks who owed more allegiance to their land neighbors in Wisconsin than to a government hundreds of miles away south across the Straits. Houghton's report of the presence of copper and mention of the possibility of iron mining in Michigan's new upper addition was exciting. In 1841, Douglass Houghton, predicted, 'There can scarcely be a shadow of a doubt that the Keweenaw Peninsula will eventually prove of great value to our citizen's and to the nation'.

"After the Chippewa Indians signed the Treaty of La Salle, ceding the mineral rights to the western half of the Upper Peninsula to the United States in 1842, the copper rush was on, six years before the more famous California Gold Rush began with the Sutter's Mill discovery.

"Speculators, miners and other stalwart individuals from everywhere in the United States and parts of Europe flocked to the 'booby-prize-turned-land-of-opportunity.' Many of those early mining ventures closed, mostly due to short financing and shoestring budgets. After the Civil War, Calumet & Hecla Company dominated Michigan's copper mining. C & H was formed to develop the 1864 copper discovery in the area by Edwin Hulbert. Hulbert was a nephew of Henry Rowe Schoolcraft, who impressed upon Hulbert the copper potential of the Keweenaw Peninsula.

"From 1847 until 1887, Michigan's mines produced

more copper than any other state while prices fluctuated from twenty-two cents a pound to a price of forty-six cents a pound in 1864, before sliding to nine cents a pound in 1894. Meantime, annual copper output rose from 12.492 million pounds in 1864 to over 250 million pounds in 1912. In 1887, Montana began to produce the most copper in the country. Meantime, this area's copper output began a decline, with a resulting drop in population."

"Stop" Katrina interrupted, "My head is swimming. How in the world do you remember all of these things and organize them as if you are reading from a page. With that talent, you should be a teacher."

"I don't know. I just read things and they stick with me. As for doing anything but working the mines, I can't imagine any other life, which is why I'm dedicated to bettering conditions for the miners. A few years back, I took a job on the railroad ferry running from Ludington to ports in Wisconsin. The steel ferry *Pere Marquette* was the first to begin operating in 1897 and was capable of carrying thirty fully loaded freight cars. Later such ferries were numbered. I crewed on the *Pere Marquette 18.*

"My third roundtrip voyage started in September of 1910. On September 9, twenty miles off the coast of Wisconsin, the boat sank when huge Lake Michigan waves crashed over the stern. We found several feet of water in the hold, with more coming in all the time. We began to push railroad cars off the back to lighten the load, trying for four hours to save the ship. Our captain put out an SOS to our sister boat nearby, the *Pere Maquette 17,* to come to our rescue. Then the water reached the level of the boilers and put out the coal fires providing power to the steamship.

"As we were getting ready to transfer passengers and staff from our boat to the *17*, water suddenly swept into the

18, sinking it. I was one of thirty-five survivors. But twenty-nine weren't so lucky. That was when I figured God telling me something about ignoring the call of the copper, so I came back to the mines.

"Shortly after that, the companies began use of one-man drills instead of the traditional two-man drills. This is causing a lot of controversy about safety since a single worker may be drilling in an isolated area with no back up. If he is injured, he is far from help. If he is killed, as he well could be working a drill alone, he could go undiscovered for a long time.

"Aside from safety issue, the use of one-man drills over the traditional two-man drill eliminates a job and displaces a trained driller. The unemployed driller must take a lower paying job or look for another mine to work in, likely uprooting his family to live in a new place. Nobody but the companies and their stockholders, like the one-man drill

"I lost seniority. When the layoffs started, I was one of the first to go. Then the Western Federation of Mines asked to help organize the miners in this area. That is why I am standing on the corner passing out flyers about a WFM social tonight. As a bonus, I met a delightful pretty young lady I hope will accompany me to tonight's event to hear more about what a strike here could mean."

"Well, I think Poppa has a meeting tonight so I think I'd like to come and learn more. What time should I meet you?"

"I don't think the Michigan Hotel wants the likes of me in their lobby. We should meet here about 6:30." Erik said. "We'll be at Italian Hall for the seven o'clock social.

2

Red Jacket, Keweenaw Peninsula, Michigan – June 10, 1913 - evening

"I'm sorry I've had to leave you on your own so much today." Hermann Golder said to his daughter in the parlor of their Michigan Hotel suite, "But things are more complicated this year than normal what with all this strike talk. Some of the merchants are nervous about how much to order for fear they could be overstocked for people whose income will be limited during the strike, if one comes. Many of them are joining something called the Citizen's Alliance, a group of local citizen's who oppose a strike, supporting the mine operators.

"Anyway, I won't be able to join you for dinner because some of my larger accounts still need to talk, so I've been asked to join them for dinner. These union hotheads are driving me crazy.

"You're on your own for the evening, I'm afraid. We'll have tomorrow evening for dinner after we pack to go home next day."

"That's all right, Poppa. I made a new friend today. We made plans for this evening." Katrina decided it was best for the sake of peace not to tell her father that the new friend was male and she was going to a Western Federation of Mines function with him. After all, she was only going out of curiosity. There was no purpose in riling Poppa further in his present distracted and disturbed state."

"Very well, Have a nice evening then." Hermann said, having only half listened to Katrina's plans. "I won't disturb you when I come back. It could be quite late. I will see you in the morning for breakfast in the dining room at our usual time."

An hour later, Katrina met Erik in front of Curto's.

"This afternoon you talked a little about your family." Katrina said. "Will I meet some of them tonight?"

"Probably" Erik replied. "Most of my brothers will likely be there with their families. My mother may be there for awhile but she will leave early because tomorrow is a school day."

"And your father?"

"My father left us in 1897 to go to Alaska shortly after the Klondike Gold Strike. He thought he would strike it rich and take us all away from Copper country to live in luxury. He died in the 1898 Palm Sunday Avalanche on the Chilkoot Trail but we never found out about it for more than a year. A letter he wrote the day he left to take the trail came from a lawyer in Skagway, Alaska.

"If you have not heard of the Palm Sunday Avalanche, it happened April 3, 1898. There were five snow slides that day directly involving the 'stampeders', as they called those rushing to the Klondike gold fields. The trail was a solid stream of men and three of the snow slides involved 65 known deaths, where they found bodies. Pop was never found but his letter was dated April second."

"How awful." Katrina exclaimed. "But why did it take so long for you to get the letter?"

"It turns out that the attorney who forwarded us the

letter from the effects of Jefferson Randolph Smith the Second, a notorious con man in Skagway, originally called Skaguay, with a 'u'. Smith, known as 'Soapy' because his biggest swindle involved setting up a stand and drawing a crowd by wrapping $1 to $100 dollar bills around bars of soap. He then wrapped the money bars with opaque paper like other packages of plain soap. He charged a dollar per soap packages, selling the bars with the money in them only to his own agents in the crowd, who made a lot of noise while waving their winnings around, promoting more sales. One of his lesser frauds was collecting money from departing miners to assure speedy delivery of letters they had written home. He pocketed the money but kept the letters. He had operated in Colorado before coming to Skagway in 1879 and stayed there until a gunshot killed him in July of 1898. A gold miner, bilked out of $2,700 in a rigged card game with three of Smith's gang killed him. Fortunately, Smith's attorney found the letters, had a conscience and forwarded them to the addressees. I corresponded with attorney. He sent me a copy of the *Skaguay News* reporting Smith's death on the front page.

After my experience with the car ferry business, I figured I was the second generation of Catholic Koistinen copper men punished for ignoring the call of the copper..... and here we are at Italian Hall."

The original Italian Hall was built by the *Societa Mutua Beneficenza Italiana* in 1896 at 401 Seventh Street. A strong wind blew the walls down during construction. Completed, the fifty-eight by one hundred-foot wooden structure was destroyed by fire a dozen years later on New Year's Eve of 1908, just hours after the St. Joseph Society annual meeting of Slovenians, Croatians and Finnish. The next Italian Hall, Erik and Kristina's evening destination, erected with brick in 1908, was in 1913 still named *Societa Mutua Beneficenza Italiana*, the Italian Mutual Benefit Society, more commonly referred to as "The Italian Hall."

The 1913 Italian Hall's ground floor was occupied in the front by a bar run by Frank Russo and Dominic Vario in the west frontage and the Atlantic & Pacific grocery store at the east storefront. Apartments for the Vario family and A & P store manager Charles Meyer occupied the ground floor rear of the hall building. A seven-and-a-half by ten foot landing at the top of a five-foot, nine-inch staircase at the extreme west of the building lent access to the large upstairs hall. Erik and Katrina entered the stairway through the arched doorway with outward swinging doors, stopping at the ticket office at the top. Albert Lantto, Western Federation of Miners ticket taker for the day checked their identification along with members of the WFM Women's Auxiliary. The strict security was designed to discourage entry by mining operator's agents and Citizen's Alliance members from attending the union's social function.

"Evening Erik," Lantto greeted them, "and who is this lovely lady? I've never seen her before."

"She's just visiting town for a short time and is curious about our cause. I'll vouch for her."

"Good enough for me. Go on in then. Your mother and your brothers just got here a few minutes ago."

Entering the hall, Erik quickly spotted his family. As the couple made their way across the rapidly filling room, a wave of silence followed them. The nervous crowd leaped to the same conclusion Erik had made that afternoon: the elegantly dressed Katrina was a few rungs above them on the culture/fashion scale. Therefore she must be some kind of spy for the upper crust.

"Mother, I'd like you to meet Katrina Golder from

down below." Erik said. "She is in town with her father who is a wholesale grocery broker in town to take orders from the stores for winter supplies. I met her this afternoon. She is interested in what we are about here. You and she should get along well, since you are both schoolteachers.

"Katrina, this is my mother, Heleena Koistinen."

"I'm pleased to meet you, Mrs. Koistinen. I've only been teaching a year and am still trying to learn while I teach. Your son was kind enough to invite me here tonight so I could learn more about miners and their side for the strike issue."

"Never stop learning, my dear," Heleena warmed immediately to this charming stranger. "As soon as we stop learning, we begin losing our ability to teach. I hope you enjoy yourself here and leave with an understanding of the plight of the copper mine worker so that if a strike comes, you can tell our story to other downstaters.

"These are my sons and their families. My oldest is Jalo: he and his wife Mina have no children. Next are Joni and Adelina with their children Vilma and Vili, who will tell you his name means 'brother'. Vili likes to tell people this is her 'brother brother', which she thinks a great joke. Next, there is Olli with his wife Sarii and their two sons Yarjo and Antos, who boasts his name means 'thought' though his scholarly performance sometimes belies his name. Then there is Miska and his wife Paulina with their son Urho, meaning 'brave", along with the girls Brita and Kirsti. Of course, you know my youngest, Erik, who I hope has extended the highest courtesy to you.

"I guess my children must have had some mysterious insight of the future when they named their children since in the coming days we will all need both thought and bravery.

"Well, have a good time dear. I'm sure there are other people Erik would like you to meet."

Erik and Katrina began to circulate. The word "*tyttöystävä*, girlfriend", followed them. Greetings became louder and friendlier.

Throughout the evening, Katrina met the heads of the five local WFM union's leaders: John Dunnigan, William Williams, Dolpus Lewis, James Rowe, James Paull and Anton Perhaur. All had high praise for Erik's abilities as a recruiter for Western Federation of Mines membership and his outstanding performance as liaison between the out- of-state organization and the Finnish mineworkers.

"Goodness," she said. "I thought you were just hired to circulate flyers. I had no idea how important you are to both elements of this issue."

"Well, of the roughly 25,000 mineworkers in Copper country, about 5,000 of them work in the Red Jacket area. Of those, about forty percent are Finnish so my being a native and freshly laid off because of the one-man drill makes me valuable to them. If I can help keep the peace and dignity between miner workers, the union and the companies in the same way my hero Chief Red Jacket did and maybe stay friends with all, I hope to be valuable to everyone."

Talking to more people, Katrina began mentally keeping a list of their grievances, which included:

1. Blacklisting, the practice of firing worker who joined or talked of joining a union.
2. Care of the injured.
3. Poor and unsafe working conditions: In 1911, sixty-three men died in Copper Country mine – an average of over one a week. Traditionally safety condition decisions were left to the mining companies. Accidents were deemed to be

strictly due to careless work habits of the miners. The 1910 establishment of the National Mine Safety Administration began to improve working conditions some, but not fast enough to suit mine workers.

4. Delays in reaching the surface after a shift.

5. Cheating on contracts by mining companies: when a contract basis exited where a miner and a mine captain agreed on a price to be paid the miner for a fathom of a specified type of rock in a specified area, after which the mine manager measured and the miner was paid, minus cost of supplies.

6. A need for higher wages across the board for those who worked on "company accounts" (a specified monthly wage):In June 1913, average wage per shift was $2.98 for miners and $2.59 for trammers, a level deemed inadequate by the worker in view of the hard, dangerous work.

7. The one-man drill: That could halve the underground work force. Companies thought of the one-man drill as a laborsaving device, as well as a labor cost reduction method.

8. An eight-hour workday: Workers usually worked ten to twelve hour shifts with one day off each week. Contracts were juggled so all miners made essentially the same amount, after the companies deducted the cost of candles, lamps and mining materials.

Katrina already knew that in copper country, mine owners utilized a system called paternalism, in which the mine acted as "parents" to the community as a whole as well as miners and their families individually. Hoping to attract the best skilled workers, particularly from the German and Cornish mining districts, companies furnished communities with opera houses, bathhouses and libraries. Cornish and German miners were offered cheaper housing on mining company land close to the shaft while unskilled workers, generally Finnish, Croatian and others, had to find pricier homes located off company property. While beneficial to the worker beyond wages, the system put mineworkers in a position of staying "on the good side" of the mining companies lest the workers lose a lifestyle as well a job. The preferential treatment of some nationalities over others added to growing tensions.

Among the Western Federation of Miners social's attendees, opinions varied wildly about the looming strike threat.

Katrina met Ana "Big Annie" Clemenc, an attractive woman in her late 20s, more often called "Tall Annie" because of her six foot-two inch height, for her zeal for workers rights and her full support of a strike. Annie headed the Woman's Auxiliary of the WFM.

"Let me read you something" Annie said. "This is a statement made by Calumet & Hecla President Agassiz during a strike made in 1874. Little has changed in the company's attitude toward workers in these past forty years."

"We cannot be dictated to by anyone," she read. *"The mine must stop, even if it stays closed forever .... We have always treated our men fairly and honestly, they have received higher wages than from any other company. I attempted to get their good will by offering them a share of the profits. They spit in my face as it were and all we can do is sit quietly and await result. Wages will be raised whenever we see fit and at no other time. If they don't like it they*

must go and get employment elsewhere."

"There, you see what kind of arrogance we face. I say strike hard and settle some of these issues forever." Clemenc concluded in red-faced rage.

Katrina got a different view from Henrik Rytilanhti, present with his wife Kerttu and daughters: sixteen-year-old Emilia and her younger sister Heli. Dangerously wounded in a mine explosion, Henrik lost most of his sight and his equilibrium while doing battle over the extent of his injuries with Workingmen's Compensation organization. Yet he remained philosophical, though cynical.

"We are here less in support of strike talk and unions than in courtesy to our fellow Catholic friends, the Koistinen family. When the vote comes, I will vote *no*." he said. "It matters not for I am but a small minority and there will be a large majority voting to strike. But they do not know those who run the mine as I have come to. Our men have their legitimate grievances, some petty, many not, all begging for fair, ethical and just redress. There still will be no redress, they believe that they can influence management. They cannot.

"It is all about money. No one has a complaint against a fair profit. But if it is a matter of giving many a few dollars more or giving few many, many, many more dollars, then 'savage capitalism' will easily win out. We strike, but we will never win."

Rytilanhti's wife Kerttu said "I disagree. That is all I will say."

"I dunno," Mamie Tulppo, a slightly older mother said "me and my husband were both raised around the mines and my kids probably will be too. Mebbe this strike would work out, mebbe not. We've seen unions try to form for copper workers before they's all been put down. They come and go and folks like us just go on with not much change in our lives. Kaisa" she said to the young girl pulling at her skirt "Behave yourself, we'll git you a cookie soon enough."

"Kaisa," Katrina said, "what a pretty name."

"It means 'hope'" Mamie replied.

Later she listened to Frank Zawada, who had lost a leg in the mines in 1909. His two sons, scarcely teenagers, had gone to work in the mines in order to feed the family. Zawada was non-committal, perhaps from fear that active union involvement would jeopardize his injured worker sustenance. His sons were more muscular and looked more worn from working in the mines than teens should look, Katrina thought. The sons were adamant about the need for safer working condition, more liberal benefits for injured workers, along with fair, equitable wages. They seemed resentful of the loss of their childhood and spoke bitterly of the mine operators.

As the music slowed, the food became sparse and the crowd began to fade, the last person Katrina spoke with was Anna Reeve Bloor, a reporter for the National Socialist Press Association. Bloor seemed less concerned about the plight of the copper mineworker than she was about championing the socialist cause. The woman made her uncomfortable with her clothing and status as Bloor became increasingly shrill ranting about "the privileged few needing a lesson" and the "coming revolution."

Mercifully, Erik noticed her dilemma and came to her rescue, saying, "Excuse me, Miss Bloor, there are some other folks I want Katrina to meet before the evening ends."

As they departed, Katrina asked "Do you like her?"

"Can't stand the woman." Erik replied.

3

Red Jacket,
Keweenaw Peninsula,
Michigan – later June 10, 1913,

"Have there been other unions and strikes here before?" Katrina asked Erik as they left Italian Hall for the walk back to her hotel."

Erik laughed. "Oh Katrina, Katrina. Anywhere there is a heavy concentration of management and laborers in an area, class distinction is more pronounced, with each feeling misunderstood and ever wanting more. Put wealth and hard work this close together and the seeds of discontent lie around in abundance. Always there are unions about to nurture those seeds of malcontent in the gardens of the workers, to the chagrin of the operators.

Copper Country in the Keweenaw has seen labor strikes in 1872, 1874, 1890 and 1893 with varying degrees of violence but no deaths. Then along came 1906 when Quincy miner workers struck demanding a ten percent raise and were offered a five percent increase. They accepted after being on strike for three weeks. Later in the year, Finnish workers at an Ontonagon mine went on strike seeking higher wages and a chance to have Finns make their way upward into management, an unheard of demand. The strike ended with two Finns dead and dozens of others injured in a riot. These were usually isolated and localized strikes with smaller unions.

"One problem with organizing labor here is the wide divergence in nationalities imported to mine the copper during the Civil War while Americans were off fighting and population hereabouts was sparse. Besides a sprinkling of white Americans, we have Chinese, Cornish, Croatians, Finns, French Canadians, Germans, Irish, Italians, American Indians, Poles and Slovenes from varied regions of their countries living and working here,. Many do speak English. Some factions don't get along with others. Even within the ranks of the mineworkers themselves, there is a pecking order. The Cornish and the Germans, who come with mining experience from their native countries, are at the top of the pyramid, while other nationalities follow, down to the Finns, Croatians and Slovakians, who generally have the lowest jobs. 'Beasts of burden' they call themselves. Naturally, the lower down the totem pole a man is, the more he wants things to improve, making him a prime target for union organizers. The higher he is on the totem pole, the less likely he is to want to cause problems.

"We have 12 newspapers in this region, each with a point of view that fits it's readership. For instance, I might read something about an incident in *Tyomies*, one of our five Finnish-language newspapers. I read a report of the same incident in *The Mining Gazette* and get very different ideas about what happened and who was to blame. *Tyomies* means "workers", while the Gazette leans toward the miner operator's view. Then there is the *Miner's Bulletin*, the official newspaper of the Western Federation of Miners, printed in Hancock. Little doubt about the angle of that one.

"The WFM came back to the state after operating here for a while in 1902, facing some of the communications problems I mentioned. The union was formed in the western states, where there was less ethnic diversity, so our potpourri of nationalities baffled them. They gave up trying to organize here. Plus, the WFM was completely ignored by the mining companies. In 1908, they came back operated smarter, hiring local people with contacts in each of the nationalities, like me with the Finns, as recruiters of members."

"Sounds like the Tower of Babel story. However would anyone organize a cohesive unified voice for such a group?"

"Well don't forget that it has happened before .... in the formation of the United States ... and even though we have strong differences, as witnessed by the War Between The States, we've been a single national voice for 137 years.

"But that's beside the point of what you asked about previous unions. The Knights of Labor was active in Keweenaw copper country in the 1890s. They never led a strike that seemed to accomplish anything. In 1893, Calumet and Hecla fired all of the workers on strike and quickly replaced them. The Knights of Labor's strategy to meet that challenge was to urge the new workers not to go to work, without much success. So the Knights got the bright idea to educate the mining companies about the plight of the workers. What they overlooked was the fact that the mining companies had no desire to know about the problems of the miner's real or imagined complaints. So the Knights of Labor vanished.

"The Western Federation of Mines was organized in 1893. At first, they tried following the Knights of Labor's strategy of education and arbitration. Individual grievances went to court under WFM, but changed nothing with the mining companies. WFM ramped up their strategy and began to borrow pages from the Socialists by talking in terms of 'slavery' and 'the evils of management.' WFM came to the Keweenaw in 1903, ignored by the companies. With little growth in membership, they left in 1908.

"In 1910, companies started cutting mining expenses by using lighter machinery, which could be operated by one man instead of two. We thought the new drills were still too heavy to be operated by one man and that with only one man operating a drill alone, there would be extreme danger of his coming to harm without anyone knowing. Concern arose that the "odd man out" would be kicked downward to a lesser-paying job or lose his job. I know personally about that one because as I told you this afternoon, I was laid off last year.

The WFM has grown steadily since their return to the Keweenaw and, spurred by the company's adoption of the one-man drill. It has become a force, even though the company's act like the union isn't even here. Tonight they told me that out of a total workforce of about 15,000, around 9,000 belong to WFM with more coming in everyday. The WFM higher-ups were real happy with me tonight because I suggested that instead of making the event a drum beating fire and brimstone labor rally, we should just have a social and let those happily in favor of union action convince their friends who aren't yet ready to join the movement. Just before we left, they told me we had the biggest single day of sign-ups in the history of the union."

"You should be very proud." Katrina said as they approached the Michigan Hotel. "Well, here we are. We will be leaving on the early train day after tomorrow. Will I see you tomorrow?"

"I should be at the same old corner. Beginning tomorrow we are promoting a vote in early July to put the mining companies on notice that if they don't agree to a meeting with us by July 21st, we will strike. Personally, I hope they agree to meet. Strikes can get ugly."

"I'll be going to Mass in the morning, but just in case I don't see you tomorrow, let's exchange addresses now."

That done, they said good night.

"Until tomorrow then."

"Good night pretty lady."

As Katrina entered the lobby of the hotel, a firm hand grabbed her arm. Startled, she turned to see her father, looking as angry as she had ever seen him.

"Have you completely taken leave of your senses," he growled, "fraternizing with these union thugs while I am trying to soothe the nerves of people terrified of their threatened strike? We will discuss your shameful behavior when we get to our suite. Come."

Silently they made their way to the suite. Katrina was shocked into silence at her father's rage and red-faced Hermann was too angry to trust himself not to burst into a rampage in public if he said another word.

Closing the door behind them in the suite, he ordered her to the parlor settee, taking a seat facing her in an over-stuffed chair.

"I cannot believe that you would embarrass me in this manner when you know how important this trip is to my business. We were still having dinner when a man one of the storeowners had hired to monitor the union gathering tonight at Italian Hall came to make his report. He said that there was not much new going on except he heard there was to be a vote on whether to strike early next month. Then he mentioned casually that the most excitement at the social seemed to be presence of an elegant young woman who seemed completely out of place but it was rumored she was the girlfriend of one of the Western Federation of Mines local organizers. Then he went on to describe you in detail. No one seemed to know the identity of the young woman but my hosts talked derisively about how scandalous it was that a woman of breeding would lower herself to associate with those people. I stayed silent and was secretly glad I had not mentioned that I had brought you with me.

"I will not ask you why you did such a thing because I already know you go out of your way to defy me. I tell you this; I excused myself and left dinner early before my shock made them suspicious enough to connect me with you. I have already hired someone to follow you until we leave here and report to me what you do and to whom you talk. As of now, you are forbidden to see or contact whoever it is among these rascals who fascinates you so much. If you want to continue living in my home, you will obey me in this matter."

"Father, you have greatly misinterpreted this situation. I was interested in what is going on and I met a very well spoken young man who invited me to tonight's event. I learned a great deal about what is going on and the issues are not as simple as you portray. I resent very much being treated like a child and I detest the narrow minds of the people you think are so important. Most of all, I am disappointed in your failure to give me the benefit of the doubt. I …."

Hermann rose quickly, said tersely "Good evening Madame", then walked into his bedroom, slamming the door behind him.

Next morning, after a frosty silent breakfast with her father, Katrina made her way to St. Josephs Catholic

Church, noting a man in a bowler hat following her and making no effort to disguise his interest in her.

■■■

She was a little relieved not to see Erik on the corner where they first met yesterday and was glad they had exchanged addresses the night before. Entering the church, she had just kneeled in a pew close to the front of the church when Erik Koistinen slid into the pew beside her. After a quick glance at him, she returned her attention to the altar in front of her, whispering, "Do not act like you know me. I am being followed and I don't know what might happen to you if we seem to be acquainted."

"All right" Erik whispered in reply "but I got a look at the guy following you and I don't think I need to fear that little pipsqueak but I'll honor your wishes. I will leave a note for you in the hymnal rack."

After Mass, Katrina lingered in the pew. Hauling out her rosary, she knelt and began enumerating the beads in one hand while retrieving Erik's note with the other. Unfolding the note with one hand, she read it in quick glances while bowing her head periodically, feigning reverence.

Dear Katrina, she read, *I hesitated to write this since I fear my boldness so shortly after meeting you may be met with your shunning of my strong feelings for you.*

Until yesterday, I thought love at first sight was the stuff of sugary romantic novels and the nonsense of stage plays. Meeting you changed all that. I have now thought of you most of the night. The beauty of your smile, your ease of interaction that makes everyone you meet an instant friend even if you don't particularly like them. Your kindness and patience in dealing with people as well as your warm dignity and endearing quest for knowledge have already made you precious to me; and yes, I love you.

I hope at worst we can be friends from a distance and at best, you share my feelings. I look forward to seeing you again.

Erik

Katrina rose and left the church, giving her fathers hired stalker a frown. Erik was on the same corner as yesterday She approached with apparent indifference, then kissed him full on the lips while slipping the note she wrote early that morning among the flyers in his hand.

"We cannot see each other today but I will carry you home in my heart and write you often, my love."

She hurried away.

He read her note expressing nearly the identical feelings for him he had written about his love for her

The next morning Erik watched from afar at the Red Jacket depot as Katrina's father paid the little man in the bowler hat as the Golders boarded the train.

Part II: ERIK

4

Red Jacket, Keweenaw Peninsula, Michigan – July 10, 1913

"I say to hell with the greedy bastards, let's vote to go on a strike tomorrow." Abram Niemela, echoed by a chorus of "Damn right" and "Let's show the sons 'o bitches we mean business."

Erik Koistinen sat close to the front of the crowded Dan's Hall Western Federation of Miners meeting waiting for an opportunity to speak. Koistinen had come to the meeting hoping to cool some of the heated anger that was fermenting throughout Copper Country along the Keweenaw Peninsula before the situation became violent.

Erik had studied the history of the WFM, created in 1894 by a merger of many silver, copper and lead miners' unions in Colorado, Montana, Idaho, Utah and South Dakota following decades of unsuccessful attempts by hard rock miners to organize. Koistinen had come to believe that while WFM was undoubtedly the largest of miners unions aligned to the copper men's cause, it failed to use its size effectively. Having built its reputation by inciting discontent among miners coining phrases like "wage slave" and "complete revolution of social and economic conditions is the only salvation of the working classes", then rushing to dramatic strikes, WFM continued to act like a bunch of ruffians spoiling for a fight.

Further, the WFM's close association to the Socialist movement, while sometimes advantageous in terms of moral support and some financial aid, often alienated mine owners at the offset so the companies ignored the tendering even the sincerest of olive branches. Approaching management defiantly was, in Erik's opinion, the equivalent of gorillas pounding their chests and beating the ground with a stick before even trying to get the group to share their bananas ... it seldom worked.

He knew that in 1894 at Cripple Creek, Colorado; 1897 in Leadville, Colorado; 1899 at Coeur d'Alene, Idaho; and 1903 again in Colorado, WFM-led strikes had quickly deteriorated into violence, bloodshed and death without much result. A lot of ill-will still festered on both sides of the strikes. He was determined to avoid a repeat of those episodes here in Keweenaw Copper country.

"The chair recognizes Erik Koistinen," the meeting's chair, Bill Rickard, president WFM Calumet local said.

"I still think we should try to meet with the mines' management to discuss some of these issues before we rush into a strike vote." Erik said "I ….."

"That's the same bullshit the Knights of Labor tried twenty years ago." Francesco Pierotti said, ignoring the out-of-order gavel. "Me and a lot of the rest of the guys are tired of all this talking and no action. Hell, even the federal government thinks we have a case. In the last twenty years, the companies have gradually reduced the number of service they used to provide us miners with only small increases in pay. Some of us are tired of seeing the Cornish get all the benefits just because their miners come here straight from the mines in their country while the rest of us have to suck hind tit because we weren't born wearin' a miner's helmet.

KAISA

One of the first things that new U. S. Department of Labor Secretary William Wilson did when the department formed back in March was to assign that guy John Moffit to work on our problem.

"But so far, it's just been talk, talk, talk. I say we vote today and strike tomorrow"

"As I was saying," Erik continued. "My family has been here almost from the start of copper mining here and has seen many changes. In the beginning these mines were way out in the backwoods with no towns nearby so in order to get and keep miners, the companies had to supply such things as doctors, hospitals, houses and schooling for miners and their families. The mining companies took care of their miners, particularly those with families. In exchange for those services, in addition to wages, the companies expected the miners to, for lack of a better phrase, behave themselves. Excessive drinking, fighting, boisterousness and other improper behavior by miners were cause for instant firing at any time.

"Now towns have grown up here and the companies have gradually discontinued most of those company-paid services now furnished by private providers, or made miners pay for them just as they would pay any provider of the same services. There are seventy-eight bars in town and since miners are less concerned about what the companies think about their behavior, they are more careless about it themselves. At the same time they have raised wages at rates they see as appropriate but some miners feel are inadequate. It is a growing problem and has been addressed a number of times in varying degrees of success and rancor. Neither miners or companies want the other telling them their business..."

"Geeze, Koistinen," someone in the back yelled.

"You talked me into joining this damn union. Now you talk like a company mouthpiece. All that readin' you do must have made you forget who the hell you are."

"No." Erik replied. "I just keep thinking about a quote I read in George Santayana's *Reason and Common Sense*, a book that interprets a lot of great thinkers for our modern world. He said 'Those who cannot remember the past are condemned to repeat it.' That in mind, I would like to suggest that a letter to the companies be drafted and delivered today from WFM requesting a sit-down of companies, miners and Citizen's of Copper Country to discuss some to the issues in the open instead of one or two elements holding closed-door sessions."

"How many times have you heard of a miner's disputes with the companies that you know of have been settled by talking?" Pierotti asked.

"About as many as I have heard of that went to strike without somebody getting killed or hurt or ended with anybody getting what they wanted." Erik replied. "I think we should, as my granddad used to say 'Make haste slowly' before we rush into a strike.

"I move that we take a vote on a resolution that if we have had no reply to WFM in five days, then we go on strike."

A number of voices from around the hall seconded the motion and the resulting vote favored delaying a strike unless WFM's request for an open meeting with the company was granted by July 21, 1913.

Erik left the hall relieved he had been able get something resolved, however tenuous, but stinging slightly from the gentle rebuke he had received from WFM Calumet local president William Rickard.

"Whose side are you on Koistinen?" Rickard asked.

"Here we are pushing for a strike and you sit here tearing at the heart of what made this union grow."

"I thought the object of the exercise was the welfare of the miners and I had to express my thoughts."

"Well, I'd watch myself if I were you. I'm pretty sure headquarters is not going to be happy with my report on tonight's meeting and vote."

"Why not" Koistinen said "It just tells them that as local president you have a group that is doing its best to reason with management and is going into this after exhausting all other options so if there is a strike no one can ever say WFM was trigger happy."

"That's the way I'll tell it. But I'd still watch it if I were you."

No sense worrying about it, Erik thought. Regardless of what happens, I have to follow my conscience.

His other big concern now was Katrina. After a month, there was still no letter from her, despite his having sent her more than a dozen letters. Had their quick meeting and her mutual feeling just been a spur of the moment action, put backstage in her life when she returned home?

He fretted more about that than about where the Red Jacket miners' dilemma could lead.

■■

July 21st came and went, with no reply from the mine managers. The mining companies followed the lead of James "Big Jim" McNaughton, president of the powerful Calumet & Hecla Mining Company and Chairman of the Houghton County Board of Supervisor. McNaughton stated categorically he would not recognize the Western Federation of Miners, or any other union representative of C & H employees.

A vote taken by the next day WFM locals declaring Western Federation of Mines members would strike all 25 mines in Keweenaw Peninsula Copper Country effective July 23, 1913.

The strike began without the authorization of the cash-strapped national WFM organization, still financially reeling from supporting major western states strikes. Once the Michigan strike was declared. However, national WFM realizing it was the first to hit all Michigan Copper Country mines at once, immediately rushed to collect fees and donations from members in other states to support the Michigan strike.

The first day of the strike began quietly, with the peoples of Red Jacket looking forward to a fireman's tournament opened by a parade led by a band marching down Fifth Street. At the mine shafts, strikers blocked entrances to the shafts to discourage those bent on going to work despite the strike from entering, Adding to the tension, Houghton County Sheriff James A. Cruse hastily recruited deputies added to the gatherings at the shafts "to protect the mines". This motley crew of hangers-on was mostly composed of derelicts spoiling for a fight they would be paid for, with a few genuine law enforcement professionals thrown in for appearance sake.

By early afternoon, hundreds of Upper Peninsula fireman and eight bands paraded through the community to the delight of onlookers. Nearby, shows and rides were provided by the Miller Carnival Company. At the same time, in an auditorium in the adjacent village of Larium, WFM Executive Board members Guy Miller, John C. Lowery and Vanco Terzich met with strikers, promising them financial aid from the Western Federation of Miners and the American Federation of Labor. At 4:30 p.m., the meeting broke up and Larium strikers began an impromptu march toward Red Jacket, where the march became a riot and the peaceful, orderly marchers transformed into a mob.

As rocks were thrown, clubs swung, thumps resounded from fist blows to flesh and curses filled the air, Erik Koistinen stood on a street corner sadly watching his hopes for quiet resolution die on the sidewalk.

"Cm'on, join the fun," someone yelled as he ran by Erik, leaving a trail of blood dripping from a gory pipe in his hand. "Let's go get some 'o these sum'bitches." Erik neither knew, nor cared, whether the man was striker or deputy, peace lay shattered in the streets of Red Jacket.

****

By the end of the first day of the strike, strikers attacked anybody who tried to cross picket lines. The Houghton County Board of Supervisors gave Sheriff Cruse authority to hire the Waddell-Mahon Detective Agency of New York to furnish reinforcements to his band of ruffians "security force". The agency was famous for furnishing men who made the Cruse delegation of "deputies" look like daffodils when it came to violent handling of situations. At the request "Big Jim" McNaughton, Michigan Governor Woodbridge Ferris sent 2,000 Michigan National guardsmen to attempt to restore order and protect the mines. About half of the National Guard troops were withdrawn three weeks later as more Waddell-Mahon "security force" hires arrived from New York.

Practically from the beginning and throughout the strike, women and children paraded in support of the strikers, often pelting the non-union workers with all sorts of things, including "brooming" the slop from their outhouse pit at them, screaming "scab". Feeling safe from harm behind their shield of gender and age, the "broomer squads" were often led by Ana "Tall Annie" Clemenc.

On August 14 in Copper Country's Seeberville, two strikers, John Kalan and John Stimac, walked across mine property, taking a shortcut home. A deputized guard told them to stop. They did not stop. The deputy notified his supervisor. Soon a contingent of guards, deputies and "Waddell men" arrived at Kalan's residence with orders to bring them to the supervisor. Kalan said he would not go and went back inside the boarding house where he and Stimac lived. When the cadre of "deputies" started shooting at the house, wounding Stimac and another boarder, Standko Stepic. Two other boarders not connected to Kalan, Stimac or the strike, were shot: Ali Tijan and Steve Putrich died of the wounds they received.

The funerals of the two victims was attended by an estimated 5,000 people with a procession afterwards led by "Big Annie" Clemenc, who would lead countless processions throughout the strike and become known as the "Joan of Arc" of the strike. The Seeberville incident brought the first deaths of the strike and ramped up the intensity of worker/"security force" confrontations. In February, 1914, a "deputy sheriff" and three Waddell men" were convicted of manslaughter.

On Labor Day, in the Copper Country village of Kearsarge, a parade of about 200 women and children was organized to protest the anti-union workers who had returned to work in the Kearsarge shaft. They were accused of illegal assembly by the deputies. Women among the protesters yelled they had as much right there as the deputies. Rocks were thrown. Nervous deputies shot guns in the air hoping to disburse the marchers. Fourteen-year-old Margaret Fazekas, a Hungarian girl, whose family had moved from Wolverine a decade before, was struck in the head by a bullet from the deputies' volleys of gunfire that scattered the protesters. Fazekas recovered, but news of her shooting became a rallying cry for WFM-frenzied strikers as typical of the police brutality hallmarking the strike.

While union, company, state and federal groups fought a war of words in court, a real war of bitter confrontations escalated in streets and at mineshafts in Keweenaw Copper Country.

Violence continued. On October 23, 1913, three months after the strike began, Michigan National Guard General Perley L. Abbey, sent a telegram to Governor Ferris, reflecting the frustration deciding who was victim and who transgressor; *"Lawlessness broke loose throughout district today."* The telegram stated. *"Northwestern train windows smashed with rocks. 30 men broke into workmen's homes at Quincy. Row with deputies at Quincy. Paraders at Calumet armed with clubs. Three fights, 2 deputies badly cut up. 13 strikers arrested. 4 arrests near Ahmeek for shooting up workmen's premises. 2 arrests at Allouez. Picketing throughout entire district."*

Abbey, who commanded the National Guard troops along the Copper Country front, had arrived in the summer to protect the mines on the premise that mineworkers were the enemy. By autumn, he found himself in sympathy with those who wanted to go back to work. He often complained of the harsh treatment non-union and union citizens received at the hands of "law enforcement" and, sometimes, each other.

In the ensuing three weeks, over four hundred people were arrested. Waddell men were often "taken on" by "Tall

Annie" Clemenc's "crew".

The weather got colder as the strike got hotter while autumn went to winter in Copper Country. Strikers intimidated union and non-striker workers alike, attacking facilities and strikebreaker mineworkers. Law enforcement, hired deputies and the presence of the National Guard intimidated strikers. Rumors were rampant including one that at first seemed bizarre until one afternoon Erik confirmed it in Vairo's tavern. A Michigan game warden for Keweenaw County early on said wildlife had been slaughtered, animal dens flooded, streams poisoned and trees cut down in copious quantities further north. The trees were burned. Slain deer and other game were allowed to rot on the ground, allegedly by mining company hires and contractors in order to starve and freeze out the strikers. Little could be proven, the game warden said, because every time he found someone who could affirm who was behind the stripping of wildlife from the area, that someone would disappear.

Townspeople and some deputies, like many of the mineworker's families, were split in their feelings about the strike.

Most just wanted it over.

Merchants, recognizing that the mines were the linchpin to their economy and the reason they existed here in the wilds of northern Michigan, generally supported the mine owners, particularly in public. Privately, however, the merchants, specifically grocers, also recognized the workers by far represented the majority of their customer base and for a time extended credit to strikers. WFM members collected strike pay from the union. The storekeepers thought the strike would be short-lived.

Stores quit extending credit when the Western Federation of Miners began shipping food and clothing from out of state to aid Copper Country strikers. In early November, WFM had thirty railroad cars filled by McNeil & Higgins wholesale grocers in Chicago, destination Hancock, Michigan for distribution to WFM store locations in Copper Country towns. A corresponding massive jump occurred in new memberships of the Citizen's Alliance, a group formed in November 1913 opposition to the strike and notably the WFM, took place following the union's upstaging of local merchants. The Alliance began publishing a newspaper called *Truth* to present a point of view opposite that of the WFM.

The Jane brothers, Arthur and Harry, had left the Keweenaw Peninsula for Canada before the strike. They continued contact with Thomas Dally and his wife, who ran a boardinghouse in the Copper Country village of Painsdale. When they learned that things were apparently improving, with the Champion Mine up and running again and seeking workers, the Jane brothers wrote the Dallys that they would be returning for Christmas. They arrived Saturday, December 6, 1913, to an enthusiastic welcome at the Cornish boardinghouse. They took a walk around their home village and renewed old acquaintances, impressed by how normal things seemed, despite seeing patrols of "deputies". At supper with twelve boardinghouse tenants and the Dallys at their home, they all agreed to go to the Methodist Episcopal Church Sunday as a group. All retired to their rooms for the night, except Mrs. Dally, who went to an evening concert at the church and returned late to read in a front room. About 1:30 in the morning, she looked out and saw a man across the street from the boardinghouse but thought nothing of it, thinking he was probably one of the patrolling deputies.

Suddenly the nighttime quiet echoed with the sound of rifles fired. Bullets ripped through the boarding house, killing Tom Dally in a downstairs front room, along with Arthur and Harry Jane upstairs. Next-door was the home of Eldred Nicholson and his family, which somehow took more bullets than the Dally's house, wounding a 13-year old girl. Deputies rushed to the sound of gunfire. One deputy, approaching the scene, saw the flash of rifles and shot at the attackers. A search of the surrounding woods, found nothing.

Outrage over the murders seethed. In the middle of a storm, hundreds of people boarded a train in Houghton to attend a mass meeting at the Armory in Calumet on Sunday, December 7th. The Citizen's Alliance had already slated simultaneous mass meetings for Wednesday, December 10th in Houghton and Calumet. At the Sunday meeting, the assembled angry Citizen's drafted a statement condemning the early morning murder of three miners and wounding of an innocent girl as "….. but a repetition of the numerous outrages that have been perpetrated at the instance of non-resident agitators of the Western Federation of Miners during the past four months." The Alliance called for the law to be enforced and for Sheriff Cruse to use his powers to "rid this community of these murder inciting mercenaries as people want absolute enforcement of the law."

Erik went from place to place trying to find some solution that would defuse the conflict, being rebuffed by the union, disgruntled union members and implacable representatives of the mine owners. He grew more morose with each act of violence. In addition, each day of Katrina's prolonged silence by mail brought more depression.

5

Red Jacket, Keweenaw Peninsula, Michigan – December 23, 1913

On the morning of December 23rd, Erik was invited to lunch by a group of Finnish businessmen, much to his surprise. At lunch, they made a proposal that seemed an answer to his prayers.

"We will not identify ourselves, but if you recognize us its fine, I guess. This meeting could be so dangerous to all of us; it probably makes no difference who knows who." The apparent leader of the group said. "We've asked to meet with you because we are a kind of an unorganized group of like-minded conservative Finns who are very concerned about our people. As you already know, Finns are a large part of the area population, mineworkers, strikers and otherwise. We think this WFM strike thing could backfire on the Finns when the strike is over. This union is so closely associated with socialism that we think Finns could be penalized for their participation in both the union and the strikes. At a meeting of all Finns last month, Socialist Finns made the most noise but a lot of us are afraid the repercussions on all Finns could be dangerous."

"So what do you want from me?" Koistinen asked.

"We have had some indication that you might be becoming disenchanted with the radicalism of the Western Federation and be looking for a change. If we are wrong, this conversation ends here; we have a good lunch and say good-bye, hoping you don't report this to anybody. If we are right, we have a proposition for you. Which is it?"

"You're putting me in a dangerous position too. If I say yes, I could be having my loyalty to the union tested, and God knows what would happen. Also, if I say yes and you are sincere, I think we may all be way too close to a potential shitstorm. If I say no, I could be shutting the door on a chance to help my people"

"I can assure you this is not a setup and we all know the menace we face if we proceed. Our homes, families and businesses will be at risk, perhaps from fellow Finns.

"Our reports were right, you are extremely cagy."

"Look, no offense, but I've had it with meaningless conversation from everybody over the past four months, so if you have something to say, let's get to it." Erik snapped.

"All right sir. Here goes. We are taking a long view toward re-establishing the Finns reputation as good workers and good citizens. Our people's involvement in too many unions and unsuccessful strikes, mainly because we represent such a large portion of mineworkers, has left many people with the opinion that we are un-American slackers. Already we are seeing traces of discrimination against Finns in housing and some licensing. Do you agree?"

"I've heard of some situations, yes. I agree with you this could not bode well for Finns if the attitude is not fought."

"Astute and well spoken. Our reports were right on. Anyway, we are looking to form a group of Finns to combat the notion that we are undesirables, to promote our people and combat socialism, which we view against the American way."

"Isn't that what this new Citizen's Alliance is all about?" Erik asked with growing interest.

"Citizen's Alliance is a puppet organization of the mining companies designed to wrap a flag around the cause of their strikebreaking. The stated goal of the Alliance is to destroy the destructive seeds of socialism, which is an admirable goal in our minds. The Alliance feels the entire community economy will suffer long-range harm from a prolonged strike. We think that is a ploy to fire up the strikers to push for a quick end to the strike and toss out the Finns.

"For some strange reason, some strikers have begun wearing Citizen's Alliance buttons and still more are prancing around flaunting American flags while going along with the WFM's socialist agenda. It's confusing to everybody but especially to our people. We think an organization is needed that indentifies we Finns as dedicated Americans in opposition with the social doctrine that undermines the system that built America and welcomed us to work within her shores. We are not ready to announce or formally incorporate before the strike ends, however it ends, but it looks like the union's hold is beginning to slip. More people every day want to go back to work. We want to do something to keep the Finn's from being the fall guy."

"So again my question, what do you want from me?"

"We'd like to hire you to feel out the attitudes of Finns in the area and give us a report about the feasibility of such an organization. We're willing to pay you a salary while you prepare your report. If it looks doable, we'd like you to help us organize. We'd like to think about incorporation early next year, perhaps with you as our founding director.

"That is quite an offer. You realize what you're asking me?"

"We do, and I hope you realize we have just placed our lives in your hands."

"I will give you an answer after the holidays."

His mind was racing. He would have to leave the union and go to work in the mines since Calumet and Hecla was already rehiring any man who would tear up his union card. He knew that he would be starting at the bottom of the underground worker's pecking order again, tramming, the ignominious job of breaking rocks manually and lading them into railed cars. This after working his way up the line from trammer to the timbering crew to being allowed on a two-man drilling team, a rarity for a Finn. His "Finnesss" of course had led to him being among the first laid off when the company started using the one-man drill. He also knew he would be branded a traitor by some of his friends, neighbors and family. He might even be in physical danger, but his anonymous potential employers, more than half of them he recognized, had promised personal protection if necessary. Those who knew him knew he did not make decisions lightly and many would go along with him. He could not help what others would think

Maybe he could even hop a train and go to Holland to see Katrina before he started canvassing fellow Finns. Maybe he could discover how he could have misread her and her declaration of affection. No, he decided, his life was about to be full enough without adding another rejection by Katrina Golder.

6

Italian Hall - Red Jacket, Keweenaw Peninsula, Michigan – December 24, 1913

Late in the morning of Christmas Eve, 1913, Ana Clemenc looked at the Christmas Trees and other holiday decorations adorning the main hall of the Italian Hall and declared it nearly ready. Turning to Erik Koistinen, she said, "After you and the others finish setting up the chairs along the sides and straighten the tables, would you mind going down behind the hall and start bringing up the presents from my sled and putting them by the tree on stage."

"Right away, ma'am." Erik replied. He arrived early morning with his mother so she could oversee preparation of baked treats and candy for the WFM children's Christmas party. Now Erik found himself appointed Big Annie Clemenc's Captain-In-Charge-of-Party-Preparation. It was assumed that when Heleena Koistinen volunteered for something, the whole family had volunteered, he thought as he watched his brother Olli bring another load of chairs from the storeroom. Other brothers Jalo, Joni and Miska were elsewhere on strike picket duty, leaving Erik and Olli to help Momma at the Hall.

As he went toward Clemenc's wagon, he decided he

was being too rough on Annie. After all, she was giving her all to the strikers and the miners in organizing marches of striker's women and children, along with other demonstrations highlighting the miners' plight.

It was her idea to have this party so that the striking miner's children of Western Federation of Miners members could have a happy holiday in the shadow of the bitter strike. She had traveled all over the Keweenaw Peninsula; buttonholing everyone she met to contribute to the party to let the blameless children have a happy Christmas, despite the bleakness of the strike. She talked Associated Charities into donating $3,000 clothing, nuts and candy for the children in need. It was rumored that other funds were donated to be sure each striker's child was remembered with a Christmas gift had come anonymously from "Big Jim" Mac Naughton, C & K President. When Ana Clemenc heard that rumor she had wanted to send the money back, but others convinced the "Joan of Arc" of the miner's strike that the cause was nobler than the giver. She relented, using the money for children's gifts. Word spread and money came from outside the area for the party.

Now beginning its six month, the WFM-led strike was putting strain on everyone as the mine owners staunchly refused to recognize the union and was, putting strikers back to work in the mines alongside strikebreaker hires, if the striker turned in this union card. WFM stores were starting to run short on some items in their inventory and strikers pay from the union was erratic to non-existent.

Some Copper County firms and merchants had to lay off their workers as their revenue dropped with the fortunes of the strikers. Though the brightly decorated downtown in Red Jacket, even more stunning at night, showed scant evidence of being a strike town, Erik noted that the

Christmas shopping crowd was abbreviated from previous years, as he rounded the corner of the Italian Hall to take a load of presents upstairs. At least there are some people in town with enough for Christmas presents, he observed, managers and company officers were scarcely affected and stores catering to them seemed to be doing well. Erik knew that the wrapped hats, mittens and socks he carried would probably be the only presents the kids at the party would see this Christmas, other than stuff homemade by loving relatives. Even among his own family, he could see the grip of the union beginning to slip, greased by violence and deprivation. It was as if everyone was waiting for someone else to make the first move to break the deadlock and return to normal.

He thought again about the offer he received the day before.

He had already said he would give them his answer after the holidays. He had several days to think, though he was already mentally doing a checklist for organizing his new job.

Maybe I am the one, he thought. Maybe if I return to the mines, the Finns who trust me would follow and become the nucleus for rebuilding the fine Finnish worker name.

Maybe .....

"Hey Bub, watch were yer goin'" a man in the anteway at the base of the stairs up to the main hall said as Erik nudged him with a package as the stranger stood at the door to the right, ready to go into Dominic Vairio's tavern. "Fella can't even go get a drink in this damn town without some miner with an attitude tryin' to knock 'im down."

"My apologies, sir." Erik proceeded up the stairs, thinking it was one thing the man needed, it was not another drink "and a Merry Christmas to you too."

"Smart aleck sum bitch." The mustached, slouch-hatted stranger said to Erik's retreating back.

As he reached the top of the stairs about noon, Eric paused to look inside the main hall. He had to admit it was beautiful. Three Christmas trees adorned with cotton to appear as snow sparked with tinsel while pink and blue paper streamers were strung everywhere. *The Mining Gazette* was wrong in predicting "a cheerless, presentless Christmas", while the *Calumet News* was more on point with the headline "*NO CHEERLESS FIRESIDES IN CALUMET*".

He smiled.

The first group of parent and child partygoers arrived behind him. Pete Lantto, official doorkeeper, with other WFM members, checked identification. Only union members or non-union members accompanying members were admitted to the hall.

By two o'clock it was impossible to guess how many people were in the hall. Estimates said about 500 children and around 200 adults sang, played games, greeted one another with happy voices and in general moved around in a merriment belying their circumstances. The noise was deafening. Chatter in German, Polish, Finnish, Slovenian, Croatian, Hungarian, Chinese, American Indian, Irish, French and English wafted along over waves of laughter as people found soul and language mates in the chaos.

Toward three o'clock, organizers tried to form lines of children to receive their gifts in an orderly manner. Bringing order about was a stiff order because the revelers clung defiantly to prolonging the spontaneous festive nature of the event.

Realizing he hadn't eaten since early breakfast, Erik decided to go downstairs to Vairo's tavern for a quick sandwich. As he left, Erik saw Elin Lesh leave her post on the landing by the door where she had been watching to be sure only the children of strikers entered the party. She smiled as she passed him and shouted something, which was drowned by the party noise except the word kitchen. Erik smiled back and headed down the stairs.

At the bottom of the steps in the vestibule, he noticed the door to the outside was left ajar by some hurried partygoer. He pulled the outside door closed and turned left to enter Vairo's tavern. By some measure, the noise level inside the smoke-filled bar would seem extreme but to Erik's ear it was fairly quiet after the roar of the upstairs crowd. Some of the noise from upstairs could be heard in Vairo's but the main sign of the party was the thump of more than a thousand feet shuffling and dancing about while chairs and occasionally tables were shifted about.

The tavern was only partly filled, mostly by single men with no one to share Christmas Eve with and drowning that knowledge with newfound bar buddies alongside married men who were having a drink before going home to be dragged out shopping or spending the evening in the hubbub of "move the tree a little to the right. No, back a bit".

Erik was no sooner seated at the bar and was about to order a sandwich when a gravelly voice, apparently speaking loudly for his benefit, spoke out. "Listen at that damn ruckus up there. Them people ain't got the pot or the window and yet they're up whoopin' and hollerin' like the second coming is here. If the stupid bastards'd go back to work they wouldn't need that damn Clemenc troublemaker out beggin' so they could have a party."

He glanced over his shoulder to see the man he'd met in the hall smirking back at him, puffing his chest out to be sure Koistinen could see the Citizen's Alliance button pinned there. "Somebody oughtta go up there and shut those brats up."

"Come on" Dominick Vairo said. "I don't want any trouble in here on Christmas Eve. What can I get for you, Erik?"

Shoving away from the bar, Erik said "I don't guess I'm hungry anymore, Dom. I'm going back upstairs where the company seems to know what the season means." As he headed for the door, the slouch-hatted man stuck his leg out in front of him. "Sure Finn, go back where the women can protect you. Bump me in the head will ya'? Well I'm not some snot-nosed miner's kid so try hittin' me when I'm lookin'."

It took a good deal of restraint not to drag the loud drunk out of his chair and show him what several years of tramming in the mines could do for the muscles. Erik wrote the man's ranting up to the booze and honored his friend Vairo's request for peace.

At the top of the stairs, he noticed Elin Lesh had not returned and no one was checking identification. Must be they think everybody that's coming is already here, he thought as he scanned the crowd and saw his brother Jalo waving from the back corner of the room. He joined the rest of his brothers and their families so their children would be close to the stage when the gifts were distributed.

A few minutes later, as he talked to the brothers Koistinen, or tried to over the roaring din of the partygoers, he glanced toward the door and saw the drunk from downstairs enter and make a beeline for the stage, where Annie Clemenc and other WFM ladies were sorting gifts. Mumbling, the man struggled with something in his pocket and Erik noticed the hammer of a gun peeking from the man's jacket.

"What are you doing?"

Erik blocked the drunk's approach.

"Gonna' shoot that socialist troublemakin' bitch Clemenc," the man mumbled "An' you too if ya don' get outta my way."

"You'll do no such thing," Erik said, grabbing the hand the intruder still had in his pocket and squeezing tight, crushing it against the gun to make it impossible for him to draw or fire the weapon. "Now, you and I are going to go outside and talk about this thing."

"Sum bitch" the man grumbled as Koistinen steered him across the floor back toward the entrance. "They got me stuck in this godforsaken hole protectin' the mines from the likes of you, when I could be where it's warm. But the money is so damn good, getting' paid to beat up guys like you. Don't make any dif'rnce. It's all going to be over soon and you bastards are all gonna be fired." His voice rose as they reached the door to start downstairs. He broke loose and ran down the stairs yelling louder with each step. "Did ya hear me I said Fired....FIRed.... FIREd .... FIRED."

Erik chased the drunk down the stairs and through the doors and vestibule and second doors to the outside. Grabbing troublemaker by the front of his shirt, Erik reared back a fist to give him what he'd been looking for all day when the strangest sound he had ever heard erupted from the doors to Italian Hall, stopping him in mid-swing.

The intensity of the combination screams, cries, curses, grunts and thumps increased as he swung open the doors and stepped back in shock. In front of him was a huge seething lump of humanity stacked nearly to the ceiling as more people piled on to the back of the heap in the jammed stairway.

"Help me." A little boy cried from his place jammed about eye-high in the mob, extending a free arm. As

JACK R. WESTBROOK

Koistinen reached for the boy, a strange gurgling sound came from near the floor and he looked down to see a life leave the bulging eyes of a girl exhaling her last, unable to inhale because of the bodies on top of her. Screams for help in a dozen other languages needed no translation.

"Erik, Erik, here come help me," he heard and thought at first the voice had come from the growing heap of writhing bodies, but realized it was coming from his right and turned to see Dominick Vairo standing in the front doorway of his bar. "Come, maybe we can help from the side."

Koistinen ran into the tavern, where the door to the staircase vestibule was open and a few customers were struggling to pull children sideways from the crush. After trying in vain, they soon realized the sound of popping bones meant they were doing more harm than good to the wedged people.

"Erik" Vairo shouted. "I have a ladder in my apartment behind the bar; we can go up the back and try getting them back from upstairs."

Running out the back of the building, they saw a few people running down the fire escape while other people hung out the windows shouting "Come back …. There is no fire."

Placing the ladder on the sill of one of the upstairs windows, Erik and Vairo scaled it quickly, helped through the window by Eric's brother Joni. Happily for him, all Erik's family was still in the same corner of the hall as before.

"What the hell is going on?" Olli asked "somebody started yelling 'fire' and there was a quick rush to the door. Then the rush stopped when people realized there was no smoke or flames or anything but now there's all this scream-

60

ing commotion over by the stairs."

"All you guys come with us, "Erik said, "Women and kids stay here. Where's Momma?"

"Still in the kitchen, far as we know."

"Let's go."

As they reached the door and looked down the steps, they were paralyzed at first by what they saw. From the bottom of the steps to halfway up the stairway, a stack of human bodies was crammed to the ceiling. Erik had seen the front of the mass below and it was apparent that the panicked party-goers had pushed the frontrunners down in their haste to escape and those who followed were pushed into a growing heap by others trying to flee the non-existent fire. As the pile of humans grew, the people upstairs pulled back in confusion to find that, other than their own panic, there was no threat to life in Italian Hall.

At the edge of the mass, arms and legs groped for purchase as people tried desperately to extract themselves, while would-be rescuers tried to help without hurting those jammed in the human morass. As they were removed from the pile, bodies of all sizes, moving and inert, were passed bucket brigade style to the main hall at the top of the stairs. Screaming in the stairway diminished, replaced by crying, moaning, gasping and whimpering as life departed the cruelly pinned, until finally there was an eerie silence, punctuated by an occasional muffled cry of "go back .... go back" by those at the downstairs doorway who could not grasp the enormity of tragedy.

"*Hyvä Jumala auta minua.... Minon lapset .... Minon lastenlapset.* My God, help me. My children. My grandchildren. Oh my God." The Koistinen brothers heard as they realized their mother was at the forefront of the wedge of rescuers, slipping back and forth from Finnish to

English as she did when she was excited. Ollie pushed his way down to her and took her arm, which she hysterically jerked away. "Momma, Momma" Olli yelled, "It's me. Everybody is all right and waiting for you upstairs. Go to them in the back corner of the hall. We will take your place here." Heleena Koistinen tearfully ran upstairs and the brothers joined the rescue effort.

In a short time the last of the bodies was removed from the stairway the air inside was chill from broken windows where some of the 700 from upstairs had broken windows to jump to the snowy street below during the fire scare. Many of the partygoers were evacuated by fire escape and ladders while the body-littered stairway was cleared. Many others stayed in the upstairs main hall looking for loved ones, some of whom had made it outside and were waiting there unbeknownst to those upstairs. The stairway reeked of sweat from the rescuers mixed with the noxious stench of body wastes released at the moments of death. Bodies were laid out in a makeshift morgue on the floor of the main ballroom, then moved to the fire hall nearby. Only grieving families and the most ghoulish of curiosity seekers remained while outside on the sidewalk, deputies held back people trying to enter the hall. Later speculation would claim that the deputies who kept outsiders from entering the building were also the cause of blocking exit doors at the ground level of the stairway.

Official body count listed the dead as:

CHILDREN:

Aaltonmen, Sylvia, daughter, 5, Finnish female;

Aaltonmen, Wilma, daughter, 7, Finnish female;

Aura, Lempi, daughter, 12, Finnish female;

Bin, Will, 7, Finnish male;

Bolf, Ivanna, 9, Croatian female;

Burcar, Victoria, 12, Croatian female;

Butala, Joseph, 8, Slovenian male;

Giacoletto, Jenny, 9, Italian female;

Gregorich, Katarina, 10, Croatian female;

Heikkinen, Edwin, brother, 5, Finnish male;

Heikkinen, Eino, brother, 9, Finnish male;

Heikkinen, Eli, brother, 7, Finnish male;

Isola, Paiva, baby daughter, Finnish female;

Jelic, Rosie, baby daughter, Croatian female;

Jokipii, , Uno, 13, Finnish male;

Kallunki, Anna, daughter, 9, Finnish female;

Kallunki, Effia, daughter, 8, Finnish female;

Kiemaki, Johan, 7, Finnish male;

Klarich, Christiana, sister, 5, Croatian female;

Klarich, Katarina, sister, 7, Croatian female;

Klarich, Mary, sister, 9, Croatian female;

Koskela, Johan, 10, Finnish male;

Kotajarvi, Anna, daughter, 4, Finnish female;

Krainatz, Mary, 11, Croatian female;

Lantto, Hilja, daughter, 5, Finnish female;

Lauri,Sulo, 8, Finnish male;

Lesar, Mary, sister, 13, Slovenian female;

Lesar, Rafael, brother, 5, Slovenian male;

Lindstrom, Arthur, 12, Swedish male;

Loumi, Lydia, 5, Finnish female;

Lustic, Alfred, 7, Finnish male;

Manley, Wesley, son, 4, Finnish male;

Manttanen, Ella, sister, 8, Finnish female;

Manttanen, Mathais, brother, 10, Finnish male;

Manttanen, Yrjo, brother 13, Finnish male;

Milelchich, Agnes, cousin, 3, Croatian female;

Mihelchich, Elizabeth, cousin, 9, Croatian female;

JACK R. WESTBROOK

Mihelchich, Paul, cousin, 5, Croatian male;
Murto, Walter, 9, Finnish male;
Myllykangas, Edward, brother, 3, Finnish male;
Myllykangas, Johan, brother, 5, Finnish male;
Papesh, Annie, sister, 6, Slovenian female;
Papesh, Mary, sister, 14, Slovenian female;
Raja, Saida, 10, Finnish female;
Renaldi, Teresa, 13, Italian female;
Ristel, Elma, 6 Finnish female;
Rytilahti, Emilia, sister, 16, Finnish female;
Rytilahti, Heli sister, 13, Finnish female;
Saari, Yrjana, 5, Finnish male;
Saatio, Elida,16, Finnish female;
Smuk, Mamie, 7, Slovenian female;
Staudohar, Antonia,7, Croatian female;
Taipalus, Elisina, sister, 6, Finnish female;
Taipalus, Sandra, sister, 5, Finnish female;
Takola, Edward, 9, Finnish male;
Talpaka, Lydia, 10, Finnish female;
Tulppo, Kaisa, daughter 10, Finnish female; and
Wuolukka, Hilja, 8, Finnish female;.

ADULTS

Aaltonmen, Sanna, mother, 30, Finnish female;
Aura, Herman, father, 50, Finnish male;
Bronzo, Katarina, 21, Italian female;
Cvetkovick, Nick, 33, Croatian male;
Isola, Aina, 30, mother, Finnish female;
Jelic, Barbara, mother, 25, Croatian female;
Kallunki, Briita, mother, 42, Finnish female;
Kotajarvi, Anna, mother, 39, Finnish female;
Lantto, Maria, mother, 40, Finnish female;
Manley, Elina, mother, 26, Finnish female;

KAISA

Niemela, Abram, husband, 24, Finnish male;
Niemela, Maria, wife, 22, Finnish female;
Petteri, Kate, 66, Finnish female;
Tulppo, Mamie mother, 42, Finnish female; and
Westola, Johan, 48, Finnish male.

The original list included a little girl who came back to consciousness half an hour after she was laid with the dead. Countless injuries were attributed to the Italian Hall Disaster. Another child was taken to the hospital, unconscious, to die the next day.

Of the seventy-three people who died in the packed hallway, forty-seven were female and twenty-six male; the youngest were two infants and the oldest, 66 year-old Kate Petteri. Fifty-eight children, average age 10.24 years, and 15 adults, average age 34.46 years, died in the crush. The ethnic makeup of the victims included one Swedish, three Italian, six Slovenian, fourteen Croatian and forty-nine Finnish.

Beyond the numbers, family tragedies abounded. Eight mothers and one father died in the stairway with one to three of their offspring, including Maria and Hilja Lantto, wife and child of the evening's ticket taker. One young couple aged 22 and 25 years old perished, as well as three cousins and nineteen siblings in duos and trios.

One incident in the aftermath of the tragedy was particularly sad. Dominick Vairo, owner of the tavern on the ground floor of Italian Hall, who had struggled from the beginning to untangle people from the human mass, furnished a ladder to help evacuation of the upstairs room and worked tirelessly helping families reunite, returned to his business to find his cashbox empty and most of his liquor inventory stolen. Additionally, his baby son had been snatched from his wife's arms by a hysterical woman who claimed the infant belonged to her. Vairo's wife grabbed the child back before the other woman disappeared into the crowd of on-lookers.

Late that night, body heavy with exhaustion and mind racing with visions of the horrors of the evening, Erik headed home. For a while he despaired that his apprehension of the drunken stranger who started the stampede when he shouted "Fired" at Erik and began a panic by those who heard "fire". Then he took comfort in knowing had he not stopped the man's attempt to assassinate Annie Clemenc, the shot in the noisy crowded hall might well have caused a larger melee and increased the death toll in the stairway.

Of all the pictures in his head from the rescue efforts, the most bittersweet was snatching her baby from the upraised arms of twenty-two year old Maria Neimela, who was trapped standing upright in the mass of people near the bottom of the stairs. Maria whispered "thank you" with her last breath as she died of suffocation, a few feet from her twenty-four year old husband Abe. Erik remembered attending the Neimela's wedding as he passed the screaming baby boy back upstairs through the line of rescuers, where the infant ended up in the arms of his Heleena Koistinen. How happy Abe and Maria were then and later when they announced her pregnancy to friends and neighbors. Both their parents had departed Red Jacket for parts unknown during the strike, when evicted from their company-owned home for being unable to pay the rent.

The final life-changing moment of the tragedy came for Eric as he pushed his way through the crowd of more than 5,000 people gathered on Seventh Street in front of the Italian Hall. Physically and mentally spent, he heard a voice among the onlookers say to a companion "That union strike is mostly socialist Finns anyway. This is bad, but they brought it on themselves." The day after Christmas, Erik gave the conservative Finns a "yes" answer and a week later began work in the mines.

■■■

Aftermath

In the weeks that followed, the Western Federation of Miners saw their influence erode rapidly as starving and grief-stricken mineworkers targeted the union for their woes. It did not sit well with the workers that WFM President Charles Moyer shook off any attempts by mine owners to end the strike that did not include recognition of his union. Gradually it became apparent that the main priority of the WFM was to keep members under its thumb in the hopes that dues and assessments would fill the coffers of the union when they won the strike.

WFM membership dwindled. The union closed their store and striker's paychecks slowed to a trickle. In the spring, the Finnish Anti-Socialist League was incorporated on March 29, 1914, with Erik Koistinen as Acting President.

On July 14, 1914, World War I began. German orders stopped, but both the demand for and price of copper skyrocketed. Copper production hit a record high of 269,794,531 pounds at a price of thirty-seven cents a pound. Workers flocked to the mines. The war ended November 18, 1918. The government continued to order copper until 1921, when government orders stopped and copper prices dropped to fourteen cents a pound in the early 1920s.

The vote to end the strike came from 2,500 WFM members in Copper Country, all who remained of the 9,000 members on the union's roster when the strike began less than nine months previous. On April 14, 1914, Moyer declared the strike was over, just before he was shot at a hotel in Hancock and put on a train back west, where he'd come from. The WFM had gambled $743,454 on the strike in Michigan Copper Country and lost to retreat in ignominious defeat.

The miners' strike of 1913, saw more than 10,000 people to leave the area. Germany had been buying all the copper from Copper Country on the Keweenaw. The strike caused a reconsideration of supply by the Germans. Electrolysis treatment filtered silver from the copper and revenue from the silver was more than enough to pay for shipping across the Atlantic.

The mines had introduced the 8-hour workday midway through the strike and made moves toward higher daily wages for mineworkers. An uneasy peace returned to Red Jacket as winter turned to spring, Relief for the end of the strike was punctuated by the throbbing wound of community-wide grief for the deaths in the Italian Hall stairway.

Erik realized all his dreams but one – Katrina.

Still no letters from Holland. Two days after Italian Hall he had received a Christmas card signed "Affectionately, Katrina", curiously postmarked Grand Rapids, Michigan; other than that he'd heard nothing beyond the endearing note she handed him the previous spring. Life moves on, he thought, probably when she returned home she looked at her life there compared to what the future would be if she became involved with a mineworker and opted on the side of the good life. His weekly letters to her were likely ignored.

I can't waste my time brooding over a love that's never going to happen, he concluded. The day the strike ended, he penned his final letter to Katrina Golder.

Part III: KATRINA

7

Holland, Michigan April 20, 1914

"*Uw koninkrijk kome, Uw wil geschiede* .... Thy kingdom come, thy will be done." Katrina Golder neared the end of her prayer as she walked north on Central Avenue from her teaching job at Maple Grove Elementary School on Twenty-fourth Street.

She wanted to get to the Holland Post Office on Eighth Street to mail her latest letter to Erik before it closed, then go to her family home at 18 East Twelfth Street for dinner with mother before they went to the Women's Literary Club in the evening. This would be the Club's first meeting in their new building. Poppa, of course, would be late at the office. She couldn't remember who the meeting's speaker was but she was more interested in seeing the inside of the building that she had "sidewalk superintended" when she went downtown from her home two-and-a-half blocks away during the construction.

It's strange that I can go downtown to board the Interurban Electric Railway and go to Grand Rapids or Saugatuck but I can't get a trolley from my job on 24th to my home on 12th, she thought. No matter, today is a good day to walk, unlike many during the school year. Overall, however, she was happy to be teaching at the eight-year-old school within reasonable walking distance from home. Many teachers her age taught in a rural one-room school and lived in the homes of nearby families, seldom getting to their parents' homes.

At State Street, she turned on the northeasterly angled street and walked to where State met Michigan Street in an inverted "vee" intersection where they both joined River Street. There she turned north on River. The maneuver took her a block out of her way but took her to the southwest corner of Centennial Park, where she angled northeast through the park and enjoyed the colorful and fragrant flowers of spring.

Centennial Park, Katrina knew from teaching local history to her students, had once been an open-air market, as Center Street had once been Market Street. In 1876, the nation's Centennial year, Holland was one of Michigan's first cities to adopt a park plan, developing the seven-acre former market plot into a park, planting Maple trees and installing flowerbeds. A jail was built in the northwest corner to accommodate overzealous revelers of various celebrations. A rustic fountain of rock was installed in Centennial Park in 1904, followed by underground rest rooms in 1904, with a bandstand built atop the restrooms in 1907.

It was a gorgeous sunny spring afternoon and the early bloomers like jonquils, daffodils, hyacinths and some early tulips made the park Katrina's favorite place to be, except perhaps, being with Erik.

Erik, what is going on with you?, she thought as she passed the rock commemorating the Grand Army of the Republic, (G. A. R.), veterans of the Civil War and a stone monument similarly remembering the slain in the Spanish American War,,

When she first returned to Holland from Red Jacket

71

with her father last June, she wrote to Erik every other day. After a time with no answer, she figured that the copper mineworker's strike, which she was able to follow through her father's newspapers, was taking too much of Erik's time to expect him to write. As the strike progressed, she kept track of the strike's progress through her father's periodical grumbling about "that damn ruffian boyfriend of yours and his gang of rascals." Cancellations of grocery orders to Poppa's business came from the Copper Country, while demand dropped as economic caution about the future increased. Then when the union shipped eight railroad cars of goods they had ordered from one of his competitors from Chicago in to the copper range towns and opened stores for the strikers, Poppa was apoplectic, making a great show of sending checks to support the Citizen's Alliance.

Worst of all was her, father's scrutiny of her every activity. He interrogated her practically every night about her day: who she saw; who she talked to; where she went and whether she talked to anyone about her "Upper Peninsula dalliance." At these sessions he searched her face for traces of dishonesty, paranoid about someone discovering her association with anyone connected with the union on strike over five hundred miles away. Lately, he had begun extending frequent dinner invitations to a gawky young accountant from his business, obvious in his desire that his daughter would turn her attentions from the north country.

By summer's end, with no word from him, she cut back to writing Erik once a month. After the Christmas Eve disaster in Red Jacket, she wept when she read about the Italian Hall tragedy and found the names of people she'd met among the rosters of the dead: the Rytilahti girls, Emilia and her sister Heli; Elina Manley and her son Wesley; and the life-weary Mamie Tulppo with the sweet daughter

Kaisa. She expressed her grief in a long letter to Erik along with her relief in not finding his name or that of any of his family.

Still nothing in reply.

She continued to write, sure that the spark between them was real and somehow something she wrote might unlock his silence.

Now she was reaching the end of her second year of teaching and her father was pressuring her to begin cultivating a social life, fearing she would become a "damnable old maid schoolteacher" in his words. If she didn't hear from Erik now that she knew the strike had ended, she planned to stop writing by the end of the summer.

She looked briefly at the site of Holland's new post office at the corner of Tenth and River streets, where construction was nearly complete on the location of the old Phoenix Planing Mill. A short walk across the park to the post office will be nice, she thought.

Crossing the park diagonally, she encountered two women she knew near the corner of Tenth and Center Streets. The older woman, Lida Rogers, was the biology teacher at the high school and the much younger woman was Ruth Keppel, who had graduated high school with Katrina. The two were dividing their attentions between the newly finished Women's Literary Club building that would tonight officially become home to the fifty-year-old club and the profusion of flowers surrounding them in Centennial Park. Katrina knew them both as members of the Women's Literary Club. Miss Rogers had come to Holland a couple of years before to teach biology. Ruth, a talented violinist, would soon graduate high school, and depart for her first term at the Oberlin Conservatory of Music.

Ruth and Katrina shared a common bond in that

Ruth's great-grandfather and both Katrina's maternal great-grandparents were among the sixty Calvinist Protestant Dutch men women and children who fled economic depression and religious oppression in the Netherlands to settle on the eastern banks of Black Lake in 1847, naming their settlement Holland. Katrina's mother, Marta Golder, was the last of her family line, who had suffered sickness and the harshness of frontier life with Adolphus C. VanRaalte. Recognizing that their fledgling community could become important for turning logs to timber and shipping building products throughout the Great Lakes, they sought government money to dig a channel between Black Lake and Lake Michigan. When government aid was denied, the Hollanders dug their own channel and cleared an area near downtown, now Centennial Park, as a market square. Hundreds of Dutch immigrants flocked to the area. Those original families prospered, buying land at a dollar and a quarter an acre from the Government Land Office in Ionia and subdividing that land as additions to the expanding city. Holland as a timber finishing and commercial center, grew, and by 1914, the population of the city was nearly 11,000, with over eighty percent of the citizenry of Dutch descent. Hope College, across Twelfth Street from Katrina's home, had grown to a leading liberal arts college.

Listen to me, Katrina chided herself. Less than two days with Erik Koistinen and I spout history at the drop of a hat.

"Good afternoon, ladies." She said pleasantly. "What is so fascinating?"

"Well," Miss Rogers replied, "Miss Keppel is such a student of local history and my college minor was Botany, she is filling me in on the history of downtown and I am instructing her about the scientific names of the flowers in our park. I'm afraid we are both so excited about our subjects that our heads appear to be on swivels. Then we are going to dinner before the Literary Club meeting. Would you care to join us?"

"No, thank you" Katrina said, " I'm just off to the post office and then home for a quick bite before Momma and I come to the meeting. You know, it is too bad we can't share the beautiful flowers in our city in the springtime with the world."

"Perhaps the Women's Literary Club could play a role in making that happen." Miss Rogers replied. "Such an enterprise would take a lot of planning."

"We will see you at the meeting." the two women chorused as Katrina hurried away.

Entering the post office on Eighth Street, considered the main avenue downtown, just east of Center Street, Katrina gave the broadly smiling clerk three cents postage for her letter to Erik. She left quickly, wondering why her trips here lately prompted such blooming cordiality. Must be that the post office has a new policy of extra friendliness.

Walking down Center Street, she encountered her longtime friend Berta De Boer coming out of Centennial Park.

"Katrina," Berta said breathlessly. "I've been look-ing all over for you. I have something to tell you."

"Can it wait, Bert, I'm running late today."

"No, I think you need to know this right away."

When they were seated on a park bench, Berta began talking rapidly. "I was in the post office this morning when your father was picking up his mail from his box. A clerk called to him and he went to the window, handed the clerk some money and got an envelope. I figured it was just post-age due and didn't think anything of it." Berta's father was a rural route carrier for the post office, so her speech often was punctuated with postal jargon. "Then he walked to a table in the lobby, sorted his mail and discarded some of it, including the envelope he'd just gotten. After he left, I looked in the wastebasket and right on top was this letter addressed to you. I retrieved it and have been waiting for the school day to end to find you and give it to you. I knew you walked home but missed you earlier.

"When my father came home from his route I told him what I saw. He laughed and said it was part of the Holland central office gold mine. I asked what that meant and he said that your father placed a three-dollar bounty on envelopes addressed to you from Red Jacket, Michigan, or letters with your return address addressed to Red Jacket. He said it's turned into a contest amongst the clerks and the mail sorters and they even have a scoreboard in the back room with a total of over three hundred dollars so far. The rural carriers like my dad are jealous because they never see the kind of mail that qualifies. Anyway, here's your mail."

She extended a hand with an envelope face up. Katrina recognized the handwriting immediately from the note Erik gave her so many months ago. She took the letter and quickly opened it

Berta, the park and the world disappeared as she read:

Dearest Katrina,

You may probably never read this since it is obvious that you have ignored my previous letters. Enough time has passed that I now realize mutual feelings between us must have been in my imagination and my desire for a long-term relationship was only the mirage of a day.

Thoughts of you have filled my days through the horrendous days of the strike, which you may know has

ended.

As my fortunes have improved dramatically since leaving the union, I have hoped that conveying to you that I would soon be head of the Finnish Anti-Socialist League, in addition to being promoted to a full-fledged miner (rare for a Finn), would raise your estimation of me. However, it is obvious that the cold light of reality set in with your return to the privileged life as daughter of a rich city merchant.

Only a dispassionate Christmas card since last June is enough of a signal for me. (Katrina was baffled for a moment, then remembered a friend said she was going to the post office last December so Katrina gave her the hastily signed card. Later the friend apologized. She forgot Katrina's card in her purse and mailed it on a Christmas shopping trip to Grand Rapids).

So, I surrender.

This is the last you will hear from me.

I wish you a happy life and hope you will spend it with someone who gives you joy.

With love,

Erik

****

When Hermann Golder returned to his sprawling brick home in one of old Holland's best neighborhoods, he found his wife sitting in the parlor.

"How was the Literary Club meeting?" He asked.

"I did not go." Marta replied through clenched teeth.

Catching her tone, Hermann asked "Where is Katrina?"

"Gone." was the reply in the deadest tone he'd ever heard from his wife. "Gone where?"

"She caught the seven o'clock Interurban to Grand Rapids and from there she is going to Red Jacket to try to salvage her life with Erik."

He reached for the telephone. "She will do no such thing. I'll make some calls and get her stopped."

"Put the phone down, you son of a bitch." Marta in a voice so resolute he complied immediately. "You have done enough to try and ruin her life."

"But the man is just not suitable for her. He's a Finnish miner, for god sake, and a union rabble-rouser to boot."

"As it turns out, he is only one of those things. While you have been playing dictator, our daughter has shared with me his tender note from last summer and told me of his intelligence and tenderness.

"Remember how my father thought the handsome young grocery clerk that captured my heart was beneath me and my station in life. Remember how he liked your idea of a grocery wholesale business in Michigan and staked you for starting the enterprise you have today. I'm glad he and mother did not live to see what an insufferable pompous snobbish sausage of a man you've become. What you have done to our daughter is unforgivable.

"This is my home and it was my family's money that put you in business. My money has seen you through the hard times. We live in my home because you like the prestige of the address. For once I will tell you how things will be. First, you will be sure that mail addressed to me comes to the house. Second, you may continue to live in my house and sleep as far away from me as possible. Third, our religion forbids divorce, so in public and before the servants, we will continue to present the facade of a happy marriage, but our life as husband and wife is at an end. Fourth, if you ever, ever seek to do harm to our daughter's life with whomever she chooses to share it with, I will see that you are ruined.

One day you will die a lonely old man and I hope, then, your damn wealth will comfort you, I certainly shall not."

****

Two days later, Katrina reached Red Jacket. After a quick reunion, she moved into Heleena Koistinen's home for the three weeks publishing of Catholic Banns of Marriage.

"We have plenty Finnish Katerinas around here," Heleena Koistinen said "so it will be nice to have the only Dutch Katrina in Red Jacket."

On the fourth Saturday after her arrival, Katrina and Erik were married.

Exactly nine months later, they welcomed Kaisa Marta Koistinen in February 1915. Erik researched the name Kaisa and said, besides meaning "pure", the name derived from Katherine for Katherine of Aragon, who lived 1485 - 1536 and was the first wife the king tried to divorce, defying the pope.

Part IV: KAISA

8

Delaware Mine, Keweenaw Peninsula, Michigan – September, 1928

"Ya know, if da Finns and the Dutch ever got in a war over who was the blondest ...dey'd have to declare a truce when they saw Kaisa Koistinen, ey." Clyde Bails said to his fellow off-shift workers who were loafing on the porch of the store ambitiously dubbed the Delaware Emporium. Bails, forever known as Clawed Balls after an unfortunate incident with a raccoon in an outhouse, cast an appreciative eye toward the slim girl climbing the mountainside above the mining settlement.

"Ya, Clawed, and the rest of her has improved a bit during da summer too, ey?" another of the front porch philosophers agreed.

"Shuddap youse. Dat's Erik's girl." Gimp Gilmore., Delaware's storekeeper, by virtue of his injured leg that made mining out of the question. Because of his sense of propriety, Gilmore was general keeper of the peace, as well as guardian of the intellectual level of the conversation on his porch, lest a sensitive customer approach the assembled brain trust's earshot without their knowledge. "Remember, none of us would have the chance to be here without Erik so let's show some respect for him and his."

"Ya, wherever here is." Clawed clung sullenly to his imagined conversation leader role. "Sometimes I t'ink bein' laid off and starvin' in a decent town like Calumet, or Red Jacket, or whatever they're calling it this week or Houghton or any civilized place in da Upper Peninsula is better dan bein' up here working our arses off for a share of almost nothin' while we look for Erik's bullshit mother lode. Maybe we shoulda done like Erik's brother Jalo and headed downstate to drill for oil after that oilfield 'scovery at Mt. Pleasant. We'd still be makin' holes in the ground but they'd be from the top o' the ground instead of under it."

"Y'ull be singin' out the other side of your shredded scrotum if today's blastin' uncovers the joinin' of the three veins." Gilmore replied. "Your share will be enough to keep you bitchin' here on the porch for a hundred years while you send other poor damn fools underground."

"Ya, Ya. Where'd I hear dat before? You'd defend Erik Koistinen if he dipped his lantern wick in your wife's oilcan, just because he cut you in to the payoff just for storekeepin'." Bolles said, as he ducked the pan Gilmore threw his way. "

"Oh, so now there's gonna be a payoff, eh?" Gilmore replied, "Mebbie ya just been breathin' too much copper dust Clawed. But yer right about Kaisa, she's growin' up fast."

****

"Pyhitetty olkoon sinun nimesi, thy valtakuntasi, tapahtukoon sinun tahtosi, maan päällä ....Hallowed be thy name, thy Kingdom come, thy will be done, on Earth ...oh

damn, why do I feel stuck here up north 'til next spring."

Kaisa Koistinen, the thirteen-year old trigger for the Delaware Emporium front porch speculation, walked up Delaware's main street toward the mineshaft. She wondered briefly if God would get her for breaking off a prayer with a curse as she made her way through the town below the mine entrance to the Delaware Mine. She always was torn between emotions when each fall she returned from the warm downstate lakeshore elegance of her grandparent's home in Holland, Michigan. Besides the drastic change in climate from Lower to Upper Peninsula, she also had to suffer her grandfather's frosty indifferent silences as he brought her to and from between Calumet, known as Red Jacket until last year, and Holland. Here at Delaware she would stay until the following spring, when Grandfather's store supply business brought him north to take orders for fall delivery. Under protest and at the insistence of Grandma Marta Golder, he would pick up Kaisa for her annual summer visit to Holland.

It had been bad enough when the Koistinens lived in Red Jacket, twenty miles southwest of Delaware, which grew up as center of a cluster of villages around the Calumet and Hecla mine. That thriving mining town at least had lots of people and events to fire the teenage imagination.

Grandpa Golder refused to do business with the Delaware Emporium store because of Kiasa's father's involvement with the whole Delaware Last Chance Mining Company venture. She was shuttled around from Delaware to Calumet to Holland and back again like a box of tools.

Gimpy went to Calumet to place his supply order "under the table" with a friend of his who ran a store with which Grandpa would do business. There Grandpa collected her and, three months later, dropped her off without a word passing between them for the entire round trip to Holland.

The settlement where the Koistinens now lived had been reclaimed two years ago by Kiasa's father Erik Koistinen and his Delaware Last Chance Mining Company crew at the mouth of the famous Delaware Copper Mine near the tip of the Keweenaw Peninsula, northernmost point of Michigan's Upper Peninsula. The Keweenaw jutted northeast into Lake Superior like an accusing finger toward the wilderness of Ontario Canada, as if saying "why aren't you, too, swarming with miners?"

The Delaware Mine was one of the largest copper producers in the late 1800s. It closed for good after a long, harrowing road lined with fiscal disasters and short closings several times due to fluctuating fortunes of copper mining. The Delaware Mine began at the site of E. B. Wales 1845 Permit Number 222, on a one square mile tract, one of nine granted near the upper point of the Keweenaw Peninsula.

The original opening of the Delaware Mine came by way of its initial prime corporate ancestor Northwest Copper Mining Association, formally granted a charter by the Michigan Legislature in 1849 as Northwest Mining Company. Northwest boasted among its directors the eminent Horace Greeley, Editor of the *New York Tribune*. Greeley's well-known quote "Go West young man, go West!" most likely evolved from his belief in the opportunities for riches offered by the copper-rich outer reaches of Upper Michigan.

The main focus of Northwest's attentions were three fissure mines that had been found along the trap range's southern slope a little south of Lake Superior's Grand Marais Harbor near the middle of Section 15, Township 58 North, Range 30 West, Grant Township, Keweenaw County, Michigan. At this spot Northwest set up mining operations overlooking Michigan's Montreal River. Shafts were put down to each of the veins, reaching as deep as 1,130 feet. The veins of copper-laden rock were exposed by prehistoric miners in a number of pits. These veins were named the Kelly, the Hogan and the Stoutenburgh. It was thought then that they might converge into a single deposit of unthinkably large value. At first, the Northwest produced mass copper, most of the masses small, less than a ton in size. Excitement mounted for a short time with the discovery of some native silver in the Kelly and Hogan veins. Later an amygdaloidal vein was found cutting across the fissure veins.

Between 1849 and 1851, Northwest produced 250 tons of refined copper with the Delaware Mine yielding a gross of $95,000. Getting the copper out of the ground and refining it cost more than twice that amount so the goal became getting more copper out of the ground without adding substantially to costs. A steam-powered stamp mill, the first in the area had been installed, followed by two more. Financial spreadsheets grew continually dreary and Northwest went out of business in 1859.

In 1861, a second reorganization took place with the company becoming the Pennsylvania. Sam Hill, a member of the preliminary mineral assessment party that ventured into the Upper Peninsula 20 years earlier, was agent for the new company. Hill was so profane that his name became synonymous with profanity and was used as a more socially acceptable substitute for letting blue language rip, as in "what the Sam Hill ..." - when the would-be curser was in polite company." Hill also was one of the most experienced of Upper Michigan copper mining experts. Under his direction new bedded copper deposits were opened, new hoisting equipment was erected and another mill was built at Lac La Belle, the best equipped and largest in the district.

Higher copper prices came about with the Civil War. The era saw part of the Pennsylvania company split off as the Delaware Mining Company, yet no profits were made to enhance the company cash reserve.

The New Jersey Mining Company was formed in 1863; the Maryland Mining Company in 1864 and the Wyoming Mining Company in 1865, all mines being on Pennsylvania-owned lands but not much mining took place. Instead, the company sold lots nearby for a village, which first became known as Wyoming, then became known as "Helltown" when many of the lot buyers opened saloons on their property. Apparently, company management found more cash flow in real estate than mining. Concerned shareholders took over mine operations in 1866 to no avail and for many years, the mines were idle.

A passerby of the area in 1869 wrote:

"On the road from Eagle Harbor to Lac La Belle, we passed the almost deserted village of the Pennsylvania and Delaware mines where was once a village of some 2,000 inhabitants, but there is now scarcely an occupied house.

"Streets numbering nearly a hundred houses, churches, schoolhouses, stores, and every appointment for a flourishing village are handsomely situated, but no people and the only sign of life was the pumping engine of one shaft kept in operation to clear the mine of water.

"We passed scores of other mines on the road whose names I cannot remember, but we saw no deserted village so large and so expensively equipped on the surface as that of the Pennsylvania and Delaware Companies, the property of which will probably be sold under the hammer."

A short time later, at just such a sale, the Pennsylvania and Delaware sold with an Edward M. Davies of Philadelphia buying the bonds, but little mining activity occurred while he owned the company.

The needed reorganization came in 1876 when the Pennsylvania and Delaware properties combined under the name of the Delaware Mining Company with Captain A. P. Thomas of Copper Falls in charge of operations. He reopened the old Stoutenburgh vein, built a new shaft house and made railroad connections from that shaft house to the mill. The main shaft was deepened, at first with disappointing results. A conglomerate lode, thought to be the fabled convergence of the Kelly, Hogan and Stoutenburgh veins, was discovered and the area took prosperity of new heights. The lode compared favorably with the giants of Calumet and Hecla and Quincy mines. Again, the seductress Delaware promised much and delivered little. The conglomerate lode proved to be wide but its copper content poor and again the Delaware suffered a downturn until 1884 when the property closed.

For nearly forty years, the properties saw limited and short-lived mining attempts. In 1923, the Calumet and Hecla company, with their extensive consolidation of copper properties, took over the Delaware Mine from Manitou Mining Company and did some exploratory work but was unimpressed. The Delaware mine would probably have disappeared to rot with the search for the legendary convergence of its three veins abandoned with the hopes of seven decades of investors if not for the vision of Erik Koistinen.

Koistinen was one of the miners sent to the Delaware Mine with the 1923 Calumet and Hecla exploratory crew. After the 1913 copper strike, Erik had worked two jobs: one in the mines and the second as president of the Finnish Anti-Socialist League. When the League re-named itself American Finnish Clubs in December of 1914 and began to relax its anti-socialist stand, the organization lost appeal to him and he returned to the mines full-time. He remained on good terms with the mining companies and conservative Finns in the Copper Country business community.

Although the C and H experts had declared the Delaware shafts not worth pursuing, third generation Finnish Upper Michigan copper miner Koistinen heard whispers of promise on the fourth level and recognized the haunting call of what his grandfather always called the "voice of the copper". Though far away, the voice of the copper was loud, strong, and still echoed in Erik's head a few months later when he and a number of his shift mates were laid off in still another downshift in the fluctuations of the copper market.

Koistinen was able to raise enough capital investors to re-open the Delaware mine, making a "farm out" offer to C & H. His Finnish conservative business friends from his days with the Finnish Anti-Socialist League invested heavily. Erik and crew would reopen and work the mine and in exchange for their permission to do so. C & H Mining Company would receive a percentage override of the proceeds.

For almost two years the Delaware Last Chance Mining Company, Erik Koistinen President, wrestled with the fourth level of the mine, eking out enough copper to keep slightly ahead of bankruptcy. Discouragement ran rampant through Delaware. The Last Chance Board of Directors agreed the current blasting would be the last attempt before the company gave up and its participants scattered to seek employment elsewhere.

Kaisa continued her silent monologue of teenage angst as she climbed past the entrance of the mine to her favorite spot, a sunny grassy spot just below an outcrop sheltering her from the wind. She warmed herself in the protected pocket of springtime. From here, her view was that of a bird.

Like a diorama she'd seen in a museum, the houses of Delaware spread out before her with a ribbon of track for the ore cars running through, headed for the crushing plant and smelter at the base of the mountain at Lac Labelle Harbor. Beyond, she watched breezes chase each other across the rippling surface of Lake Superior, the color of liquid silver, serving as a backdrop to Lac LaBelle, the Mendota Ship Channel, the Mendota Lighthouse and *Bête De Gris* (French for grey beast) Bay. She saw the lacing of the ore car tracks from the abandoned nearby Montreal, Amygdaloidal and Wyoming Mines angling down the mountainside near the harbor. She tried to imagine them all scurrying with action like the Delaware track was now, each time the miners sent rock from a new blasting down to the plants for processing and hopefully shipping of the copper ingots that were the lifeblood of the community. She hoped to see even more Delaware ore cars soon.

She knew the importance of today's blast.

"So you're back," a voice interrupted her solitude "How was life among the other half down below."

She looked up to see a dark-haired boy about her own age smiling back at her from the edge of the outcrop.

"I thought you'd come up here as quick as you got the chance."

"Hello Eino." She replied, feeling a faint rumble from inside the mountain that let her know the blasting had begun. Eino was just sixteen and a stoker for the boiler that ran the ore crusher. Next year he would be working underground. He and Kaisa had been students of Katrina Koistinen's one-room school in Delaware together. They became friends when they discovered a mutual interest in reading history and for the past two years had been nearly inseparable.

■■

Hundreds of feet below, the smoke and dust cleared from the blasting and men rushed forward to clear the shattered rock. The lead miner looked at the wall of rock at the end of the tunnel just exposed by the blast.

"Lord 'a mighty" he exclaimed.

"What?" said the man behind him.

"Run, get Erik, quick." The head miner said "He's gotta be the first to see this."

"See what?"

"Never mind …. You just go get him." The man repeated and turned back to see three yard-wide veins of copper converging in the wall of rock. "B'god, we've done it."

Erik Koistinen came running along the tunnel, shouting, "What's wrong …. What's wrong."

"It's not what's wrong, boss, it's what right. Look't this beautiful sum'bitch."

Erik stood awestruck for a moment, then moved forward to caress the gleaming ribbons of cool copper spelling his and Delaware Last Chance Mining Company's salvation. Shouts of jubilation spread behind him as word of the copper strike spread through the tunnel.

He stepped back, stifling tears of joy. "Well boys, let's get this mess cleaned up and send some of the men down the hill to start the crushers and smelter . We ….."

He heard a faint crack above him and looked up to meet the ton and a half of pure float copper falling from the roof of the tunnel, his last moment on earth screaming with the call of the copper louder than he'd heard all his life.

■■

Up the mountainside, Kaisa and Eino Heinonen chatted about their respective summers.

Eino talked mostly about his summer job on the timber crew, cutting trees to be used for timbers in the mine. They laughed over his story of the folly in disturbing a family of skunks.

When it was Kiasa's turn, she spoke of the theaters, stores and libraries she and her grandmother visited, then turned and spoke of the exciting bit of history she had witnessed.

"It's not so bad once we get to Holland because grandmother Marta treats me like a visiting princess and I seldom see grandfather, since he spends a lot of time at the office and traveling. They kind of act like ambassadors from two warring countries asked to sit together at the same dinner table. We shopped, we traveled, we worked in her beautiful flower garden and we helped other ladies tend the flowers in the Centennial Park near their house.

"She takes me to her Women's Literary Club where I heard Miss Lida Rogers's, a lady mother said she knows, give a speech last year about how the Literary Club should spearhead a movement to urge Holland residents to grow tulips and their yards and organize a festival to celebrate the flowers that symbolize the city's Dutch heritage. Another lady mother knows, Miss Keppel, seconded a motion that the club take up the cause. Eino, it looks like they are going to do it. Grandmother told me that this year the City of Holland bought 100,000 bulbs from the Netherlands. They resold the bulbs to townspeople who planted them all over town. Next year they are having their first Tulip Festival in

Holland and grandmother is making my grandfather come up here a month early so I can be there when it happeneds. It was so exciting."

"I thought you hated being shuffled back and forth."

"I do, but this was something really big and I, a little copper town girl, will be part of it. Downstate is so beautiful, with lots of open space, grass, flowers and a big lake you can actually swim in for more than a month each year. But when I'm there, at night when things have slowed down, I miss it up here too. I wonder what Dad and Mom would think of what I've seen that day and I think how sad mom looks sometimes when I describe how Holland is today."

"And do you miss me too?" Eino asked, sidling closer to her.

"Of course I do," Kaisa replied. "How can I not miss my best friend? Who else my age can I talk to about everything? We share books, we share thoughts and we share laughs ...."

"And I'd like to share more." Eino said breathlessly as he wrapped his arms around her and kissed her in a fit of rampaging teen hormones.

Shocked at first, Kaisa felt his lips on hers and warmth she'd never known began creeping through her body. She kissed back.

Suddenly from below, they both heard the shrieking of the emergency whistle and parted just as a shadow blocked out the sun as she heard Clyde Bowles stutter, "Come quick Miss Kaisa. Th-h-h-h-h-here's been an accident."

■ ■

KAISA

They buried Erik Koistinen four days later in his favorite spot beneath the outcrop above the mouth of the Delaware Mine, the spot he had shown Kaisa when she made it her spot.

The shareholders of Delaware Last Chance Mining Company voted to give Katrina a half-share of the mine's proceeds, which assaying estimates said should be considerable. Marta Golder mourned for and with Katrina by mail and extended an invitation for her and Kaisa to return "Home" to Holland, to which Katrina replied that Copper Country was now home, close to Erik.

9

Delaware Mine, Keweenaw Peninsula, Michigan – Early Morning Wednesday, October 30, 1929

Arlin Marlich, First Bank of Calumet Delaware Branch Manager, finished hastily packing his meager personal belongings in preparation for a pre-dawn escape before angry miners stormed the bank to withdraw their money …. which was no longer there.

Ever since news of the Tuesday collapse of the of the market in the New York Stock Exchange came over his telegraph, the only one in the tiny town, Marlich pondered the danger in his future. When the discovery that much of the hard-earned money the mineworker shareholders in the Delaware Last Chance Mining Company deposited with his bank in the eight months since it opened was gone, he would be a dead man. After the richest copper discovery in decades was made in a mine thought worthless, everybody wanted to be the Delaware miners friend, particularly the First Bank of Calumet. Though the income from the mine was substantial, initial investors had to be paid, as did the monthly farm-out override to Calumet and Hecla, owners of the land and the mine. Those payments were paid promptly.

The individual miners' accounts were a different story. By paying withdrawals from a slush fund of deposits, Arlin Marlich had used depositor's funds to build a substantial portfolio of investments in the stock market for himself. The Dow-Jones Industrial average had just topped 300 when Arlin, recently promoted from Chief Teller, opened the Delaware Branch of First Calumet in February 1929. He already had a small account with Paine-Webber investment brokers in Calumet. The stock market had been good to him to that point. Nothing spectacular, but good..

When the D-J continued to rise, deposits at the Delaware Branch began to grow exponentially as residents of the far reaches of the Keweenaw Peninsula found the convenience of a bank nearer them than the larger communities further south. In June, the Dow-Jones average kissed 350 and Arvin hatched his scheme. He began buying heavy on the margin. Margin requirements were only ten percent. For every one-dollar Marlich had on deposit with them, Paine-Webber and Company would lend him nine dollars. He lunged like a tiger investing a thousand dollars of his own and bank depositors' money.

The D-J average reached 370 by the end of August and Arlin considered bailing out then. He could pay Paine-Webber, return the depositors money and still realize a tidy profit. The profit would be even tidier, greed whispered in his ear, if he waited until the D-J hit 400.

He decided to hang in there. He invested more

The market began to slip in small increments in September, but not seriously. Those who kept the faith were rewarded with a rise in early October and the brave ones laughed at the weak sisters who had bailed the month before. Marlich began considering another margin investment.

Then came the plunge.

A precipitous drop in late October was followed by a slight rise as trading and values hung on the precipice, then plunged yesterday, October 29. He got word late in the day, near closing time.

At home, he calculated his losses. He was ruined. He knew a margin call would come on Wednesday and he owed nearly $90,000. Fortunately, Delaware was so remote and the people of the town were geared strictly with the affairs of producing more copper so few paid attention to news outside the town. Radios were few, reception irratic and telephones even fewer. He knew eventually news of the stock market collapse and the resultant economic panic would find its way to Delaware. Wednesday the bank would be swarming with depositors with withdrawal slips in hand and what money that was in the tills and the vault would be gone in less than an hour.

In the darkness of the cooling small hours of Halloween Eve day, Marlich cleaned the cash drawers and vault at the bank, driving there without lights lest someone wonder why his shiny roadster was doing plying the night-deserted streets. Still without lights he accelerated up the mountain street adjacent to the ore-laden tram cars rumbling down their track from mine to processing plants along the Lake LaBelle Harbor below.

It looked like he would make good his escape.

■■

Katrina and Kaisa Koistinen were also treading the dark streets of early morning Delaware. It was part of their daily routine. Erik Koistinen's half share of the profits of the Delaware Last Chance Mining Company was sufficient to provide the Koistinen women with a sustenance living.

To augment that income and that of Kristina's pay as teacher in the town's one-room school, the pair had taken to making pasties and selling them to miner's families where the women of the household were suddenly too grand to be bothered with preparing such mundane food for their men to eat in the mines. Katrina also had developed a talent for making and selling Kroners, the ear-flapped wool hats popular in the north country. Their "pasty route" involved early morning delivery before Katrina and her fourteen-year-old daughter left to prepare the school for the day's onslaught of variously enthusiastic scholars.

They split their route into two parts, designed to each loop through and meet at the downmountain end of the village streets, where they would walk together back up the incline to the school.

Working the east side of town, Kaisa's thoughts were about Eino, now seventeen years-old to her developing fourteen and becoming more obvious in his desire for her. They had not kissed since the bittersweet day more a year ago, when Delaware lost a leader and Kaisa lost her father during the copper discovery that catapulted the town into prosperity never before known by the miner/owners. Although she had a deep affection for Eino, his talk of their someday together sometimes wearied her. She was not yet fully grown and already she felt her life was planned to the end. A miner's home in this stark north country with copper dust in the air sucking away life and the beauty of youth was not for her. The promise for a life of literature, art and gentility fading to contempt for the higher classes, again not for her.

She knew from her summers in Holland with Grandmother Golder and her taciturn grandfather that not all people of wealth and refinement were the immoral thieves that existed in the myths of the lower classes. Her contact with ladies like Miss Lida Rogers and Miss Ruth Kappel and others of the Women's Literary Club taught her that women could achieve higher education and accomplish great things with their vision and ambition. She was rapidly developing a taste for a life that would be unattainable if she grew to adulthood here. Being part of the first ever Holland Tulip Festival this year had been exquisite.

When she tried to express herself and these thoughts to Eino yesterday, he gave her a walleyed look of disapproval and said, "Why do you want to think such nonsense, we're miner's kids and that's all we'll ever be. We've got it some better than most, thanks to your dad, but you gotta be born to the kinda stuff you're talkin' about .... and we weren't. You're havin' your head turned by the fancy life you lead summers down below. This is the real world and you better wake up to it or you'll die alone an old maid like your heroes in Holland Miss Fancy This and Miss Highfalutin' That."

His words stung.

Kaisa walked along deep in thought, knowing her future held some hard decision: comfort in things familiar or the frightening reach for things unknown. A predicament, I think it is called, she said to herself.

****

On the west side of town, a side she always chose since it was closest to Wyoming, a couple of miles away, where a few remnants of that village's Helltown days still lived in sullen envy over Delaware's good fortune, Katrina made her way through the darkened streets, thinking of her daughter Kaisa.

KAISA

She was becoming a beauty. A wisp of a girl with strength of body and spirit her delicacy of appearance masked. Kaisa's near platinum, naturally blonde, hair and fairness of complexion reflected the best of Katrina and Erik. Each time she returned from summers in Holland she was more polished. Katrina saw the fine hand of her mother's gentle guidance in that. Kaisa still hurt from the chilly indifference of her grandfather, but Katrina knew he would never change and convinced her daughter that it was his loss that he could not accept love.

She smiled as she thought about her daughter's excitement over Holland's first Tulip Time Festival, which had drawn thousands of visitors to Holland. The City of Holland had decreed that Tulip Time would henceforth be an annual event. Katrina was proud of her old friends Lida Rogers and Ruth Keppel who had masterminded and ramrodded the celebration of Holland's Dutch heritage.

She thought wistfully of the life she'd left behind in Holland. How much pain leaving her mother caused both of them. Then she remembered her father's betrayal that nearly cost her life, however brief, with her true love and anger burned as hot in her heart as it had when she first discovered it over fifteen years ago. No matter how hard she tried, she could never forgive him nor stand the thought of being in his presence. Her life was here now, close to Erik and reveling every day in the success he had brought to so many in his unstinting answer to the call of the copper, a call she heard and embraced.

She turned onto the final downward bound street in the up and down zigzag of her route. This would be quick since there were only houses on the right side of the street, with the tram tracks loaded with copper ore rumbling toward the crushers and processing plants downhill on the left.

Imagine having to live with this constant infernal ruckus across the street twenty-four hours a day now that the mine was working three shifts, she thought, I don't think I could stand it.

Oh well, she thought, enough wool gathering, back to work. She reached in her basket to retrieve a wrapped pasty from the dwindling pile then raised her head to find herself hurling though the air. She was puzzled for a second, then the pain set in briefly as she piled headfirst onto the hard packed surface of the street, snapping her neck and killing her instantly.

Behind the wheel of his speeding dark car, Avril Marlich felt the thump of collision and wondered what he had struck. A deer probably, he shrugged, probably didn't hear the car because of the tram noise. Well if the deer couldn't hear the car, probably no one else could, he chuckled over his cleverness. Touching the brakes, he saw a body, an indistinct shape, lying in the road behind him. He reached the top of the town and turned south to freedom, leaving behind the economic wreckage he'd brought to Delaware ..... and the lifeless body of the town's beloved schoolteacher.

At the base of town, Kaisa wondered what was taking her mother so long to make the last deliveries and scaled the street to find her. A few minutes later, her screams nearly drowned the sounds of the thundering tram train.

****

In Calumet later that morning, a policeman pulled Arlin Marlich over, for driving erratically with only one headlight. He began blubbering a confession of his thievery and the hit and run death of Katrina Koistinen before the police officer had his ticket book out of his pocket. The Delaware Last Chance Mining Company was able to recoup the money Marlich had stolen from the bank, but not that he had used to play the stock market on the margin.

****

Three days later, after Katrina's burial service placed her beside her husband, an impromptu meeting was held by the friends and relatives of the Erik and Katrina Koistinen.

The subject was Kaisa's future.

Should she stay in Delaware to be raised by relatives?

Would she be safe from her grandfather's influence here? Should they acquiesce to Marta's grieving request that her granddaughter be sent back to downstate Holland? They knew the spirit of Katrina would not stand for such a prospect.

Erik's brothers, Kaisa's uncles, Joni, Olli and Miska, shared the duties of head of the Koistinen clan in Copper Country after the death of Heleena Koistinen two years before. Their suggestion was Kaisa should go to live and be raised in the center of the Lower Peninsula at Mt. Pleasant, where the remaining Koistinen brother, Jalo, was working in the oilfields. Jalo had recently written that he and his wife Mina had been lucky enough to buy a large house in town early in the oil boom. The childless couple was taking in boarders to accommodate the hordes of fortune seekers arriving daily, which was practically paying for the home. When Kaisa heard she would have a chance to live in the town where her mother had gone to earn her teaching certificate at Central Michigan Teacher's College, she quickly agreed to go live with Jalo and Mina. Erik Koistinen's half-share of the mine proceeds would be sent regularly to her in Aunt Mina's name.

Kaisa longed desperately to contact her grandmother in Holland, but knew such contact would not be in anyone's best interest. She loved Marta Golder and thought of the life she could have in Holland, the growing city on the eastern shore of Lake Michigan. She knew, however, the constant conflict of her grandmother's love and her grandfather's aloof distain would place a pall of discord over any potential happiness in Holland. She agreed to be placed with Uncle Jalo and Aunt Mina in Mt. Pleasant.

She was put on the train south the next day and everyone was sworn to secrecy. Hermann Golder and, reluctantly, his wife Marta, must never know where Kaisa had gone.

10

Mt. Pleasant, Michigan – Late night Friday, July 17, 1931

"*….En leidt ons niet in temptation*….. and lead us not into temptation…" Sixteen year-old Kaisa whispered a prayer in Dutch. She was tired, hot and weary of revisiting visions of her own life as she laid restlessly on a daybed on the huge screened-in porch at the south side of her Uncle Jalo's North Fancher Avenue home in Mt. Pleasant, Michigan. She turned her thoughts to the house that was now her home for almost two years. The Koistinen passion for local history surged through her veins full tilt as she recalled the things her aunt told her to augment the things she'd learned at the library.

When she first arrived here from the Upper Peninsula of Michigan, she'd expected to find an area of smallish mountains much like home, especially a place named Mt. Pleasant. What she found was flat land and learned the region was part of a delta extending from the Saginaw Bay in the forefinger-thumb of the Michigan "Mitten" to a ridge of hills roughly ten miles west of Mt. Pleasant, called Bundy Hills. Still curious about the origin of the Mount in Mt. Pleasant, she delved further.

John Hursh and his wife Elizabeth were the first settlers in the Mt. Pleasant area in 1855, when they carved a rough pioneer life from the forest in an area south of the present community with their seven children. About four miles to the north, the U. S. Federal government had recently, at the request of Methodist-Episcopalians in southern Michigan, moved the Chippewa Indians from the Lapeer area to the middle of Michigan to a place called Indian Mills on the Chippewa River. There they built a grist mill so that tribal members could make a living beyond the monies granted for their move and placed a large tract of land in trust as the Saginaw-Chippewa Indian Reservation just to the east. The settlement of Indian Mills grew as Europeans moved in to establish stores and provide services to the tribe and the local Indian Agent.

At the Hursh property, the first guests that winter were two lumbermen named David Ward and John Kinney, looking at their respective properties to estimate timber harvest. Ward's property was 200 acres on the bluff of the Chippewa River curve, where the river changed direction from east/west to north/south before turning again near Indian Mills to head easterly to join the Tittabawasee River at Midland, heading to a mouth at Saginaw Bay. The Arnold Kinney property, which son John Kinney would return to oversee timbered, was attached to Ward's property at the northeast corner.

In 1859, Isabella County came into being and a log cabin at Indian Mills, now renamed Isabella City, became the county seat. David Ward finished timbering his 200 acres on the bluff to the southwest of Isabella City, platted a village there, naming it Mt. Pleasant. Some say he named it for the area in upstate New York where Ward was raised, while others say that he wanted to sell the village to outside speculators for the offering of lots for sale and "swampy spot overlooking a river in the middle of a forest of stumps" is not a good name to encourage purchases of land. To sweeten the deal, Ward offered the newly established Isabella County government five acres in the center of his new village. The offer was accepted and a crude cabin was built on the five acres, along with another crude structure to act as a jail. Eighteen years later the county would build red brick Victorian Era-style buildings to replace both buildings.

David Ward sold the roughly platted Mt. Pleasant settlement to the Morton brothers, New York land developers, who built the Morton House hotel at the corner of Main Street and what was simply called "The Road to Saginaw" until renamed Broadway Street. The Morton House hosted prospective lot purchasers among merchants and customers from timber related service industries like sawmills. The hotel also served to host loggers each spring as they floated their winter harvest to market each spring. The long civilization-deprived loggers could tie up their rafts at the base of the bluff and climb the hill to the hotel for rooms and revelry, sometimes to the detriment of those thinking of settling in the town.

Among those who came to Mt. Pleasant were lawyer/surveyor Isaac A Fancher and his wife Althea, daughter of Mt. Pleasant's first minister William A. Preston. In 1863, Fancher bought three large lots on North Main Street across from his father-in-law's home at the corner of Main and Chippewa streets. Not content with Ward's rough plat, Fancher resurveyed the settlement and that survey was used to have Mt. Pleasant officially registered as a place in 1864.

Mt. Pleasant was established as a village in 1875 and as a city in 1889. Augmenting the timber related population growth of the area, Central Michigan Business Institute and Normal began here in 1892.

In early 1892, citizens of Mt. Pleasant, a fledgling, mountain-less, now timber-less, lumber town in Isabella County at central Michigan were inspired to establish an institution of higher learning and set about the project through an organization called the Mount Pleasant Improvement Company (MPIC). The MPIC bought the last sixty-two acres of the old Hursh farm for $8,000, platted 224 lots and sold the majority of them by chance assignment for $110 each on 52 acres, setting aside ten acres for the school they hoped would someday come to be.

On September 13, 1892 the first classes were held at Central Michigan Normal School and Business Institute upstairs over a drug store at the southeastern corner of Main and Michigan streets in downtown Mount Pleasant. A private enterprise, the school's premiere class boasted a mighty enrollment of 31 students who gathered in the rented space located in the downtown building over a store.

At September 18, 1892, ceremonies Central Michigan Normal School and Business Institute, Principal Bellows officially broke ground for the school's first building on the ten acre plot south of town. Bellows also presided over the November 19, 1892 laying of the cornerstone of that first building in ceremonies conducted under the auspices of the Knights of Pythias.

Construction of the first building on the Central Michigan Normal School and Business Institute campus was completed in 1893. The new wooden main administration building remained a focal point of the fledgling school for thirty-two years and saw the campus expansion from ten to twenty-five acres in 1894 to encompass and area from Hopkins to Preston between Main and Franklin Streets.

In private hands until 1895, Central Michigan Normal School and Business Institute became Central Michigan

Normal School, a state institution, that year. The main administration building was augmented by a wing addition to the west in 1899, with another added to the west in 1902 to meet growing space needs of the robust young school.

Dow Chemical Company drilled brine wells and established a bromide plant on the old fairgrounds property north of town just upriver from the now nearly abandoned Isabella City. The Dow operations in Mt. Pleasant ceased in 1930, a victim of Great Depression price drops. The town was home to a sugar beet processing plant, Transport Truck Company, a chicory plant, and the new refinery at the railhead on West Pickard in the northwest part of town.

Thanks to the presence of an active oil and gas exploration, production and refining industry, the Mt. Pleasant, Michigan of 1931 was enjoying a booming economy while much of the nation slogged through the economic devastation of the Great Depression. Two railroads, the Pere Marquette and the Ann Arbor served the town where United States highway US-27 and Michigan Highway M-20 intersected. Both telephone and telegraph served the town.

There were two banks, one privately owned hospital, a clinic and a hospital unit on the 640-acre grounds of the 1894-established Indian Industrial School. A daily newspaper served the 7,000 town population, as did two movie theaters. The Bennett and Park Hotels, along with the Monroe House and several other local hostelries were sold out most nights. Many local homeowners had begun renting rooms and several had converted garages to living quarters to rent. Houses were being hauled in from economically distressed Alma, twenty miles south, following the collapse of that towns manufacturing base. When Kaisa's Uncle Jalo came in the autumn of 1928, he was fortunate to be able to buy a house before the oil boom started in earnest and was renting the three extra bedrooms (one to be hers) was a bonus.

From the minute she saw her new home in November of 1929, Kaisa fell in love with the big white house. Sitting at the west end of Crosslanes Street, once called Stub Street for some unknown reason, the wedding cake of a residence on North Fancher was built in 1883 just beyond the extreme east side of the growing lumber village of Mt. Pleasant. Lansing Street, next avenue to the west, was the east edge of the original 1864 plat used for the official incorporation of the town. It remained so until pioneer lumberman/merchant John Kinney made the Kinney Addition to the town in 1877 naming the first street east of the old boundary after his good friend and fellow Mt. Pleasant pioneer Isaac A. Fancher.

Kinney was born in Clyde Township, St. Clair County, Michigan, in 1837. In 1854, his father, Arnold Kinney, one of Michigan's early pioneers employed at various times by the government to build roads through the state, bought 320 acres near what was to become Mt. Pleasant. John worked for his father's lumber interests from age 12, and was lumberman David Ward's companion who stayed overnight with Mt. Pleasant's first settler John Hursh here in 1855, as they inspected their respective timber properties. Kinney, now a lumberman, returned to the Mt. Pleasant area in 1863 with a crew of ten men to cut practically all the timber and make the Kinney property suitable for cultivation.

Since there was no store in Mt. Pleasant, goods had to be bought from Isabella City. formerly Indian Mills, nearly two miles north and across the Chippewa River. In 1863, Kinney bought the log cabin at the corner of Main and Broadway and brought in goods by oxcart and canoe to open the first mercantile enterprise in town. The "Blunt" post office, four miles south, was transferred to Mt. Pleasant with Kinney as first postmaster. The post office name was changed to Mt. Pleasant later. Nelson Mosher was appointed deputy postmaster and Cass Mosher was Kinney's assistant in the store. Mosher's home was a block away, where the "Road to Saginaw", now Broadway Street, would eventually push through to the Chippewa River and open the west side of town.

In 1865, Kinney sold the store and returned to his home in Clyde Township, where he acquired a considerable amount of property and served as Township Treasurer of Clyde. Twice nominated as candidate for a State Congressional office from that area, he refused the nomination both times. In 1877, he returned to Mt. Pleasant and made the Kinney Addition to Mt. Pleasant and Kinney's Second Addition in 1884.

When the house where Kaisa now lived had been built, the local newspaper was boastfully proclaiming that North Fancher Avenue was being "stumped" (stumps removed from the street to allow more wagon traffic). One of those conveniently located stumps, killed and leveled off, became the support for the southeast corner of the front porch of Jalo and Mina Koistinen's home. Kaisa laughed as she recalled the story Uncle Jalo told her of his surprise at finding the stump when he crawled behind the latticework to rescue their lost cat.

The original structure of the house obviously had been built before electricity and inside plumbing were available. The back section, built later, contained the kitchen and bathroom. Uncle Jalo had discovered that from the fuse box at the back of the basement, a single electrical cable leading to a two-plug panel on a beam, from which two plugs served all the wiring for both floors of the front of the house. He quickly updated the wiring.

According to the lady next door to the south, in the little Cape Cod-style home just past the hedge, this house once occupied the center of three city lots. When somebody in the family got married, the owners of the original home had a house built for the newlyweds on the north lot. They hired a builder/contactor to build a new French Provincial style house. In partial payment, the contractor, Harold Moore, had taken a half-lot from the southernmost lot, leaving the home where Kaisa now dwelled on a lot and a half. If Crosslanes Street were to be pushed through east to Main Street, the south half-lot yard would be gone, as would the porch where Kaisa tried to sleep in the humid July heat. She had abandoned the hotbox bedroom upstairs to try for relief here on the porch.

Just a block north of the house Andre Street was the widest street in town to allow two-way street access for freight wagons to the Pere Marquette Railroad Depot, built in 1879 when the railroad arrived to "take Mt. Pleasant out of the woods."

"Evenin' lass," she heard, her reverie interrupted by the lilting brogue of one of the boarders, Mickey Conroy.

If Kaisa represented the best of blonde Nordic/Netherland genes, Conroy was the poster child for the typical Irishman. The twenty-year-old roustabout worked the same drilling crew as Uncle Jalo. Mickey hailed from West Virginia, where his oil driller father had migrated from County Clare in Ireland. The elder Conroy originally headed toward the Copper Country of Michigan, but was detoured by the appeal of working aboveground instead of the dark tunnels of the mines. Red-haired, fair skinned and green-eyed, Conley was a source of fascination to Kaisa, as well as being target of her teenage crush.

11

Mt. Pleasant, Michigan – Later night Friday, July 17, 1931

"Oh God," she said, hastening to pull a thin sheet over her mostly gaping nightdress. "I didn't hear you come in."

"Came in the back door, just in from the pub at the Bennett Hotel where a bunch o' oil guy's were drinkin' and tellin' lies. Thought I'd head home since we're probably gonna drill into the Dundee strata tomorra on hardluck McClanahan's latest dry hole, no matter what he says about this bein' the big one. He's been holdin' off bottom for four days now and built two five hundred barrel tanks on the site so he can have as many of his investors as possible on hand to put on a show for when he drills in … tomorra' bein' Saturday and all.

"Din't know anybody was out here or I'da been quieter."

"Don't be puttin' a curse on Mr. Walter's well before it's even drilled in." Jalo Koistinen said from the middle of the stairway leading upstairs. One disadvantage of this Victorian-era house was that, though it boasted four bedrooms, it had only one bathroom and that was on the ground level. Careful scheduling and luck played a large role in bathroom use for the three-member Koistinen family and two boarders. "Had to go to the can and heard ya down here. Lord, who couldn't. You best be headed for bed, we got a big day tomorrow."

"Aye _{and} g'night ta ya both." Conroy mumbled and went upstairs.

"You all right, Kaisa." Uncle Jalo asked. " Just makin' sure 'cause Mick brags about the ladies a lot on the rig floor and yer not 'zactly dressed for men visitors."

"It's all right. He just came in."

"Well, watch yerself. G'night."

Jalo went back upstairs and Kaisa shifted her thoughts to the oil boom that had brought he and his wife Mina, and by extension her, to Mt. Pleasant. While the rest of the nation was languishing in the economic devastation of the great Depression, Mt. Pleasant, Michigan, was a boomtown.

One of Uncle Jalo's boarders for a time the previous year was a geologist for the State of Michigan Geological Survey Division, Oil and Gas Section, regulatory body for the oil and gas industry. George "Josh" Lindberg, the geologist, spent most of his time in the field and the rest looking for a home to rent or buy so he could move his wife to Mt. Pleasant, since his assignment here looked to be permanent. Originally from Ironwood, Michigan, Lindberg had been on the staff of the U. S. Bureau of Mines and the Michigan Public Service Commission before joining the Geological Survey.

He and Kaisa became fast friends when he discovered the Koistinens, like him, were from Michigan's Upper Peninsula. Kaisa's hereditary curiosity fascinated Lindberg and they sat on the front porch on summer evenings last year while he instructed her about Michigan oil and natural gas exploration and production history. Kaisa was delighted with his ability to translate the complex industry into words she could understand.

"The Michigan geological basin is the bowl-shaped remains of an ancient tropical sea." He told her, "The ancient seabed is layered with millions of years of younger sedimentary rock. This bowl-shaped assemblage of rock and soils extends east beyond Niagara Falls, west beyond Prairie du Chien, Wisconsin, north to the edge of Michigan's Upper Peninsula where it meets with the volcanic rock of the Lake Superior Basin and south to just beyond the Michigan-Ohio border. Strata of rock within the basin are labeled by their geological age and geological formations layered within the geological age groups.

"Formations in a geological basin are also often referred to by the location where they "outcrop," that is reach the earth's surface. In the Michigan Basin, some formation names, like the Detroit River formation, are obvious. Others are more obscure. The Salina Niagaran formation is named for the Niagara River and the deep Prairie du Chien for Prairie du Chien, Wisconsin.

"The rock under the earth varies in density. Some of the layers are quite porous, allowing liquids or gases to move them, while others are quite dense, forming natural barriers to the movement of liquids or gases. Within the more porous layers are deposits of oil and natural gas, called reservoirs, often accompanied by salt, brine, or fresh water. These reservoirs are contained by denser, nonporous rock."

"I never heard of any oil wells in the Upper Peninsula." Kaisa said.

"You never heard of any copper or iron mines in the Lower Peninsula either." Lindberg said. "The mitten of the Lower Peninsula of Michigan sits almost in the center of this bowl-shaped basin, with the deepest part believed to be in the neighborhood of St. Louis and Alma. There drillers would need to sink well bores more than 17,000 feet to reach the rock of the Lake Superior Basin you can get out of your car and look up at in the Upper Peninsula.

"The lack of sedimentary rock in the Upper Peninsula makes it unlikely that oil and natural gas in commercial quantities exist there. Despite the odds, six holes have been drilled in the 'U.P.' but none has been found in commercial quantities."

"That's pretty confusing to somebody like me, who doesn't know anything about geology."Kaisa said.

Lindberg laughed, and continued. "That's the geologist's gobbledygook version. For lay folk, here is another way to picture Michigan's geology.

"Imagine a bowl of raisin bran, with the raisins representing the porous rock containing oil and natural gas. Some of the raisins are bigger while some are smaller. The bran symbolizes the denser rock that keeps the oil and natural gas inside the raisins. There is a lot more bran than raisins. Now, imagine several such bowls of raisin bran, each bowl a little smaller than the one underneath it, stacked together one inside the other like your mixing bowls in the kitchen. Picture the whole group of bowls scraped, layered and cluttered by glacial deposits then covered with a mitten-shaped piece of graph paper. Finally, take a jeweler's drill and try to hit a raisin. A petroleum landman friend of mine, Howard Pew, once heard me use this analogy and quipped 'and in Michigan we're blessed with two scoops of raisins!'"

"Now I understand a little better." Kaisa. "But how did they know where to look for oil here in Michigan?"

"Geologists suspected in the first years of the twentieth century that there was enough oil underneath Saginaw to make oil wells profitable." Lindberg stated. "Michigan's State Geologist Dr. A.C. Lane in the early 1900s observed 'uplift and folding' in Michigan geology between Bay City and Saginaw, which he believed indicated that oil was likely present. Dr. A.C. Smith, State Geologist, in the 1920s said 'Most of the evidence indicating favorable structure conditions for occurrence of oil and gas wells in the Saginaw region was derived from numerous comparatively shallow salt wells drilled along the Saginaw River, drawing brine from the upper Marshall Sandstone .... Apparently this fold ran slightly west and north through Saginaw near the Bristol Street Bridge."

The geologist, encouraged by Kaisa's attention, pressed on as they enjoyed the pleasant spring evening.

"In 1912 and 1913, a group of local capitalists and businessmen formed the Saginaw Valley Development Company to prospect for oil. During the group's second attempt, a hole near the geographical center of the city was treated with the downhole discharge of 100 quarts of nitroglycerine. According to newspaper reports, the well *'erupted with a spout of oil forty feet high from the mouth of the well and stood solid for four or five minutes' This spurt was followed a few minutes later by a second, higher column of oil that lasted about two minutes and also included natural gas. The excitement in Saginaw was spontaneous. Predictions were freely expressed that a new era of prosperity was opening for the Valley.'*

"The discovery well, along with eight others nearby, did not pan out commercially. Ultimately the Saginaw Valley Development Company ceased operations, sold its equipment and the efforts 'determined without reasonable doubt that oil was a myth in this locality.'"

"Pretty discouraging." Kaisa said. "Sounds like

some of the people my father used to talk about. They struck out on their own to find just enough copper to encourage them but not enough to make a mine that paid enough to make a living."

"Exactly." Lindberg replied, "Oil can be as elusive to find as copper. But a well, and the disappointment of not finding anything commercial, is faster to drill than a mine is to dig."

"Fortunately in Saginaw there were those willing to try again. James C. Graves, a Dow Chemical Company chemist closely followed the progress of Dow's brine wells with oil shows. He became acquainted with many Saginaw businessmen, some of whom made him president of the Saginaw Prospecting Company, formed in 1925 to revive the Saginaw area oil search. A test well started July 25, 1925, on city-owned property known as Deindorfer Woods on the north side of Weiss Street.

"On August 29, 1925, the Saginaw Prospecting well was drilled in as a success. The well produced an average of 23 barrels of oil per day for a few days, and averaged 17 barrels a day for the first 30 days. Company records show production from that Saginaw Field discovery well was 13 barrels of crude oil per day after 90 days, eight after one year and an average of six barrels per day the second year. These were not spectacular production rates but it was enough oil to be sold commercially. Michigan had arrived as a real oil and gas producing state.

"A little less than two years later, in December, 1927, a larger producing field was found in Muskegon."

"Good for Saginaw and Muskegon." Kaisa said, "But why is Mt. Pleasant such a hub of oilfield activity and those areas are not?"

"Good question," George replied

"The largest and most important of the nine new Michigan oilfields discovered in the 1920s was the Mt. Pleasant Field located on either side of the Isabella-Midland County line, largely in Chippewa and Greendale Townships. The Mt. Pleasant Field was critical in that it proved that oil discoveries in Saginaw and Muskegon counties were not Basin-flank flukes."

"What does that mean." Kaisa asked, holding up her right hand. "Show me."

Lindberg pointed to the juncture of her thumb and forefinger. "Saginaw is here." He ran his finger across her palm to the far left. "Muskegon is here," He put his finger in the center of her palm. "and Mt. Pleasant is here."

"Returning to the stacked bowls and raisin bran analogy, if the raisins containing oil are all found at the edges of the bowls, leaving only bran in the center of the bowl, a basin flank anomaly has occurred. Saginaw and Muskegon are on the upside edges of a basin. Finding oil in the Mt. Pleasant Field was critical because it demonstrated the presence of oil "raisins" are accessible throughout the Michigan Geological Basin rather than just on the Basin's periphery."

"But the town of Mt. Pleasant is nowhere near as large as Muskegon or Saginaw." Kaisa persisted.

"Yes, but the Mt. Pleasant Field was more prolific in production than either of those two. Besides, both Saginaw and Muskegon had larger populations and more commercially diverse than Mt. Pleasant. That's why the influx of people and money flow to the smaller town had more impact than on the two larger communities with more developed diverse economies.

"The *Mt. Pleasant Times* of February 27, 1928, reported the discovery of oil in the Pure Oil Company Laura Root #1 well under a headline reading "CLAIM BEST OIL

STRIKE IN THE STATE". The newspaper reported that the strike involved "50 to 60 feet of oil sand." The story said that Pure at the time had about 80,000 acres under lease in the vicinity of the well and others had leased 25,000 acres. In point of fact the strike was the richest of the decade and the fourth largest in the history of the Michigan oil and gas industry.

"For the next several weeks Pure went about the task of getting the well ready for production, while continuing to drill in the area. Ultimately, the company would build their own drilling-housing-office complex just south of M-20, just into Midland County, so workers would not have to deal with weather and dirt roads to get to the fields that grew up on the company's vast Central Michigan lease holding. Retail operations to serve those workers began nearby and led to establishment of the town of Oil City in Midland County.

"The Mt. Pleasant newspaper later noted that local citizens Walter Russell and Fred Stilgenbauer helped Pure obtain pipeline right of way to Mt. Pleasant. Pure built a pipeline to the Mt. Pleasant railhead and on July 3, 1928, the firm started to sell oil to Imperial Refining, Sarnia, Ontario via rail shipment from Mt. Pleasant.

"Mt. Pleasant became a boomtown where oilmen were very welcome. In 1929, just before you joined us from the Upper Peninsula, Kaisa, the Mt. Pleasant Rotary Club hosted a welcome banquet with 40 oilmen as their guests. The city is known as the 'Oil Capital of Michigan.' The town flourished with new residents, new housing, new businesses and best of all, new money

"Mt. Pleasant became a hub of Michigan petroleum activity, first as an accident of geology and later as a convenience of geography. The community lies close to the geographical center of the "mitten", so it is located equal distance from anywhere in the Lower Peninsula. Primary oil and gas explorationists, petroleum supply and service companies, and drilling contractors all headquartered in Mt. Pleasant. Others soon came to try their luck in search of oil and gas."

Lindberg stood up to go to bed. "So now you know as much about why we're here as I do. For the future, well, we will see. The only certainty in this business is you can't be certain of anything until the oil's in the tank and the check for it is safely in the bank."

"Thank you." Kaisa said."I understand what's happening here much better now.

"That's good to know." Lindberg said, smiling. "because I was using you as a guinea pig. I have a speech to give at the college next week and you've been a great sounding board. We'll talk again, Kaisa."

They never did.

Lindberg found a house three days later and moved out in a week when his wife arrived from Lansing.

Kaisa thought about the nearly two years she had lived here in Mt. Pleasant, and of the friends she made at Sacred Heart Academy. Uncle Jalo had taken her to the Roman Catholic school when she first arrived in October, 1929. Though she was a few weeks late from the start of the school year, the nuns at Sacred Heart had tested her and determined that her previous schooling and self-gained knowledge was sufficient to allow her to sidestep the ninth grade enrolled her as a sophomore in high school.

She fell asleep thinking of her mother's skill as a teacher and hoping she could live up to Katrina's heritage as an educator.

Sometime later she awoke, suddenly aware of another presence on the dark porch.

"Don't start, lass" the unmistakable Irish brogue of Mickey Conroy whispered. "Shhhhh. It is but I, come to talk with ya."

"What do you want? Kaisa said in a low voice.

"You been a lot on my mind lately." Mickey said. "I never met anybody quite like ya. You're bright. You're so damn bright and mature along with bein' a lot easier to look at than any other gal I ever met. I'm thinkin' about you every minute. and don't ya know, if this well comes in tomorra Big Walt McClanahan has promised all us drillers a bonus. I never had a bonus before and I was thinkin' it might be enough to get a place a' my own an' you and me could get hitched and I could get a job in town and quit this roamin' life of a driftin' driller."

Taken aback, Kaisa whispered. "Mickey, I'm only sixteen."

"And so? I know grammas ain't got as much on the ball than you. Besides, in the old country, ye'd damn near be thought of as an old maid by now."

"Besides," Kaisa continued, "I'm planning to finish high school this coming year and go to Central State Teachers College here in town for a teaching certificate so I can teach like my mother."

"No worries" Conroy said quickly. "I can get a job with one of the oilfield supply outfits and you can go to school and we'll have a great life here." He already knew about the regular payments she had coming in from her late parents share of a copper mine up north. They could live on that if he decided daily toil was too confining to his adventurous spirit.

"Let's just wait and see what happens tomorrow." Kaisa said, flattered at the attention of the dashing man of the world, but reluctant to give up her dreams of travel and seeking a place in the wider world. She already decided she would teach here a few years then move on to somewhere bigger.

He took her in his arms, holding her tightly in a long breathless kiss as he drew her closer, then began sliding her nightdress higher. Kaisa felt her breathing shorten and her body tingle with excitement.

"Mickey ….. I've never….."

"I have," he gasped. "I know the way…."

12

Greendale Township, Isabella County, Michigan – late afternoon Saturday, July 18, 1931

The long flat swampy and scrub brush-lined twenty-seven mile stretch of road between Midland and Mt. Pleasant, Michigan was spanned by a dirt state highway designated Michigan highway M-20. A couple hundred yards south of M-20 four miles east of the Midland-Isabella County line, Jalo Koistinen and Mickey Conroy and the rest of the drilling crew on the Walter L. Mc Clanahan A. C. Struble #1 sweltered in the sun while battling swarms of mosquitoes. All afternoon, the normally isolated wellsite became crowded with townspeople, many of whom had a small interest in the well. Word was spreading that the well was a success and that "hardluck" Walter McClanahan was about to see his luck change.

"Damn mosquitoes are bad enough," Jalo Koistinen said as he, Mickey Conroy and the rest of the drilling crew, stemmed the flow of the "gusher" of oil with a valve at the wellhead and prepared to divert it to the storage tanks. "But these lookie-loos are cloggin' up the lease road and beginnin' to get in the way."

"Oh calm down." Mickey replied "T'was not so very long ago ya were tellin' me not to put the curse on this hole and now yer complainin' that it looks like McClanahan is going to get his due. Don't ferget, so are we, with the bonus he promised us fer bringing' this steamin' she-devil in. It is lookin' good and could end this short spell 'o dry holes they been havin' around here lately." Conroy went back to his work, whistling to himself and smiling at the thought about his encounter with Kaisa in the pre-dawn hours of the day.

People continued to arrive. It was customary for big crowds of investors, potential investors, townspeople, reporters and petroleum explorers' families to turn out to see a well "come in". A recent shortage of good wells made the rumored impending success of McClanahan's Struble 1 a larger attraction than usual.

Following the 1928 Pure Oil Co. oil discovery of the Mt. Pleasant Field in Section 18 of Greendale Township, Midland County, about four miles southeast of the McClanahan location, drilling in central Michigan proliferated. Offsets were drilled farm to farm in Isabella County's Chippewa and Denver Townships as well as in other Sections of Greendale Township. The success ratio on the 10-acre locations was extremely high in the 3,500 foot Dundee Formation wells, with initial flows from 800 barrels to 4,000 barrels per day. State proration, which would limit daily oil production to conserve reservoir dynamics and extend the productive life of wells, was still eight years away so the only limit to daily flow rates was the size capacity of the pipeline.

Overproduction became such a problem that oil prices fell steadily, at one time reaching twenty-nine cents a barrel. Operators attempted a "driller's holiday," a period in which it was agreed no new wildcat wells would be started, but few kept the agreement. In September 1929, Mt. Pleasant Field production was reported at 6,000 barrels per day.

Drilling slowed appreciably in the Mt. Pleasant area by the end of 1930, with activity moving northeast and southeasterly from the discovery well and its offsets. Speculation began the two year drilling boom near Mt. Pleasant was ending.

Then an oil discovery was made in Section 15 of Greendale Township, extending the oil field three miles to the east. The 800 barrel per day well revived drilling activity and caused many to take a second look at areas that had fallen short of initial test expectations, places like Jasper, Yost, and Porter Townships, southeast of the Mt. Pleasant Field.

One of those early 1931 wells drilled in the aftermath of the Section 15 discovery was the A.G. Struble 1 in Section 10, Greendale Township, Midland County, about thirteen miles from Mt. Pleasant. Drilling Permit No. 1164 was issued to Walter L. McClanahan on May 15, 1931, when the Michigan process of issuing oil and gas drilling permit was only four years old.

McClanahan, a tall Tennessean with a southern drawl and engaging nature, was among the independent operators who were attracted to Mt. Pleasant in the early 1930s as development slowed down in the 1925 Saginaw and 1927 Muskegon Fields, where he had no luck. At 45, he had made the rounds of oil country in Mexico, Oklahoma, Kansas, Kentucky, and Texas without much success. In fact he was often referred to as "Hard Luck Mac" in newspaper stories and oilfield parlance of the time. Despite the hard luck moniker, he managed to have a summer home near Grayling, Michigan, and a winter home in Sea Island, Georgia.

In putting the Struble prospect together, he had attracted investment monies from some of the Roosevelt Refinery people and a good number of local Mt. Pleasant interests. As Mt. Pleasant's *Isabella County Times-News* reporter Norman X. Lyon said of the middle of Michigan drilling boom *"It is a time when lawyers, shopkeepers, doctors and schoolteachers were eager to invest. Many had already taken a flyer in oil deals and were winners before McClanahan arrived in town."*

The Struble #1 commenced drilling on May 27, 1931 and by mid-July had reached a total depth of 3,545 feet in the Dundee geological formation. Two 500-barrel tanks had been erected on July 16 and by the July 18, the rig floor was crowded with well-wishers and investors. Once oil started to flow to the tanks, at an estimated rate of 100 barrels an hour, the crowd moved toward the storage tanks to better view the gauge.

High natural gas content accompanied the oil and settled in the sultry heavy atmosphere around the Struble site. Cars were parked far away down the lease road, most metal surfaces were covered with cloth and, naturally, smoking was prohibited, lest a spark ignite the errant gas.

On the rig floor, the excitement was infectious. Walter McClanahan hosted several of the most prominent investors close to valve that would send the oil rushing to the tanks. Jalo and Mickey prepared to open those valves.

"Hoooray!" Mickey Conroy yelled as he opened the valve. The crowd surged forward, toward the tank, to watch the of oil level climb on the outside gauges measuring the level of fluid in the tank. Mickey and Jalo were almost alone as all attention shifted to the tanks.

"We're in the money, Jalo old sock." Mickey shouted, "Bonus money for me to shake the dust 'o the oilpatch off me feet and head for friendlier climes."

"Man, I'm glad Mina and Kaisa decided to go shopping today instead of coming out to be part of this mess. Mina pegged it right: 'hot, sticky, loud and stinkin' she said.' Told me I could tell her all about it when I get home tonight. What's all this talk about hittin' the road. Thought you had oil in your veins," Jalo replied. "I even heard you were thinkin' of settling down here."

"Not me, laddie." Conroy replied. "That's just some blarney I sometimes lay down to get the ladies to do the same. Soon as I got my bonus money, there's places to be seen, beer to be drunk and women to love in far better places than this."

"So that's why you've been grinnin' like a dieter with a *paistettuti hoistoon*, a baked treat, all day."

"That's part of it, m'lad, that's part of it."

"It better not be havin' anything to do with Kaisa. I know she's taken a shine to you and she's young enough to be led astray, even if she looks and acts like a woman. You best be leavin' her alone"

"Too late, me bucko," Conroy smirked, "That ship already sailed ... early this very morn."

"*Senkin narttu*," Jalo Koistinen growled, "You son of a bitch." He lunged toward the Irishman and swung a fist toward his smiling face. Conley ducked, slipped on the deck and fell, his belt buckle clipping an uncoated bolt at the edge of the valve, striking a spark.

Natural gas blanketing the crowded well site erupted into a flash ball of flame.

Jalo Koistinen and Mickey Conley died instantly and more than thirty people were injured in the flash blast that lasted only seconds. Within twenty-four hours, nine more adults, including two pregnant women and one child succumbed. Eleven more were injured.

Official victim list from the tragedy included:

DEAD:

Conroy, Mickey, 22, Mt. Pleasant, driller.

Fugate, Marion, *28*, Mt. Pleasant oilfield scout associated with Mr. McClanahan and brother of Mrs. W. L. McClanahan.

Gorham, Arwin E., *63*, prominent Mt. Pleasant manufacturer, who had come to town with the original Gorham Brothers in 1888 when they transferred their business interests from Ohio to Mt. Pleasant.

Guy, Mrs. E. J., *45*, wife of Mt. Pleasant's Roosevelt Oil Company Superintendent.

Guy, Mrs. Robert C., *18*, Mt. Pleasant., wife of Roosevelt Oil Company employee and **her unborn baby**. Daughter-in-law of Mrs. E. J. Guy.

Koistinen, Jalo, 45, Mt. Pleasant, driller.

Lamb, Thomas, *28,* Mt. Pleasant, oil worker.

Lamb, Mrs. Thomas, *25,* Mt. Pleasant, wife of oil worker, and **her unborn baby**.

McClanahan, Mary Lucy, *35*, Mt. Pleasant, wife of well owner Walter Lee McClanahan.

Melvin, Ruby, *13,* Greendale Township, Midland County.

Whittekind, Mrs. H. E., *35,* Mt. Pleasant, wife of oil worker.

CRITICALLY INJURED:

Guy, E. J., *45*, Mt. Pleasant's Roosevelt Oil Company Superintendent.

Guy, Robert C., *20*, Mt. Pleasant., Roosevelt Oil Company employee and son of E. J. Guy.

McClanahan, Walter Lee, *45,* Mt. Pleasant, oil well owner and operator.

Melvin, John, *40,* Greendale Township, Midland County.

INJURED:

Cropsey, Charles, Mt. Pleasant.

Cowden, Harry, *30,* Mt. Pleasant.

Fitzgerald, Paul, *32,* Mt. Pleasant High School Teacher.

Hobson, Glen, *22,* Mt. Pleasant, employee of Roosevelt
Refinery and brother of Mrs. E. J. Guy.

Kelley, George, Mt. Pleasant oilfield worker.

Kelley, Mrs., Mt. Pleasant, wife of oilfield worker

Luce, Don, *25,* Mt. Pleasant.

The flash explosion left chaos in its wake. Most of
the workers who would know what to do were dead or injured and the great stampede to escape in case the well itself
exploded blanked out reason.

Later McClanahan's daughter would tell of the day
in her small green notebook journal entitled *Schoolbook
Memories bringing back pleasant memories of happy hours
spent in work and play.* Marion told of her mother picking
her up at a movie theater in town that afternoon and rushing
her to her father's latest well thirteen miles away, while telling her excitedly "This is the greatest day in our lives. No
more moving all the time. No more driving all over Oklahoma. Your daddy has brought a well in …. It's a big one
…. It's a huge one …. We're rich!"

Mary Lucy McClanahan continued babbling about
the glorious future ahead for the family as they arrived at the
site of the well. The sound of shouting and the smell of oil
and gas was everywhere. "I don't want you going up that
road, sweetie, it's a sea of mud. You might slip and you'd
get all filthy. I am going to go up the road and get your dad-

dy so we can drive back to town and have our own private celebration." She went off up the muddy road with the drilling superintendent's wife behind her, waving and cheering."

Minutes later, restless sitting in the hot car, Marion opened the car door and was stepping out when the well blew.

There was one great roar like thunder and the sky turned bright orange, Marion recalled. Then a fierce gust of wind came through and there was smoke everywhere in thick black waves while the branches of the trees suddenly sprouted blossoms of flame. People came running out of the trees with flames on their hair and clothing, howling, screaming, stumbling and falling. The daughter of a drilling crew member came out with her new dress aflame.

Walter McClanahan came out of the copse, looking around wildly shouting "Where is Mary Lucy?", then turned and ran back into the melee to look for her.

Mary Lucy McClanahan staggered out of the woods, all on fire, pleading "Don't let Marion see me like this." She fell and died later at the hospital in town.

Mary Lucy's brother, Marion Fugate, ran up to his niece and said "Sweetie, beat the fire off the seat of my pants." Marion picked up a dead leafy branch to beat out the flames. Fugate fell down near his sister and, like her, died later at the hospital in town.

There was little sleep in Mt. Pleasant that night with the streets filled with people, Mina and Kaisa Koistinen among them, wandering, asking for the latest news, crying, praying and speculating on how many names of friends and relatives would be in the Sunday newspaper as victims of the explosion. Some wondered how much the investors would make out of the well when it came into operation and what it would mean to the community.

Marion McClanahan wandered almost ignored among them until Kaisa recognized her from school and she with Aunt Mina offered a room for the night to get some rest. Later in the evening they confirmed the deaths of Jalo and Mickey. In the morning they told Marion of the death of her mother and uncle and offered to take her to her father, who was burned all over and not expected to survive. Wrapped in bandages except for part of his face blackened by the tannic acid used for treatment of third degree burns, McClanahan told his daughter "I know I've killed your mother and a lot of other people .... and I know they have told you I am going to die. But I am not going to."

He didn't.

In the aftermath of the blast, no one thought to shut down the oil flow to the tanks. Sometime during Saturday night, oil overflowed the two 500 barrel storage tank and the fire gnawed its way along the lead lines to the well head and ignited the well. By Sunday morning, smoke climbed hundreds of feet into the air, supported by a column of raw flame a hundred feet tall. The steel rig was a melted, twisted pile of steel lying around the hole.

McClanahan and Roosevelt employees, along with volunteers from other companies working in the area comprised a hastily assembled firefighting crew. They brought in steam boilers, water pumps, a field tractor, farm tractors, cutting torches, cables and hooks. It took three days to extinguish the flames by playing streams of steam and water across the "blowtorching" well control head.

A coroner's inquest ruled that the explosion was an accident. Recovered, Walter McClanahan settled generously with families of the victims. No next of kin for Mickey Conway was ever located.

Aunt Mina received survivors' benefits from the fire

for Uncle Jalo from McClanahan's company. A few weeks later, Kaisa's claim for survivors benefits as Mickey's wife fell on deaf ears of McClanahan, his attorneys and accountants, because of a lack of legal papers. Besides, thehe McClanahan company said, the claim was filed too late.

When she found herself pregnant with Mickey Conroy's child, Kaisa and Mina had concocted the story of a secret marriage two weeks before the Struble well fire after she discovered her pregnancy with Mickey Conroy's child. after he and her Uncle Jalo died.

Kaisa's life changed dramatically.

Obviously, there was no returning to Sacred Heart Academy to complete her senior year in high school in the 1931-1932 school year. Her son Mickey Erik arrived February 17, 1932, with a mix of her blonde and Mickey's red hair crowning his little head with a strawberry fuzz.

She was enraptured in motherhood.

She was also fascinated with a tender emotion she'd never felt before. Aunt Mina laughed when Kaisa described the feeling to her.

"You poor silly girl." Aunt Mina said "You are feeling love. I am so sorry it's taken this long in your life to feel it."

She was right, Kaisa finally realized. All of her life she had observed, laughed, gathered information, analyzed and felt affinity to some things and people, but this warm feeling of wellbeing she felt holding her baby introduced her to a new spectrum of feeling.

So this is love, she thought. Not bad.

That autumn, while she cared for her son, a new boarder arrived at Aunt Mina's boarding house to change her life again.

13

Mt. Pleasant, Michigan – morning
Monday, September 23, 1935

"Good morning, Michigan Oil & Gas News," twenty-year-old Kaisa Conroy, Office Manager, said into the telephone as she watched a crowd gather in front of the South Main Street offices of the weekly Michigan oilfield reporting magazine. "Yes, the parade is at noon."

This was probably the fiftieth time she had answered that question this morning. If she didn't put up the *"Closed for opening day of the First Annual Michigan Oil and Gas Exposition"* sign on the front door soon, she was going to miss the opening parade of the exposition she and her company had been helping co-ordinate for more than a year. If the publication still headquartered upstairs at 106 ½ South Main, as they were until last month, she would be able to see the parade and the entire main intersection of downtown Mt. Pleasant, Michigan, from the front windows of the office. But the bosses had moved downstairs to this temporary address to be more visible during the Exposition and to make the upcoming move to their headquarters in a house at 214 North Franklin easier when it came at the end of the year. The presses for the publication had already moved from upstairs to the new building. Two years of printing in the sixty year-old historic downtown brick building began extracting a toll on the structure with each press run and there was fear by the building's owner, as well as her bosses, that the floor would collapse if printing upstairs continued. So the *Michigan Oil & Gas News*, MOGN for short, headquarters office was temporarily jammed between Minto Bolton Clothing & Shoes and Butts Drug Store.

"Closed" sign in hand, she headed toward the door, just as the telephone rang again.

"Good morning, Michigan Oil and Gas News. Yes, it is a proud day for Mt. Pleasant to be celebrating the tenth year of Michigan as an oil state. Yes, the parade is at noon. You're welcome. Good-bye."

The phone no more than hit its cradle than it rang again.

"Good Morning ...."

"It's me." Kaisa's friend Ruth Collins, secretary for the year-old Oil and Gas Association of Michigan, officed down the street in the Hersee Building at the corner of Broadway and Franklin streets, said quickly. "I'm leaving right now. I'll meet you at the corner of Broadway and Main. The streets sure are decked out with bunting and I can hear the band warming up over by the high school so we'd better hurry."

"I'm on the way."

Kaisa grabbed an armload of the thirty-six page tabloid *Oil & Gas News "Exposition Number"*, which replaced the normal eight page weekly issue for the current week. In its two short years in publication the "Oil News", as everyone referred to it, had become the "bible of the Michigan oilpatch". The newspaper reported weekly on every hole drilled in the state from the time a drilling permit was applied for with the State Department of Conservation Geo-

logical Survey Division until the well was completed and
the result known. If a the resulting well came in as a "producer", MOGN reported oil and/or natural production vol-
umes. Additionally, the newspaper reported pipeline construction, legislative action and regulatory happenings af-
fecting the Michigan and national oil and gas exploration
and production industry. In the "Man About Townships"
weekly column, the Oil News got gossipy with items including everyday happenings such as new business openings;
industry related organization news; comings and goings (vacation and otherwise); how many and what kind of fish a
member of the "oil fraternity" caught; sometimes births and
marriages, but always deaths.

All-in-all, the founders of the *Michigan Oil and Gas
News* met their goals, turning the weekly publication into
the "hometown newspaper of the statewide oil industry."

Kaisa mentally reviewed the past three years.

James Patrick Dunnigan was a round-faced Irishman
of twenty-two years old who had recently graduated from
Wayne State College near Detroit. Dunnigan served as Editor nearly every publication on campus, including the *Daily
Collegian* during his four years at Wayne State. He had become fascinated with the oil industry while working the last
two summers of his college years in the oilfields of Oklahoma and Texas with his friend and classmate Danny Miller. Miller's father, was head of natural gas development for
Carter Oil Company, a subsidiary of Standard Oil Company,
active in Michigan's fledgling oil and gas exploration and
development industry. The elder Miller closely followed
news of the 1931 Struble 1 well fire, appalled by the lack of
knowledge of the oil industry reflected by the press coverage of the disaster. He urged his son and classmates Jim
Dunnigan and Lou Aaronson, whose family owned a print-

ing company in Detroit, to start an oil reporting paper when they graduated Wayne State. They began to discuss the idea of a Michigan oilfield reporting publication. There had been a couple of short-lived attempts at such a venture by under-financed itinerants, some of which left a bad taste in the mouths of many in the industry.

With so many oil field exploration and development projects proposed and underway throughout the Michigan "oilpatch," oilfolk needed a way to keep up with the action. Local newspapers filled some of the information gap but local papers were, by their nature, not interested in the broader, statewide story. Moreover, local reporters lacked real knowledge of the industry to help filter true happenings from the promoter's hype.

Through a friend of a friend, Dunnigan made contact with John P. Murphy. Murphy, a Mt. Pleasant local whose early thoughts and training were about a career teaching or in the priesthood, quickly developed an interest in creating an oilfield reporting publication.

In late 1932, Dunnigan came to Mt. Pleasant, the "oil capitol of Michigan", to discuss the venture with Murphy on behalf of a number of potential investors. Finding the hotels full, Dunnigan shopped other lodgings until he found a room at Aunt Mina's. Through conversations with Kaisa during his stay, prompted by the blatantly Irish appearance of her son in contrast to her obviously Nordic visage and name, they became friends. He was impressed by her quick intelligence, ambition, sense of history of the oil business, and determination to raise her child and finish high school. He kept the plucky Finnish/Dutch girl in mind as plans for the oil reporting publication took shape.

Jim Dunnigan, Danny Miller, Lou Aaronson and John Murphy, created Petroleum Publishers, Inc., on a shoestring. All were reporters, with Dunnigan as editor and publisher, Aaronson as Business Manager, Miller as a Production Manager, Murphy as advertising Manager and new Mt. Pleasant High School graduate Kaisa Conroy as office manager. They published the first issue of the Mt. Pleasant, Michigan's weekly *Oil & Gas News* on June 20, 1933. Besides a number of field stories, the front page of that first issue, carried a message from the owners saying *"We want to give you a service that you need; in return we expect but moderate compensation and your enthusiastic support. An honest living and the feeling we have served, and well, are all the rewards we seek."*

At first the start-up publication was headquartered in a hotel room at the Park Hotel, where the three out of towners lived and produced the publication, trading advertising space in their newspaper for a room at the hotel owned by Bert Creed. It was a year before they could afford to rent office space in a building half a block south of the hotel.

June, 1933, had been life-changing for Kaisa. She graduated from Mt. Pleasant High School and immediately put her study emphasis skills, typing, mathematics and business to work as Office Manager for the fledgling publication. She organized data for the publication, made countless calls to drilling contractors and oil producers to help assemble the weekly drilling report, answered the telephone, took subscription and advertising orders and delivered copies of the paper to local retailers.

For a while, Aunt Mina watched Mickey while Kaisa worked, but she fell ill and died suddenly, many said of a broken heart, pining for her beloved husband Jalo. Having no children of her own, Mina left the house on Fancher Street and her financial assets to her niece Kaisa. At eighteen, Kaisa owned a boardinghouse with property, was deeply involved in an exciting new business reporting to a rough and tumble fascinating business of underground explorers and was a working mother.

She hired a slightly older woman, whose oil driller husband had run off with a waitress at the Rathskeller in the basement of the Bennett Hotel, as a live-in housekeeper, cook, boardinghouse manager and babysitter for room and board and a small salary. Sarah Boranski was a gem. Kaisa and her new hire were close in age and quickly became friends. Kaisa's monthly check from the Delaware Last Chance copper mine continued to arrive, though growing smaller as the price of copper dropped. It was enough to pay Sarah with a little left over. Revenue from the boardinghouse and her job enabled her to keep a respectable balance in her savings account.

The first issues of the *Oil & Gas News* were "farmed out" for printing with the local newspaper and were printed in the broadsheet newspaper format. Early in the game Murphy decided the future of the oil and gas industry looked good enough to expand the publication. Incorporation and stock sales followed in order to purchase a printing plant that would enable them to print not only the weekly publication but to become a specialized printer of oil leases and other forms used by the oil exploration business. In due course, the printing press was purchased and installed in upstairs quarters downtown, changing the size of the weekly publication to an eight-page tabloid format.

The publication, with the Michigan oil and gas industry, continued to grow. Local newspaper reporters Lindy Davis and Norman X. Lyon, who had diligently reported the 1931 Struble fire for the local newspaper as well as state and national newspapers, began to contribute articles to MOGN and reporting "stringers" were established in "hot" development areas throughout the state. Lyon, from southwest Michigan, had taken the local reporter job at the local paper to "fill in for a while" in 1929, "A while" was still going strong in 1935.

"Booo! Welcome back to the world." Ruth Collins said as she caught up to Kaisa at the main corner of town. "Whew what a crowd. I was going to suggest we go to lunch before we go down to the park but the Snow White Bakery, the Olympia and the Downtown Restaurant were all packed when I came by. We'll have to take our chances on concession food at the Exposition."

Both Ruth and Kaisa would be spending the rest of the day and evening in their respective organizations' booths at the exposition. Ruth, who had been a year behind Kaisa in high school at Sacred Heart, had remained her friend through school and beyond. Ruth had used Kaisa as a reference when she applied for a secretary's job at the newly established Michigan Oil and Gas Association early last year.

Prior to the founding of the present Michigan Oil and Gas Association, a group of petroleum folk in the Muskegon area formed an organization in a 1928 attempt to establish higher crude oil prices. E. J. Bouwsma, a Muskegon Oil Company employee, was the group's president. However, as the boom at Muskegon subsided and the 1928 Mt. Pleasant Field became the industry's focus, the Muskegon-based association faded away.

The problems that bedeviled Muskegon oil producers, particularly overproduction, caused slumping crude oil prices, soon became a problem in the Central Michigan oil fields. To deal with these problems, producers in Central Michigan, along with those from Muskegon and Saginaw, met in Mt. Pleasant and formed the Oil and Gas Producers Association in 1931. Newly arrived oil attorney Haswell Grant became the group's President. That association was phased out when its leaders decided to reorganize with a broader member base and a better dues structure.

This broader, better financed organization, the Michigan Oil and Gas Association took shape. At a November 27, 1933 meeting, the newly formed MOGA elected Gordon Oil's Howard D. Atha President. Harry G. Hunt left the Saginaw News to become the first Michigan Oil and Gas Association Executive Secretary. He in turn needed a secretary and came to the Oil & Gas News to place an advertisement of the position. Kaisa suggested her friend Ruth, who was hired immediately.

Together they crossed Broadway north on Main Street so they would have easier access to the 401 North Main Street entrance to Island Park at the west terminus of Lincoln Street. For almost two weeks the 50 acre park had been alive with activity as more than seventy-five exhibitors assembled their exhibits for the Exhibition.

Island Park was in itself a tourist attraction to Mt. Pleasant. Within the town, the Chippewa River followed the bluff where downtown was located. In doing so, the river described a huge backward "C" two-thirds surrounding a meadow-like flatland to the west toward the Ann Arbor Railroad grade and another bluff containing the city's Riverside Cemetery. The flatland, owned by Isaac A. Fancher in the city's early days, was at one time used to graze Mt. Pleasant's urban cowherd. Fancher paid a boy to gather and herd city residents' cows in the morning, graze them on the Flats and have them back home for evening milking.

H. Edward Deuel was the 11th – 1903-05, 15th – 1909-10, 17th – 1912 and 19th – 1914-1915 Mayor of the

City of Mt. Pleasant. The flatland known alternately as Fancher's Meadows, Fancher's Flats and Fancher's Grove, served by a wooden bridge, was purchased by the City in 1909. A canal dug at the west side of the newly acquired lands made it "Island Park". A cement span bridge replaced the wooden bridge, moved to the southwest boundary of the park, now known as Oak Street Bridge.

Deuel pushed for a grandstand and racetrack for the new park and persuaded the Isabella County Fair Board to move their event there. The Fair had been homeless since selling their grounds on the north end of Fancher Street to Dow Chemical Company in 1900. The annual Isabella County Fair had now taken place at Island Park each August for twenty-five years. The venue now boasted several ball parks, tennis courts and was used for family outings and re-unions. The Grand Army of the Republic (G.A.R) for a number of years used the Fancher Flats/Island Park property for a week-long annual encampment of Civil War veterans and their families called Camp Sheridan. Families of the local Civil War veterans formed the Women's Relief Corps.

Leading the Wo-ba-no Chapter of the G. A. R. contingent in the parade was Kaisa's neighbor eighty-eight year-old Daniel Buckley, walking hand-in-hand with his wife, forty-eight year-old Nan Buckley, a leader of the Mt. Pleasant Women's Relief Corps.

The Buckley family lived three houses south of Kiasa and she had heard their story several times. Dan Buckley, born in 1845 in Ontario, ran away to Michigan early in life. He apprenticed to a tailor, a trade he hated. After driving horses to St. Louis, Missouri with a crew he joined at Detroit, Buckley was hired by the U. S. Government as a teamster. After the Civil War, in the U.S. Army, Buckley fought frontier battles while on garrison duty in the

American West. He served as a scout of the famous Seventh Cavalry, under the command of General Custer during Custer's first trip to the western plains. Buckley left the army in 1872, missing Custer's Battle of the Bighorn by six years. Working several lumber camps in Michigan, Buckley bought property in Isabella County, cleared it and started life as a farmer. His first wife died in 1905 and in 1907, at sixty years-old, he married twenty year-old Nancy "Nan" Ann McClain. Daniel Buckley's second family started with the birth of her son Herman. In 1914 he sold the farm and bought the house on Fancher Street.

Kaisa and Ruth watched the parade advance west on Broadway, led by a horse-drawn hearse with drivers in full livery. The hearse bore an effigy of "Ole Man Depression" to symbolize that an active oil and natural gas exploration and production industry had shielded the area from the Great Depression. Kaisa knew that at the bridge at the Main Street park entrance three blocks away, "Ole Man Depression" would be committed to a watery grave in the Chippewa River. The hearse paused beside them while *Isabella County Times News* reporter Norm Lyon took a picture. Kaisa looked forward to the time the Oil News would have a photographer.

Behind the hearse, the Mt. Pleasant High School Band led a procession of vehicles bearing local and oil industry dignitaries, supply and service equipment, floats from Mt. Pleasant and other Michigan towns in areas where the oil industry flourished, an assortment of politicians and exposure-seeking organizations, with the Central Michigan Teachers College Band bringing up the rear. As the parade turned north on Main, the crowd disassembled, Kaisa and Ruth rushed to their booths.

14

First Annual Michigan Oil and Gas Exposition opening day, Island Park, Mt. Pleasant, Michigan – late afternoon Monday, September 23, 1935

"Michigan is today first in the production of oil among all the states east of the Mississippi, outranking even Pennsylvania and Ohio." The booming amplified voice of P. J. Hoffmaster, Director of the Michigan Department of Conservation (official oil and gas industry regulatory body) reached Kaisa from the podium of the stage set up at the head of the Oil & Gas Exposition Midway. She heard most of the speeches from her vantage point in a specially built five hundred barrel tank fashioned into a kiosk for the Michigan *Oil & Gas News*. She listened as closely as possible as she handed out copies of the special Exposition edition, containing a subscription form, of course, and chatted with excited first day attendees.

The Exposition opening ceremonies were taking place just a few yards from her.

"Since 1925, approximately 3,000 wells have been

drilled in the state." Hoffmaster continued his welcome address. *"The year 1929 set a record for drilling permits issued by the Department. In 1934, this record was almost equalled. We confidently expect this year will see a new record established.*

"October 1, just one week hence, Michigan will have produced fifty million barrels of oil in its ten year career as a petroleum producing state...

"Michigan today has eleven oil fields and five natural gas fields and the experts tell us we can expect at least twenty more based on our present knowledge of Michigan geology, which grows daily. The oil industry today is Michigan's fastest growing industry ..... It has been of great importance not only in communities where the development has taken place but to the entire state. Farmers and other landowners have been aided by royalties and lease rentals. The industry has helped villages and towns through the construction of new homes and businesses.

"It is estimated that somewhere between forty-five hundred and five thousand people are directly employed in the production and refining oil and gas in this state. This means that about twenty thousand people supported by the industry. I submit to you this is a substantial number ...."

Kaisa's speech listening was interrupted by the approach of the smiling countenance of a tall smiling man and his entourage.

"Good afternoon, little lady." Walter McClanahan said in a soft southern accent. "Are your employers about? I have another announcement they may find interesting."

Kaisa smiled through gritted teeth. Despite the fact that she was the publication's office manager and handled as much field news and rig calls and statistics as any of her bosses of reporters, McClanahan continued to dismiss her as lowly hired help...... and she hated being called "little lady."

"I'm sorry, Mr. McClanahan, this is a very busy day for all of us but I'll let them know you have something important for them. Mr. Murphy and Mr. Aaronson are here somewhere."

"Did Jim Dunnigan come up from Detroit for this event? I'd really like to discuss some issues with the big boss. Things get done so much quicker when I deal with the top man."

Walter L. McClanahan received hero's treatment over the significant oil discovery flagged by the Struble #1. The Struble well flowed oil at a high rate of more than 500 barrels per day without letup from July 18, 1931 drill-in until May 27, 1932. McClanahan drilled three more wells on the Struble lease, all of which were successful.

As was his wont. McClanahan apparently "jumped the fortune gun" by taking a cash in advance deal with Socony White Star Refining for a quarter million barrels of oil from his Greendale Township, Midland County leases. But production declined and he was forced to default before full delivery. By that time his other ventures were apparently successful enough for him to stand the hit.

Nonetheless, his fame and fortune were made and he was involved in a number of wells in the Porter, West Branch and Crystal fields. During his moneyed days, he was generous and quick to host industry friends and groups at his homes near Grayling and on Sea Island, Georgia. A master of public relations, the charming McClanahan loved to see his name in print.

"No matter," McClanahan said, moving on with the troupe of followers, "in a few weeks I'll be able to shout out my back window to get 'hold of Mr. Aaronson." McClanahan's offices were in the 200 block of North Court Street and were, indeed, just a block west of the new Oil News building.

"Oh, goodie." Kaisa sarcastically muttered to herself before returning her attention to the speeches of the opening ceremonies. Though she knew McClanahan knew who she was and that she had lost her uncle and alleged husband, he had never once expressed to her any sympathy for her dual loss in his Struble well fire four years ago.

Returning her attention to the stage at the entrance to the exposition, Kaisa noted that Conservation Director Hoffmaster was wrapping up his speech and she watched as he took his seat among the dignitaries on the platform. Seated there were: Hoffmaster; Harold Atha, President of Gordon Oil Company and the Oil and Gas Association of Michigan; Joseph P. Carey, Central State Teachers College Geography Department head, Chair of the Mt. Pleasant Planning Commission and Secretary of the Oil and Gas Exposition; William Cline Vice President of Lupher Drilling Company, Mt. Pleasant; Harry Gover, Mt. Pleasant retailer and President of the Mt. Pleasant Chamber of Commerce; and Roy Taylor of Taylor Oil Company, Mt. Pleasant and Chairman of the Exposition Committee.

Taylor was concluding the final welcoming speech before formal opening of the Exposition. *"Mt. Pleasant has opened its gates to the throngs who fill our town from throughout the state and nation. Michigan crude oil, its products and its interests are rising to great national importance. It is to the public that the Michigan Oil and Gas Exposition addresses itself. For not only has the industry in our state become of great interest to all sorts of businesses and services unique to the oil and gas exploration and production industry, but what is called the oil fraternity of*

Michigan wants to demonstrate who we are and what we do. As represented by the Oil and Gas Association of Michigan, cosponsor of this Exposition, the oil and gas industry seeks to be good neighbors in the state and communities that host our activities.

"So welcome to Mt. Pleasant!

"I now declare the First Annual Michigan Oil and Gas Exposition officially open!"

Big deal, Kaisa thought. People have been crowding in here since mid-morning to see the seventy-five exhibits by oil and gas supply and service organization from all over the nation, without all the "official opening" fal-de-ral. The road circling Island Park was a constant stream of cars as exhibition-goers sought to park as close as possible to the show's midway action. To get into the park, they had to pass Atha Supply Company's new building at the top of the hill on Main Street, which had made headlines the year before as the first air-conditioned building in Mt. Pleasant. Already the day was beginning to warm so she imagined Atha Supply would get plenty of visitors and maybe even a customer or two during the Exposition.

"No person can afford to miss this gigantic exposition of progress made by the state's oil industry the past ten years. " The local newspaper declared. *"Here you will see one solid mile of displays and demonstrations including oil wells in actual operation. The price of admission (twenty-five cents) is within the reach of everyone. Don't deny yourself and your family this great educational treat."*

The Exhibition was alive with a variety of displays. Highlights included:

The *Michigan Oil & Gas News* booth she occupied boasted a huge replica of a front page of the publication, headlined "The Biggest Oil Reporting Paper In The

World."

At the head of the midway were two oil trucks, one built by Gorham Brothers and the other fabricated by Thompson Brothers drilling contractors of Mt. Pleasant, parked diagonally nose-to-nose to form a mobile "gate" to the Expo. Near the entrance, with an Atha Supply rotary drilling rig, Lupher Drilling Company was drilling a well, dubbed "The Fairgrounds #1" powered by twin diesel engines manufactured in Kansas.

In a huge tent nearby, Mt. Pleasant's Franklin Tool Company featured products from seven companies inside and a pumping unit by Stork Engineering of Saginaw outside the tent. J. Walter Leonard, Jr. of Mt. Pleasant's exhibit displayed a large map of his present holdings and exploration plans for a Genesee County, Michigan, township. Leonard and company planned to give away a prize of oil property by drawing each of the six nights of the Exhibition. L-France Republic Company of Alma, Michigan, displayed five trucks of their manufacture expressly designed for oilfield use. The Muskegon Separator Company exhibited oil and gas separators of the style commonly used in Michigan. Halliburton Company displayed a pumping unit mounted on a truck while Black, Sivalls and Bryson of Bartlesville, Oklahoma, whose Mt. Pleasant office had fabricated the Oil News booth, also exhibited oil and gas separators and tanks. Baroid Company of Los Angeles, Tulsa and Houston displayed Aquagel, an innovative chemical compound that made the specific gravity of fluid in the hole sufficiently dense enough to prevent caving of the holes walls.

Dowell, a division of Dow Chemical Company which occupied a building north of Mt. Pleasant on the grounds of the abandoned Dow Chemical Bromide plant north of Mt. Pleasant, demonstrated the effectiveness of its acid compound used to extract oil from limestone formations which was first demonstrated in the Mt. Pleasant Field.

The largest and most elaborate display of the Exposition was that of Roosevelt Oil Company, who had an exact replica of the Roosevelt Refinery in Mt. Pleasant, demonstrating how crude oil was refined into six different products (gasoline, kerosene, distillate, gas, oil and fuel oil) in exact detail. The Roosevelt Refinery miniature had a capacity of seven to ten barrels a day. In the same tent as the refinery model, a map of the Roosevelt Simrall Pipeline Division showed a map of the Simrall pipeline system that brought crude oil from the area's oilfields to the refinery. The refinery itself, just through the trees across the river to the north and west of Island Park, suffered a fire the previous Friday. The refinery expected to be up and running by the end of the Exposition.

The Geological Survey Division of Michigan's Department of Conservation exhibit showed the location of Michigan minerals and their economic value.

On the west end of the Exhibition grounds, the Fairgrounds #2 well drilled, using a cable tool rig, operated by Bell Drilling Company. The contrast of the faster rotary drilling technique, which grinds through the earth, compared with the cable drilling technique, which pounds through the earth, detailed for the fascinated crowd as both wells actually "made hole." There had been some debate as to whether these holes would need drilling permits from the State, but it was ultimately decided that the wells would be "held off bottom" from any potential oil or natural gas bearing zones here in the center of the geological basin so no permit was necessary. Despite that decision, wary State geologists kept an eye on the drilling proceedings.

These displays were augmented by over fifty more exhibits of everything from oil tools, to automobiles, to office equipment to mapping services and work clothing.

In addition to the *Michigan Oil & Gas News* thirty-six page tabloid Exhibition Number, the Mt. Pleasant-based weekly *Isabella County Times-News* had published a forty-page Exhibition special issue the previous Thursday. The Exhibition issues illustrated the stark contrast between the two publications.

The Oil News edition coverage dealt with statewide industry drilling activity, all of its customary field reporting, of semi-technical drilling statistics and regulatory updates in addition to touting the Exhibition. The *Isabella County Times-News* reported the overall ten-year old industry history and articles aimed toward general public consumption. It emphasized the importance of the oil and gas industry to state and local economies as well as other "nice to know" oil and natural gas exploration and production feature articles with personal profiles of industry dignitaries.

Thanks to the Times-News ace oil and gas reporter Norman X. Lyon, that edition crackled with excitement about the industry reflected by the writer's love of explaining the complicated in a simple manner. This contrasted with the Oil News rather dry compilation of drilling rig locations, drilling progress and semi-technical recitation of production runs and things more of interest to industry insiders.

Kaisa knew that Lyon's recent visits to the Oil News offices had been punctuated by closed-door discussions with her bosses and secretly hoped their weekly oilfield newspaper would be graced by the full-time talents of the jaunty, salty Lyon.

Besides oilfield-related shows, live music, food and

a dull roar of voices in awe and laughter of amazement lay like a heavy blanket in the brilliant sunshine of opening day. An air of exuberance over this island of promise in the midst of national economic despair prevailed, encouraged by Michigan petroleum geologists writing articles with headlines like "We've only just begun."

In front of the grandstand for the race track, Mayor Deuel had insisted be part of the fairgrounds when the city established Island Park two decades before, entertainment varied with each day of the Exposition. Smith's Diving Ponies, billed as the only act of its kind in the world featured ponies leaping off a high platform into a tank of water. The Fuller Duo of acrobats would appear afternoons and evenings, accompanied by the McDonald Trio of bicycle daredevils, who performed "a sensational exhibition of daring and skill on bicycles and unicycles." Add half a dozen singing acts, bands, and softball games with the state champion Roosevelt Oil team taking on all comers and the million dollar Exhibition was complemented by thousands of dollars of entertainment." Among others, the 125 voice Mt. Pleasant Civic Chorus was slated to perform Thursday evening in front of the grandstand, presenting their first concert of the season

It was already late afternoon and Kaisa began looking for her son with Sarah Boransky, who was bringing her son, three-and-a-half year old Mickey, 'M. C.', as she called her son for short. The plan was for them to have some food before the evening performance of Smith's Diving Ponies. After the show, Sarah and Mickey would join her at the Oil News booth and, hopefully, they could all walk home together. She smiled, remembering how excited Mickey had been when she brought home a child-sized hardhat with his name painted on it for him to wear to the exhibition. Big machines fascinated him, the noisier the better. He loved to watch the Oil News printing presses in action and she knew he would like the cacophony of machine roars that occasionally climbed the knoll of background noise at the Exposition.

"It's nice to meet you, too" Kaisa said for the hundredth time that afternoon, "now I can put a face to the name when we speak on the telephone."

J. Walter Leonard, Jr. walked by and waved to her, smiling. "Where's the lad?" he called.

"He'll be down in a little while." She answered, smiling. Mr. Leonard was one of her favorite people and had taken an interest in her and her son. If she had a question about any aspect of the oil industry that she did not want to let her bosses know she was ignorant of, she could count on "Call me Walt" Leonard to explain the answer patiently to her.

"You stop by our booth when he gets here. Maybe you'll win a piece of one of our leases that'll come through and you can get in the business yourself."

"Thanks. We'll see you later."

Leonard moved away into the crowd and she grinned, thinking of a story her friend oilfield welder "Red" Utterback told her recently. To supplement his welding income, Utterback was part of his brother-in-law Charlie Breedlove's four piece country band. Sometimes, Red and his group entertained on Friday nights in the upstairs dance hall, where the bar was, over the Blackstone Café at 112 South Main two doors down from her office.

"We love it when Walt Leonard and Walt McClanahan come up with their wives after dinner and a couple of drinks" Red said. "Because they always get into a contest to see who can tip us the most when we play a tune they like.

We have a whole folder of 'two Walts' music. McClanahan always wins but I think Leonard just goads him to see how much money he can get him to spend."

It was amazing how many little tales like that people liked to confide to people from the Oil News, usually accompanied with a wink and a prelude of "I really shouldn't tell you this. But ....."

Lou Aaronson, *Michigan Oil & Gas News* Managing Editor joined Kaisa in the booth. "You look busy," he said "if you want to take a break, I'll spell you. There's a lot of interesting things to see. Over in the Merchant's Building a guy by the name of Bill Burden is showing off a full working wooden model of a drilling rig with lights, working draw-works and the whole shebang, strictly on his own. Roosevelt's miniature refinery is something to see too."

"They're on my list." Kaisa said. "People been telling me about the displays they like all day so I have been keeping a list of the things I think M.C. will want to see. 'Course he'll probably want to be down here every night. Sarah should have him here anytime, then I'll take a break. Did Walter McClanahan find you? "

"Yeah he did. His major announcement of the day is that the McClanahan Marchers, a Drum and Bugle Corps he finances up in Grayling, is going to come down here Wednesday, all 30 of them. Walter says they are going to parade through downtown, and then do an afternoon program here at the Exposition. Then in the evening, they are going uptown again to play patriotic music and sing ballads specially written in praise of McClanahan. Then Walter's got them slated on the stage that night to repeat their downtown performances."

"Did the Expo planners know anything about this?"

"No. Walter just had one of his inspirations this

morning. I'll bet they're tickled pink to have their evening show extended. I keep telling you, the man's a legend in his own mind. Can you imagine the other Walt pulling a stunt like that?"

She looked up the midway toward the bridge over the Chippewa River up the bluff to Main Street, trying to catch a glimpse of Mickey's shiny little hardhat. The traffic circling the park in a steady stream of cars and trucks seemed to have stopped on her right, where vehicles climbing toward the park exit would normally be streaming. Apparently the policeman directing traffic had halted the flow, to the horn-blowing displeasure of the drivers. In the distance, she could see the approach of another of her bosses, John P. Murphy, with Norm Lyon, elbowing his way through the crowd with grim-faced determination as a path began to open before them.

"Miss Conroy," Murphy said with slow and uncommon formality, "you must come with us now. Close the booth if you have to but come with us."

"What's the matter?" she said as she joined them as they escorted her through the crowd shouting "Coming through", "Out of the way" and "Make a hole."

The throngs of exhibit-goers seemed to sense emergency and parted to let the trio pass. As they reached the "gate" to the midway formed by the two oilfield trucks, Kaisa noticed a knot of people crouched across the park's ring road. The traffic was stopped and, at the road's edge, the sun glinted off a shiny hardhat tagged "M. C."

All sound dropped away except for the weeping voice of Sarah Boransky "Kaisa, I'm sorry. He took off his hardhat because it was too hot with the sun shining on it. Then he got away from me. He got so excited when he saw the drilling rig he ran ahead Oh my God, I'm so sorry...."

153

The group of men kneeling on the ground shifted and she glimpsed the little body on the ground with a bloody forehead."

"Sweet Jesus" she screamed, "not again. I can't have somebody else taken away from me! Mickey! Mickey!"

"Don't worry." someone said, "he's still breathing. He wasn't hit by a car .... he ran into the side of one. We've sent somebody down Main Street to Doc Gardiner's house. He'll be here in a minute, he only lives a couple doors down from the park entrance.

Traffic resumed, the noise level climbed and the First Michigan Oil and Gas Exposition continued undaunted.

As word of the accident spread throughout the exhibit, an impromptu team of oilfield workers was organized and a bridge over the traffic lanes around the park was quickly designed for the base of the park entrance hill. Oilfield pipe and planks were assembled and a sturdy footbridge constructed overnight. The footbridge became a fixture of Island Park, to be known for a long time as "the Mickey Bridge".

Other than a profusely bleeding forehead cut and a scuffed knee, Mickey Conroy was uninjured in his collision with the automobile at the Michigan Oil and Gas Exposition, except for some wounded pride and disappointment at missing the first day of the Exposition. After a couple days of rest, Mickey was able to attend the exposition and see the diving ponies. He loved being the center of attention with his bandaged forehead and custom hardhat, signed by the men who built the footbridge. He swelled with pride when the announcer at the Smith's Diving Ponies show acknowledged his presence, prompting a round of applause.

Kaisa continued working long days at the *Michigan*

Oil & Gas News downtown office in the morning and the newspaper's booth at the Oil & Gas Exposition afternoons into the night. As a reward, and to compensate for her anxiety over her son, James P. Dunnigan had arranged with a Detroit industrialist friend for she and Mickey to spend a week at the friend's Mackinac Island East Bluff summer cottage called *Yononte*, one of the elegant summer homes of the well-to-do overlooking the harbor. Dunnigan said though most of the summer residents were gone, most of the tourist businesses did not close until mid-October, He gave her round trip train tickets for the following Thursday and arranged for provisions at the cottage.

She held the offer at arm's length for a while. Dunnigan was semi-wealthy and another handsome young Irishman. Her suspicions were assuaged when she discovered he and his family would be on a St. Lawrence Seaway cruise ending in New York City the same week she would be on Mackinac Island

Leaving early in the morning the following Thursday from the Ann Arbor Railroad depot on West Broadway, she and Mickey had jostled by rail to Cadillac, Michigan, where they connected with the Grand Rapids and Indiana Railway. Then there was a long stop at Walton Junction where a group of Traverse City conventioneers boarded the train on the way to a meeting at Petoskey, where there was another delay while they found their luggage and unloaded the libations they brought to sustain them on the trip. Ogled for that portion of the trip, she was relieved to leave Petoskey for Mackinaw City. Along the way, she began to notice new signs along the track and on some depots saying "Pennsylvania Railroad." When she asked the conductor, he said the Grand Rapids and Indiana line sold to Pennsylvania Railroad Company, who would take possession at the start of 1936. The new owners had begun changing some signage rail side, he said.

She arrived just in time to board the last ferry of the day to Mackinac Island, having worked off a schedule for the Memorial Day to Labor Day, rather than the abbreviated offseason ferry schedule. To top it off, it had rained steadily all day.

15

East Bluff, Mackinac Island, Michigan Friday, October 4, 1935

*"Thy koninkrijk Komen, thy zal gebeuren…..*Thy kingdom come, thy will be done…"* Kaisa muttered to herself as she watched a Great Lakes freighter slip through the channel between Mackinac Island and the Michigan Lower Peninsula mainland seven miles away, foghorn singing a mournful call, answered by screaming seagulls.

From her vantage point on the front porch of an East Bluff cottage *Yononte*, Kaisa Koistinen Conroy watched the freighter, rendered silent by distance, churn through the rippled surface of the straits separating Michigan's two peninsulas and wondered about its source, destination and cargo. She watched as it cleared the Round Island lighthouse and disappeared in the fog beyond the wooded northwestern end of Bois Blanc Island. She realized she had just watched it leave Lake Michigan and enter Lake Huron. The laden ship could be headed anywhere between here and America's East Coast from as far away as Chicago, an intriguing thought. The peaceful scene was a balm to her mind after the frantic past two weeks.

She hadn't thought so when she arrived last night after a nearly all day train trip .

"Not a very cheerful place to visit in the rain." One of the Arnold's Ferry crew said to her last night on the way across the Straits of Mackinac, "Looks like you're going to pret' near have the place to yourself, this bein' off season and almost time to close the place down except for year-round residents. Been kinda quiet here with Depression and all. Used to be we'd run full up 'til the middle of October but everybody's strapped in the pocketbook. The Mackinac Island Commission had a regular appropriation from the State legislature of $40,000 a year in the '20s that dropped to $14,000 and some change by 1933. Without much budget, they haven't been able to promote the island and visitor traffic dropped like a stone. Then two guys from downstate names o' Roger Anderson and G. A. Hendricks were able to start the Mackinac Island Bureau and convinced the Commission to 'stablish a State Park Press Bureau with just one guy runnin' it, fella named Jean Worth. Worth started out sendin' weekly newsletters to newspapers all over the place.

"Andrews organized a big festival for the dedication of the reopening of Fort Michilimackinac in 1933 at Mackinaw City. He held a re'nactment of a 1763 Indian attack on the fort. That drew a lot of people to the area, so they've repeated it the last two years on Memorial Day weekend and it looks like it's going to be an annual doin's.

"Last year Anderson and Hendricks organized a summer long celebration of the tricenten'al of Jean Nicolet's 'rival here as the first European to see the Straits. That celebration started with the annual summer long Mackinac Island State Historical Fair at old Fort Mackinac, drawing thousands of folks. So it's pickin' up some but nothin' like it used to be.

"Nice talkin' to ya." The ferryman finished. "We're comin' into port so I gotta get out on deck to tie up. Have a nice visit."

"Thanks for the information." Kaisa said, thinking the island would likely survive in spite of this man's cynical observations.

Exhausted, she had hired a horse-drawn taxi at the ferry dock to the doorstep of the East Bluff Summer Cottage *Yononte*. Jim Dunnigan had arranged their stay as a reward for her work on the Oil and Gas Exposition, and to help them both recover from the trauma of the three-year olds ("almost four, Momma") near-fatal experience at that exposition. She was happy to find the caretaker for the cottage had left her a strong fire in the screened hearth. She and Mickey were soon in bed while the random creaks of the unfamiliar house accompanied the steady fall of rain on the roof. No drips, thank goodness.

This morning it was still raining and slightly cool when they arose and fog pretty much obliterated the scenery so they read children's books and practiced Mickey's word identification and spelling skills until lunch.

Now he was napping. Kaisa, ever the one to want to know the history of the places where she located, sat on the expansive front porch with a light blanket on her lap. She was reading a book of Mackinac Island history she found in the cottage's full width living room at the front of the elegant Shingle-Style cottage. Because of the damp heavy air, she decided to stay downstairs on the porch rather than climb the stairs to the railed balcony and octagonal open cupola that would give her a spectacular view of the Straits when the fog cleared. The railing, called a balustrade, and the cupola a belvedere, she learned from her dictionary after reading a description of the cottage.

Nearly almond-shaped, Mackinac Island's eight-mile coastline, she learned, encompassed almost four square miles, rising 890 feet at its highest point, where the remains of Fort Holmes commanded an unobstructed near 360 degree view of the Straits of Mackinac. Both Mackinac, a French spelling, and Mackinaw, the English spelling, were pronounced "Mackinaw." Pronouncing them differently immediately labeled the utterer an outsider, she'd learned quickly from last night's taxi driver.

Year-around population of the island was about five hundred people, with an estimated five thousand visitors daily during the summer season.

Official location of the island is in Lake Huron at the east end of the strait known as Mackinac between Michigan's Lower and Upper Peninsulas. For centuries before the arrival of Europeans, the strategic location and height of the limestone cliffs of Mackinac Island in the area called "Mitchimakinak", or "great turtle" by the American Indians, made it an easily defended gathering, trading and sacred place. Likewise, French, British and later, Americans, found the Mackinac area valuable commercially and militarily. The British built Fort Mackinac on a bluff overlooking the harbor in the southeast quadrant of the island, but there was never an attack. The fort surrendered peacefully to Americans after the American Revolutionary War, though the British did not leave the area until after the war of 1812.

The island was the scene of two battles during the War of 1812. The first battle of that war was no battle at all. The British smuggled a cannon from the northwest end of the island to its highest point along what was later called British Landing Road, a spot behind Fort Mackinac. At dawn, the troops at the fort found themselves under the barrels of the British cannon from what was named Fort George, and surrendered the fort. Later in that war, American's tried unsuccessfully to take back the island, which was given back, along with surrounding mainland, under the terms of the 1815 Treaty of Ghent. Americans renamed Fort George as Fort Holmes, in honor of the slain commander of the failed attempt to recapture the island. The fort remained under United States government control until 1895, serving as a prison for three Confederate sympathizers during the Civil War years. This answered a question for Kaisa, who had wondered why she had seen pictures of the troops at the fort in Civil War era garb and wondered what possible threat the Confederacy could be to an island in the Great Lakes.

In the latter half of the 1800s, Mackinac Island was a popular resort and a cruise line stop. In 1875, it became the second American National Park, behind Yellowstone three years before. Cruise lines, to promote destinations for cruise ship companies and railroads, built lavish hotels, like Mackinac Island's world famous Grand Hotel. Seasonal souvenir shops sprang up as village residents figured out how to cash in on the throngs of tourists flocking to the island.

Finally, Kaisa came to the part of the island's history she was most interested in, the cottage developments.

As early as 1835, wealthy vacationers who wanted to live on the island all summer began petitioning for building lots on the island, where growing pressure on accommodations was increasing yearly. What island homes for rent on private property in the city were rapidly placed under permanent lease by wealthy full time summer residents and soon none were available for the casual visitor. Gurdon S. Hubbard in 1855 bought eighty acres on the southern bluff of the island. Here he built "The Lilacs", a small cottage overlooking the Straits of Mackinac in 1870. Following financial reverses in his hometown of Chicago, Hubbard surveyed and platted Hubbard's Annex in 1872, hoping to open a luxury resort. Instead, a popular cottage community grew rapidly, in which Hubbard sold lots just three years before lots in the national park were made available. Hubbard's Annex later became part of the Mackinac Island State Park.

Because of lacking funds, proposed building lots in the national park were unsurveyed and so unstaked from 1875 until 1884, despite frequent requests for lots submitted to the park superintendent. In 1884, the areas east of the fort and west of the new Grand Hotel on bluffs on park property were surveyed by the U.S. Army and leases were let by lottery from the requests. Leases were for ten years with rental's at $10, $15 and $25 a year, with the front lots worth the most. The park superintendent could use lot rentals for park improvements.

In 1885, eleven leases were let for lots in the park and three cottages were built on the East Bluff, the first of which was the cottage Kaisa was staying. Built on Lot 17 of the East Bluff for $2,000 by Detroit attorney John Atkinson and his wife Lida, _Yononte,_ a derivative of the phrase "on the hill", was constructed in the fall by a local builder named A. G. Couchois.

The cottage was sold in 1887, to General Henry Martyn Duffield, attorney and Civil War hero from Detroit. Michigan and his wife Frances Pitt. The Duffields had six sons: Divie B.; Francis; Graham; Henry; Morse and Pitts. Henry Duffield was admitted to the Michigan Bar when he was discharged from the Army at the end of the Civil War and practiced law from 1865 until 1898, when he rejoined the Army at the start of the brief Spanish-American War, where he was made a Brigadier General in charge of volunteers, then became a Major General in 1903. In 1904, Duffield sold the _Yononte_ to the present owner, Jim Dunnigan's friend.

KAISA

Eighteen ninety-five saw the federal government leave the island and turn over all federal land on Mackinac Island to the State of Michigan, making it the state's first State Park, placing the island under the jurisdiction of the appointed Mackinac Island State Park Commission. The Commission's stated charge was governing private development in the park and it required houses be built in the Victorian-era style.

Mackinac Island's world famous ban on automobiles stemmed from a movement begun in 1896. Carriage drivers, who made their living with tours of the island, horse-drawn taxi drivers and horse drawn freight-hauling draymen, all of whom were licensed and a large economic force, felt their livelihoods threatened by the newfangled "horseless carriages". They organized and petitioned the Mackinac Island Village Council. Maintaining that the noisy motors frightened their horses and endangered their passengers and pedestrians, the organized horsemen asked the Council to refuse licensees for motorized vehicles. The petition was approved. Three years later motorized vehicles were banned from park property, about eighty percent of the island's land area. The ban survived to modern times.

A sudden burst of sunlight took Kaisa away from the book on her lap to the vista before her. In a stunning display of fickle Straits of Mackinac weather, suddenly the island was bathed in sunshine with the rain-washed air. A postcard sunlit view of the Straits lent extra clarity to the sharpened panorama of the village, as well as the channel between Mackinac and the much larger Bois Blanc Island to the south. Another upbound Great Lakes freighter wended its way between the two islands, seemingly larger than life and only an arm's length away in the bright afternoon.

"Boat! Boat!" She heard the cry of a juvenile voice.

and turned left toward the voice, thinking her son Mickey was awake. She quickly realized the voice was coming from the elegant white cottage next door, where she saw the top of a dark-haired head bobbing above the balistraded front porch railing and down the two-tiered railed stairway to the front lawn. Without pausing, the child darted with raised arms and on legs churning with excitement through the partially open front gate and across the dirt Huron Road in front of the cottages. Looking for an accompanying adult and seeing none, Kaisa jumped to her feet and ran toward the child, who was now scaling the bottom rung of the rail fence between the road and the sheer limestone cliff above the village.

"Jared!" She heard a hysterical cry as she pulled the protesting child, still screaming "boat ... boat .... play ... play", back through the fence.

"The boat is too far away" Kaisa said, standing him upright and holding his shoulders to hold his attention.

"Oh my God! Thank you so much." A stylish young woman with tears in her eyes and voice said as she came runniung across the road toward Kaisa and the boy, lifting her long skirt from the muddy roadbed. "I fell asleep in the front room while he was napping and never heard him, slip out. Iamsuchagoose ... thenannyusuallywatcheshimbut welostherjustbeforewecamehere.... OhmyGodOhmyGod..."

"Calm down" Kaisa said sternly in the same voice she used when her son got agitated and ran his words together. "He is all right. So calm down. Take a deep breath. I am Kaisa Conroy. Who are you?"

The fashionable woman, who looked slightly older than Kaisa, leaned against the fence and watched the freighter round the southeast edge of the island beyond the Iroquois and Windemere hotels. Slowly the wild-eyed panic left her eyes and she began to speak normally.

"I'm sorry." She said "Everyone says I am flighty and I guess they are right. My name is Evangeline Maurice, but everyone calls me Evie. We are visiting here from Pennsylvania. A friend lent us the use of the cottage for a couple of weeks. We came up here last weekend and my husband Mark has gone back to Detroit until tomorrow. He is an attorney with business in Detroit so he is here on weekends. This is my son Jared. He's almost five and you can see he is a bit unruly."

Even calm, the woman with what Kaisa felt was an infantile nickname spoke rapidly, as if in fear of contradiction.

"I am also visiting." Kaisa said. My boss arranged for my son Mickey and me to use this place for a week to relax after we completed a big project."

"You work?" Evie asked, as if the concept of a woman who was not a servant working was alien to her.

"Yes. I am office manager for a weekly newspaper about oil and gas exploration here in Michigan. We are located in Mt. Pleasant, where I live."

"I don't know where that is."

"Right here." Kaisa put her left index finger in the center of her right palm. We all carry a map of Michigan in our right hand."

"Momma?" Mickey called from the front porch of _Yononte_ as the screen door slammed behind him.

"I'm right here, sweetie. Come on down and meet our neighbors. Look both ways before you cross the road."

Mickey joined them and after a brief inspection of one another, he and Jared were examining a pile of horse manure, the hallmark of the island's horse-based culture.

"Poopie!" Mickey proudly pronounced, as if he had

done the job himself.

"Poopie." Jared said solemnly, nodding in agreement.

Jared pointed to Mickey's bandaged forehead.

"'happened?"

"Hit car."

Their bonding complete, Jared started to move away.

"No," Mickey said, touching his bandage ."We can't go 'til Momma says."

Kaisa smiled, happy her son had paid attention to her stern instructions after his accident at Island Park.

Jared stopped, thought the order over a moment, and returned to his mother's side.

After a moment of stunned silence, Evie exclaimed "My goodness, Jared never listens to anyone!"

They talked for a few minutes more.

"Your job sounds so exciting!" Evie exclaimed. " I have never worked outside the home. For me it was tutors, finishing school, and marriage and three miscarriages before Jared arrived. We have always had servants, so I'm afraid I don't know much about how to do much of anything. Where is your husband?"

"He was killed a few years ago in an oil well explosion." Kaisa replied, adjusting to Evie's speech and thought patterns in thought and speech. "What is your husband doing in Detroit."

"Oh, it has something to do with two automobile parts companies wanting to merge. His client came to our place in Newport, Rhode Island, in August and asked Mark to negotiate the deal for him. The Philadelphia company has a contract with Ford for some new part it just patented, but has no facilities in Detroit. The Detroit company has equipment and workers who are about to be laid off because the part they were building was phased out. That's all I understand. What is your accent?"

"I didn't realize I had one but my father was Finnish and my mother Dutch and I speak both. I've been teaching Mickey to speak both also so maybe I have some blend of languages bouncing around in my head."

"Would you like to come over for tea?" Evie asked.

"Certainly." Kaisa replied.

When they were seated on the covered wraparound front porch of _Buena Vista,_ two flights of stairs from ground level, Kaisa admired the view from the next cottage east of _Yonante._ She knew from the book of cottage histories she read that afternoon this one was built by a Zanesville, Ohio, schoolteacher turned attorney Tilson F. Spangler and his wife Mary. Spangler had used his legal training to successfully venture into banking and real estate

"So what have you and Jared been doing since you have been here?

"Oh nothing. really. We sit on the porch and I do my needlework while he reads. We have hired a local lady to come in to clean and take care of our meals. So we just lounge around here waiting for Mark to come back to us. He said he would be on the last ferry out of Mackinaw City tonight."

"I'll bet you've been getting a lot of reading done, if last night's weather is any indication."

"The weather has been beautiful, but I don't read. History gives me a headache and made up stories just confuse me. I know lots of people who enjoy reading but I have never taken to it. I don't think I have ever read a book all the way through."

"I can't even relate to that. I have read all of my life

and as a result have been places and met people past and present that I will never meet on this earth. My father used to quote. Mark Twain, who said 'Those who don't read have no particular advantage over those who can't'."

"I don't know what that means."

"I know you don't, but we will work on that. You have been in one of America's most historic places for a week and haven't seen any of it? I have an idea. Why don't we walk downtown and have dinner, then meet your husband's ferry when it pulls in tonight."

"I don't know. Emily will be here to prepare dinner later. What if my husband changes his timetable and I am not here? They will worry."

"Well, leave them a note saying where you've gone. You do write don't you?

"Of course."

"Come on girl, let's live a little."

"If you're sure it will be all right."

"Why not. What are we? High school girls?"

Evie wrote her notes and posted them on the door, which Kaisa had to remind her to lock after first being sure the cook/housekeeper had a key, and the four walked along the ridge of the East Bluff. Instead of going a little east to take the wooden stairway down to Bogan Lane on a route to Huron Street, the village main street, they went west through the woods on the Anne's Tablet trail toward Fort Mackinac along the top of the bluff, bypassing the steep root-entangled Crow's Nest Trail down the rocky face of the cliff

16

East Bluff, Mackinac Island, Michigan Friday and Saturday, October 4 and 5, 1935

While Jared and Mickey wanted to climb over the limestone boulder-like rifts in the myrtle trimmed Anne's Tablet Trail, Evie and Kaisa more prudently walked around them, admiring the surrounding forest of buttonwood, cedar and basswood. Suddenly they came on a small clearing on their left offering a breathtaking view of the harbor and town spread below them. In the myrtle-carpeted clearing, stone benches arranged in a semi-circle faced a large stone upon which rested a large bronze plaque, emblazoned on the right with a raised figure of a young woman in a flowing dress reaching for a tree branch. To the left of the woman, in raised type, were the words: *She loved the island and island trees; she loved the wild larches the tall spires of the spruces bossed with lighter green, the gray pines and the rings of the juniper. Hear the rustling and the laughing of the forest and the waves of water on pebbly shores.*

Below these poetic words were inscribed: *"In memoriam, Constance Fenimore Woolson 1840-1894, Author, Traveler, who has expressed her love of this island and its beauty in the words of her heroine Anne – 1916."*

The blanket of trees surrounding the clearing seemed to insulate the small alcove from other sounds as Kaisa read the words from the plaque.

"My God, that's beautiful." Evie whispered. "Who is Anne?"

"Tell you what. There are books about the history of this island on the shelves of my cottage, and I noticed some at your place. Why don't you look them over and you tell me who Anne was, and who Constance Fenimore Woolson was too. We are going to both be here for a week, so you can educate me."

"I'll just do that." Evie answered.

From Anne's Tablet, they wended their way a short distance northwest before coming to a meadowlike expanse of grass alongside Fort Mackinac and there rejoined the western leg of Huron Road again, behind the fort.

"I was looking at a map of the island this morning." Kaisa said "and I think there is a road down to town just the other side of the fort."

As they crossed behind Fort Mackinac, they looked up the hill to their right to see what looked like a fort and a lot of white tents at the top of the hill.

"That would be Fort Holmes."Kaisa said. That is the place where the British secretly brought a cannon in the night and captured Fort Mackinac without a shot on the second day of the War of 1812, a war the Americans on Mackinac Island didn't even know they were in."

"Are sojers up there?' Mickey and Jared asked almost in unison.

"No. No soldiers." Kaisa laughed. "Those are for the men of the Civilian Conservation Corps, or CCC, the U.S. Government program President Roosevelt started to put men to work on public projects. I read in the *Mackinac Is-*

land News, the island newspaper, that the CCC is working at reconstructing the fort and expecting to reopen it next year."

"Can we go up there?" Mickey wanted to know.

"Not today ... maybe later."

Proceeding beyond the fort, they followed a steep road, aptly named Fort Street, between the fort and a huge home dominating a hill overlooking a golf course. Across the course, they could see the magnificent white expanse of the long porch of the Grand Hotel.

Treading their way carefully down the hill, they came to Trinity Episcopal Church on their right and the huge "front lawn" of Fort Mackinac, Father Marquette Park to their left. In the center of the park, a pedestal bore a statue of Father Jacque Marquette, a Seventeenth Century French Jesuit missionary and explorer stood in caped dignity.

"I've heard his name. but I don't know much about him." Evie said, and catching Kaisa's look, added quickly. "I suppose that is my second assignment."

"You've got it." Kaisa replied.

They had dinner at the Hotel Chippewa in a dining room overlooking the harbor and marina adjacent to the Arnold Line dock, then walked around the nearly deserted downtown waiting for the arrival of Evie's husband's late ferry.

When Mark Maurice alighted from the ferry, his son Jared ran ahead to greet him. Confusion, concern, and then relief hopscotched across his face as he looked up to see Evie coming toward him.

"What's wrong?'

"Nothing."

"Why are you here?"

"We just came down to meet you."

"How did you get here?"

"We walked."

"We?"

"Jared and I. Oh and our new neighbor Kaisa with her son Mickey."

"But you never walk."

"Well we did. Come meet Kaisa."

Mark, Kaisa noticed, was a few years older than Evie and seemed to address her more as a child than an adult. He took her hand firmly as his penetrating attorney's eyes probed hers to evaluate her strengths and weaknesses."

"Very pleased to meet you, Miss…"

"Mrs. Conroy. Forgive me if we've violated any protocols but we've been on a small walking tour of the village coming to meet you."

"Not at all …. Not at all. I was just surprised to see my family here at the dock. Evie seldom wanders from places she knows and is comfortable. …. and this lad must be Mickey."

Mickey looked to his mother, then extended a hand and said in his best grownup voice "Pleased to meet you, sir."

"What's this …. Manners? I hope some of that wears off on my son. Well, I can tell you I'm not going to lug my bags and briefcase to the top of that hill, so will you join us for a cab ride back to the cottages?"

"Yes. Thank you."

Saturday

Next morning, Kaisa and Mickey rose early and , armed with jackets against the morning cool, took the stairway to the base of the bluff. Kaisa carried a child's wagon, big enough to hold Mickey and their jackets later, down the stairs. She'd found the wagon on the back porch of the cottage and knew this first part of the hike would be tough, but after reaching lake level, the going would improve. They made their way down and followed Huron Street east into the rising sun. They visited St. Anne's Roman Catholic Church and checked mass times for the next morning. From there they continued on a northerly curve on Huron (also called Main Street) out of the village and around Mission Point on Lake Shore Road, to begin the hike circumventing the island on the 8.3 mile long Michigan Highway 185. M-185, she knew, was the only state highway in Michigan that did not allow motorized traffic.

To their right, gin-clear water lapped lazily against a shoreline of rocks from pea to near person-size, while at the left fall color of tree leaves on the nearly perpendicular bluff face gave the impression God had spilled a paint box.

They took it slow, pausing to crane their necks to view Arch Rock, an imposing limestone bridge between two outcrops at the top of a forest-strewn cliff. On the "back side" of the Island, they watched a hilarious sideshow as a mother Common Loon tried to teach her young how to dive for food. The lesson took for all the chicks but one. That one's little legs would churn him to the top of the water where he would run a few steps and sink back to the surface of the Voyageur's Bay. After several attempts to show the chick the proper diving procedure, the mother shook her head and swam off with the rest of her brood. Her attitude seemed to say "Catch up when you get it right, buster, the rest of us are going for breakfast." They never saw the loon family again so never knew if the dullard loon got the hang of diving.

After a long northwestern stretch of solitude, punctuated by an occasional rustling of small wildlife and the

throaty trill of birds on the forested steep hillside, they came
to Point St. Clair, where the road curved slightly to the
south. They reached the most northwest place of the island
at *Point aux Pins* (Point of Pines), marking the halfway
point of their trek around the island. Angling southeasterly
on an erratic shoreline route they had a spectacular view of
the Upper Peninsula's St. Ignace on their right. A little to
the north, the pale tan pinnacle of Castle Rock was prominent. Passing what looked like a shipping dock, they soon
came to a road making a semi-steep ascent into the interior
of the island, labeled British Landing Road. Kaisa knew this
route would take them all the way to Fort Holmes at the island's highest point, but decided to continue on Lake Shore
Road to the village after pausing briefly for a snack and a
visit to the newly built primitive toilets, disliked vehemently
by Mickey.

Bicycle traffic began both directions as they reached
the two-thirds point. The younger and slimmer, the bicy-
clists were, the more enthusiastic their greeting, Kaisa noted. Those riders coming toward them were fresh from the
village, were smiling and pedaling vigorously as they said
things like "Good morning" and "Beautiful day." Those
coming from behind them were slower, heralded by gasping
and grunting and nodding breathlessly as they nodded word-
lessly in passing. People in self-driven rental or hired driver
carriages were consistently the most cheerful.

Now their view embraced the vast expanse of the
Straits of Mackinac, dotted occasionally with fishing boats,
ferries and another freighter in the distance, with the north
shore of the Lower Peninsula and Fort Michilimackinac in
Mackinaw City as a backdrop. Encountering another steep
road called Forest Driveway, they stayed on the flatter road
they trod. Further down the shore, they enjoyed a roadside

park where Brown's Brook trickled out of the limestone and ambled under the road to join the Straits. Following another bulge in the island's coastline, Kaisa was relieved to catch a glimpse of an occasional roof peeking through the woodlands upslope. Mickey, finally bored with too much outdoors, napped on a bed of their jackets, rousing with the clip-clop of horses, which he loved almost as much as heavy machinery.

They passed the chimney rock called Sunset Rock and proceeded to the crumbling cliff face at Lovers Leap and the rocky potpourri of Devils kitchen at Jacker Point, places Kaisa resolved to learn more about. The forests gave way to the palace-like so-called Summer Cottages along West Bluff Drive, their second floors and ornately decorated rooflines visible from the shoreline road. Then a thick patch of cedar trees granted privacy to the lakeside frontage of the Grand Hotel, discouraging climbing toward the luxury hostelry. Kaisa knew from the ferryman some West Bluff Cottages were boarded up and closed due to the Mackinac Island State Park Commission's foreclosure on the lessees for default of rental fees by cash-strapped former wealthy occupants.

Then another expanse of open lawn another curve and they were at the village with more run-of-the-mill houses on both sides of the road. An open space framing the Round Island Lighthouse across the narrow channel, then they were on Main Street in the village, bracketed by the Windemere Hotel on the shore side and the Iroquois Hotel on the waterside.

Off-season, many of the fudge shops and souvenir businesses along Main Street were closed, shuttered against weather and interlopers. They walked along the sparsely populated streets until they found a small cafe, where they ate a late lunch, then hired a taxi to take them back to their East Bluff quarters.

Kaisa and Mickey looked forward to a nap on the front porch of _Yanonte_. "Momma, I'm tired" had been the mantra of the last hour.

An envelope bearing Kaisa's name was jammed underneath the doorknocker on the front door of the cottage. She opened to a sweetly wafting wave of lavender scent ("Why do people do that." she thought "By the time you get your breath back your eyes are watering almost too much to read what's inside."). She waved the note around in front of her to dissipate the lavender odor, then read the note inside:

Dearest Kaisa,

Mark, Jared, and I would be honored if you and Mickey would join us for dinner this evening at seven.

By the way, Anne was the title character in Constance Fenimore Woolson's Anne: A Novel, _an 1881 story of Anne Douglas, who lived here on Mackinac Island during the fur-trading era at what is now the restored Indian Dormitory and fell in love with a soldier from Fort Mackinac._

Altogether Woolson, who was a grandniece of James Fenimore Cooper. wrote seven novels, 65 poems and 30 nonfiction and travel articles in her writing career

Born in New Hampshire in 1840, the same year her three sisters died from scarlet fever, infant Constance Fenimore Wilson was brought to Cleveland, Ohio, when the family moved to start over. She grew up in "the West" and saw the area transform from frontier to industrial center. She wrote Great Lakes-themed travel articles and poems until she moved to Florida during the Civil War, then after her mother died in 1879, shifted the focus of her work to wealthy expatriates in Europe. She lived in England and

Italy. In 1894, she fell from the balcony of her apartment in Venice, Italy and died from her injuries..

The Anne's Tablet memorial was erected in 1916 by her wealthy nephew Samuel Mather, a Cleveland industrialist whose family were East Bluff cottagers on lot 13 ½ (you are on lot 17 and we are on lot 18) and descendants of Cotton Mather of the Salem Witch Trials.

I'll know more about Father Marquette when next we talk.

Until this evening then, your friend

Evangeline Maurice (Evie)

The language of the historical part of the note contrasted with the more informal part and Kaisa suspected was lifted wholesale from a book in the *Buena Vista* library. She didn't really care. She was so pleased Evie had made the effort.

She glanced next door, where Mark and Evie sat on the front porch, him using his briefcase as a makeshift desk and she reading A BOOK !!. Mark waved and Evie looked up to see Kaisa pointing to the note and nodding her head "Yes".

■■

Kaisa and Mickey arrived at *Buena Vista* just before seven that evening, to find Mark and Evie waiting in rocking chairs on the front porch. Evie stood and, taking Mickey by the hand, led him inside saying she was taking him to the playroom where Jared was waiting.

When she was gone, Mark looked at Kaisa appraisingly and said "What have you done to my wife and son Mrs. Conroy?"

"I beg your pardon?"

"I left here last Sunday afternoon with a wife whose only interest in life was our son and her needlework. A woman who couldn't go around the corner without three people giving her directions and certainly never among strangers. Who wouldn't read anything more complicated that a label on a can. We came home last night and she went to the bookshelves while I was eating dinner, then looked at several books throughout the evening, taking notes.

"This morning she got up chipper as you please and after breakfast said 'Let's go for a hike, I want you to see something'. A hike, for God's sake. So we go down the street and she points at an abandoned cottage and goes on about who built it and the shrine they built to their aunt, some writer woman. Then it was off we go down this trail through the woods with Jared sticking close to us like an actual child instead of a peripatetic demon. We went down to this beautiful little notch in the woods overlooking the harbor, where she quotes me chapter and verse about the woman memorialized. After we came back home, she found the book this woman wrote about somebody named Anne and she's had her nose stuck in it all day. I actually was able to get some work done.

"I understand this is after being with you only one day. So I repeat .... what have you done to my wife and son?"

"Nothing, except took them a couple places and we discussed a little of the history of the island. Have I done something to offend ... and it is Kaisa by the way."

"Oh no." Mark replied. "I think it is wonderful to see her come alive and actually have something to talk about. Whatever you're doing, keep it up. I wanted you to know that I have arranged with the livery in the village to have a carriage at your disposal anytime over the next week so the four of you can go anywhere you like. I'll settle up with them when I come back Friday."

"That is very generous of you. There is a lot to see here."

"So where were you most of the day? Evie asked as she returned to the porch with lemonade.

"Mickey and I walked around the island. It's beautiful."

"Mickey walked?"

"Not all the way. I found a wagon in the back room ... it was great."

"I think there's a wagon here too. Maybe we can go with you next time. How far is it?"

"A little over eight miles."

"Wonderful! We can make a day of it."

Mark stared speechless at his wife, astounded at how far she'd come out of her shell.

17

Mackinac Island, Michigan
Sunday through Saturday
October 6 - 13, 1935

Sunday, Mickey and Kaisa went to Mass at St. Anne's Catholic Church. They stayed for the social in the basement, where a display of the church's history was displayed, then returned to their cottage and lounged the day away: Mickey playing and dozing while Kaisa studied Mackinac Island history as she planned the upcoming week.

She waved goodbye to Mark when the taxi picked him up to take him to the ferry late Sunday afternoon.

Monday

The week sped by in a dizzying flourish of sightseeing and dipping from the vast well of historical knowledge about Mackinac Island. It seemed as though every spot on the Island symbolized or memorialized some piece of American, British or French history.

On Monday morning, Evie stood in front of the Father Jacque Marquette's statue in Marquette Park next to the water in front of Fort Mackinac. She began with a brief summary of the Jesuit priests' evangelization of the new frontiers of Canada and the Great Lakes area. She described how the priests often traveled with voyageurs, whose large canoes plied the waters from the St. Lawrence River to the western reaches of Lake Superior and the southern end of Lake Michigan. Voyageurs hauled trade goods into the wilderness and freighted furs out to a ready fashion market on the "civilized" New England coast of the North America and shipping points to Europe.

Father Marquette was a former schoolteacher who spoke six languages and applied for a North America missionary post often before 1666 when he arrived in Canada to relieve Father Allouez at Sault Ste. Marie, she explained.

A few years later, he was assigned to a post at LaPointe on the western shore of Lake Superior to minister to a population mix of Chippewa, Ottawa, and Huron Indians. In 1870, the Chippewa were at war with the Sioux, neighboring to the west. The other Indians were anxious not to get caught up in the Sioux/Chippewa fight and began to move east to the Straits of Mackinac, where the French had made peace with the Iroquois. Marquette moved with them, where he met Father Claude Dablon, who in 1669 built a bark chapel on a slope near the water on the Island of Michilimackinac, now Mackinac Island, calling it the "Mission of St. Ignace." Named for the founder of the Jesuit Order , St, Ignatius Layola, The mission seemed perfectly located on the island, where in the summer months, tribes met to trade, fish and hunt. Besides, in the Indian mind the island was already associated with religion as a sacred burial place. But for many Indian crops, the growing season was too short on the island and winters isolated it too much, with not enough wildlife to support a population.

Evie paused, realizing that tourists had gathered

around and were listening.

"Go on." Somebody said, "This is really interesting."

"Well," Evie continued. "When this island turned out to be unsuitable for a mission village, Father Marquette moved the Mission of St. Ignace to the Upper Peninsula to what is now the town of St. Ignace in 1671. Two years later, he and Louis Joliet left this area to begin their voyage of discovery and reached the 'Father of Waters' at the mouth of the Wisconsin river a month later. They canoed as far south as the mouth of the Arkansas river before returning to Michilimackinac. Marquette made another voyage down the Mississippi River before dying in May of 1675 at age 38 as he made his way back from that adventure.

"This statue was dedicated in his memory in 1909."

Evie finished to the enthusiastic applause of the onlookers. Kaisa felt like she had just seen a flower burst into bloom. She now realized that what she thought was just mimicking a textbook in Evie's note to her on Saturday was really an example of the woman's ability to organize facts into an understandable narrative. Her flawless verbal delivery of Father Marquette's history supported Kaisa's belief that Evie had a far greater mind than Evie herself knew.

Flushed with excitement, Evie could hardly believe the acceptance of her mini-speech.

"Did you hear them?" she asked "One person wanted to know if I was a guide here and another asked if I am a teacher. I've never spoken to an audience before and it's wonderful."

From Marquette Park, they went across Fort Street to where Market Street intersected a block up the slope from Main Street to see the McGulpin House, reputed to be the oldest house on the island, with a sign declaring it as an example of a working-class frontier home believed to have been built before 1780.

On down Market Street they looked at the abandoned John Jacob Astor Hotel, where it was Kaisa's turn to show off her research. "A three-story New England Colonial structure built in 1817, this building was once the home of Robert Stuart, the northern department manager of the American Fur Company. The structure next door to the company's warehouse, had served as home to Stuart and his wife Elizabeth," Kaisa said, "where they entertained the cream of island society. It also served as company offices and had rooms to accommodate visiting company men. The Stuarts lived there for twenty years. In 1840, it was converted by new owner Robert McLeod to a seventy-room hotel, the first on the island , catering to traders and ship captains. During the 1870s, new owners remodeled the building and renamed it the John Jacob Astor Hotel, adding a three-story porch. It was a popular hotel until the late 1920s when the Great Depression spelled its doom. Now the building and porch was in dire need of repair.

"And the porch is scheduled for demolition." Evie quipped as a footnote "I read that in the *Mackinac Island News* too."

They walked further along Market Street, past City Hall and the police and fire departments to the Biddle home, preserved as an example of what a prosperous family's home on the island was like in the Eighteenth Century.

They lunched at the Iroquois Hotel before making their way back to the East Bluff, looking in what stores were open and stopping at Doud's grocery store Fort and Main to buy a treat.

"Tomorrow, let's get the carriage and do a partial circle of the island, then take British Landing Road up to

Fort Holmes." Kaisa said.

"It's a date." Evie replied, already making mental notes about her evening subject of study.

Tuesday

After their carriage was delivered, they circumnavigated the island Tuesday morning on the same route Kaisa and Mickey took the previous Saturday. Kaisa laughed, watching Mickey trying to explain to Jordan what he had seen when the mother Loon was teaching her chick to dive, his little fingers aping the way the chick's legs churned the surface of the water.

When they reached British Landing Evie related the story of the British trip through the center of the island in the night to surprise Fort Mackinac on the morning of the first day of the War of 1812. They turned in-island at British Landing Road. "And now we'll see the place where the American's tried to take back the island two years later." Evie proclaimed in what Kaisa was beginning to think of as her "best tour guide voice."

They climbed steadily until they came to the Wawashkomo Golf Course on the right and, a little further up the road on the left came to a small monument commemorating the Battle of 1814.

"The golf course and the open space on the left were once all part of the same farm." Kaisa began. "A man named Michael Dousman received this land as part of a grant by the British after the 1812 invasion of Mackinac Island. Here he raised grain to produce rum, which was a very lucrative enterprise. The Americans landed at British Landing and instead of coming up the road, made their way this way through what is now named Crogham marsh for the American troops leader, south of us here. The British were waiting just about where the golf course clubhouse is now, with their cannon placed on a slight rise to the north and Indians lying in wait in the woods on both sides of the marsh. When the Americans emerged from the marsh, they charged the troops and cannon to the north, unable to see across the open field that the Indians in the woods were flanking them. The battle took place on both sides of this road with the Americans outnumbered, outflanked and outgunned.

"By the time the Americans retreated to their boats at British Landing August 4, 1814, fifteen Americans lay dead and fifty were wounded. The dead included the expedition second-in-command Major Andrew Hunter Holmes, for whom Fort Holmes is named. We'll see that fort later today."

A plethora of tents housing Civilian Conservation Corps workers who were restoring Mackinac Island attractions surrounded them as they looked at a marker showing a diagram of the battlefield and the lines of march. Later they ate lunch at the Cannonball Snack Shop. The place was busy but the owner was happy to engage two young women in conversation rather than the group of men, obviously CCC, who crowded the small but neat eatery. He told them the story of how Michael Early had bought the farm to use for raising hay and vegetables years after Dousman sold it in 1819. When Michael Early died, he left the farm to his sons Peter and John, who divided it. Peter passed on twelve years ago and his heirs sold Peter's property to the State of Michigan for $17,500 while John had received $50,000 for his larger portion. John retained a small parcel of land along British Landing Road and built the Cannonball Snack shop the owner said. "And I am John Early's grandson." he concluded.

As they boarded their carriage to continue up the road, Evie said ruefully "I knew most of that."

"I figured as much."Kaisa empathized.

At Crooked Tree Road, British Landing Road changed to Garrison Road and they continued to the Mackinac Island Cemetery. There they turned on the shabbily maintained Fort Holmes Road and made their way to the highest point on the island. Workers worked to reconstruct the fort that had been allowed to fall into disrepair. Fort Holmes was determined no longer vital to the security of the island and the fort no longer manned after 1817, Evie said. The British lost their last hold in the area when Drummond Island was declared United States Territory in 1828 and United States Federal troops had left in 1895. Bad roads and difficulty in accessing the location led to the demise of Fort Holmes as tourist attraction. The Mackinac Island State Park Commission was hoping reviving the fort would help to revive sluggish island tourism.

After viewing the breathtaking views of the Straits of Mackinac, along with the Upper and Lower Peninsulas, they traveled back down the hill. They marveled over birth and death dates on tombstones in both the Mackinac Island and St. Anne's Catholic cemeteries. They followed Garrison Road and came to Skull Cave, at the base of a thirty-foot rock located where Rifle Range Road met Garrison. "Wave action of an earlier higher lake ate away softer rock surrounding this tower of limestone and wore away some at the base to form this cave." Evie recited. She then thrilled the boys with the story of Alexander Henry, who was hidden here by some friendly Indians after the massacre at Fort Michilimackinac. He spent the night sleeping on what he thought was a bed of rocks until dawn revealed he was in a cave littered with the bones and skulls of hundreds of years accumulation of Indian burials. They picked up Huron Road beyond Fort Mackinac, bringing them back to their cottages in time for dinner.

"Thank God for accurate tourist maps." Kaisa said as they she and Mickey said good night to Evie and Jordan. When Evie's cook/housekeeper showed up to prepare the Maurice's' dinner, they hired her to watch Jordan and Mickey the next morning so they could rent bicycles and explore more of the island interior.

Wednesday

On Wednesday morning, the two women walked to the village to rent bicycles and, armed with their tourist map of the island, proceeded up Market Street to Lakeshore Road. They retraced in reverse the route Mickey and Kaisa had traveled the previous Saturday so that Evie could see Lover's Leap, Devil's Kitchen, Sunset Rock and Brown's Brook along the way to British Landing. Evie briefly recited a bit of history of all these sites to Kaisa and, sometimes, small knots of sightseers. By now the pair of young women had been dubbed "the history gals" by the islander and tourist rumor mill as word spread of the informal "history lesson contest." As they boarded their bicycles, some of the tourists asked "where ya goin' next?" ... a question they politely ignored.

They turned in-island again on British Landing Road, but about five hundred feet up the hill followed the right fork up State Road. About two-thirds of a mile later, Kaisa signaled that they should take a right turn on a small road into the woods, which changed quickly to a trail. Securing their bicycles to a tree off the path, the two stepped gingerly along the narrow path called Crack in the Island Trail until they came to Cave in the Woods and the nearby so-called Crack in the Island. Kaisa had spoken about neither to Evie so she doubted it was part of the other's research so she took the lead.

"Cave in the Woods is one of the oldest rock formations on the island" Kaisa recited as they looked in the small entrance at the long low cave. "During the Lake Algonquin Period, this cave would have been on the beach, even though it now sits a hundred and forty feet above Lake Superior." They walked a few feet further along the thickly wooded trail. "And here is what is called the crack in the island" Kaisa continued as they looked in a narrow shallow leaf-filled fissure in the rock." Local oral legend has it that the Great Sprit Git-chi Man-i-tou stamped his foot to create a giant crevice here and gave it magical power before he fled to the Northern Lights. The crevice was so big that rumor has it horses once fell into this fissure and if you dropped a rock in here, you would not hear it hit bottom. Regardless of what is the truth, it makes no difference now. Island residents and Indians themselves used the fissure as a convenient garbage dump for nearly two centuries before it was decided it could be a tourist attraction. The fissure has practically disappeared but the myth of its origin lives on"

"Someday future archaeologists and anthropologists are going to treasure this spot." Evie said.

Retracing their steps to State Road, they followed it to rejoin British Landing Road and proceeded to Crooked Trees Road, where they followed the curvy crooked route to another natural feature of Mackinac Island. This one was one of Evie's subjects.

"Sugar Loaf was once a part of the cliffs over there."

Evie said "but soil and the softer rock were worn away by the same Lake Algonquin wave action that formed the Cave in the Woods. As the Algonquin receded, it left this cone-shaped monolith standing alone. This is the most ancient part of the island. The seventy-five foot Sugar Loaf is two hundred eighty-five feet above the water and is seventy-five feet high. If you look closely on the north side of the rock about halfway up you can see a small cave that indicates where the highest shoreline was on this side of the island" She curtsied to her small audience, queued for refreshments at one of the oldest concessions on the island.

They took Sugar Loaf Road, then Rifle Range Road and proceeded to Arch Rock, another natural wonder of limestone at the top of the cliff, carved by the persistent sculpting power of the waters of Lake Algonquin, agreeing to return here with the boys, they started home.

After a dizzying ride, alternately pedaling and coasting, down Arch Rock Road to Huron Road to Cadotte Road, they walked their bikes down a steeper slope. They enjoyed lunch at the pro shop dining room for the Grand Hotel Jewel "Grand Nine" Golf Course before returning the bikes to the rental shop and taking a taxi home after arranging with the livery for a horse and carriage next day.

Thursday

Thursday morning found the four of them again in a carriage with Evie and Kaisa doing a repeat of their trip the day before to Arch Rock, to the delight of Jared and Mickey. Kaisa related the Indian legend that on this spot, the Great Spirit arrived each morning with the rising sun so that departing souls could find their final resting place on the island. A slight mist obscured the horizon as the voices of bicycle riders below on Lake Shore Road added an eerie air to the place. Naturally, the boys wanted to climb out on the wide archway of limestone, undercut by ancient wave action. The scheme was denied in unison by their mothers. The boys quickly became fascinated by another great adventure, solo trips to the primitive men's toilet, while their mothers read the plaque commemorating John Nicolet, the first white man known to enter the Straits of Mackinac. Kaisa and Evie's entourage departed down Rifle Range Road, where the boys had another opportunity to chatter excitedly when they passed Skull Cave for the second time as they turned on Garrison Road.

They looked at the new Scout Barracks, completed near Garrison and Huron road's intersection in 1934 by CCC workers. Mickey and Jordan were impressed by the possibility that they might someday be able to live on the island for a week with other Boy Scouts garrisoned there to help with trail maintenance and aid Park Commission interpreters at historical exhibits. They were more impressed that they could have a bonfire and raise the flag if they were good scouts and behaved themselves. At Huron and Cadotte roads, they stopped at the huge stable complex where workhorses for the island were housed and fed. Biggest attraction for the boys was the straw-laced dung heap, gleefully acknowledged with whoops and giggles and loud whispers "poopie pile". So much for impressing history into very, very young minds.

Huron turned to Annex Road at Cadotte and a short distance town Annex, they turned on Grand Avenue to West Bluff Road, where they passed deserted West Bluff Cottages shuttered and abandoned in wait for new tenants since the old lessees had been foreclosed upon. They crossed in front of the Grand Hotel with its magnificent 800-foot porch, left their bicycles near the golf course and entered the hotel at the northeast doorway. They entered the long hallway leading to the hotel's front desk, admiring the elegant furnishings as they peeked at the hotel's historic displays in two museum rooms. They had a late lunch at the Tea Room on that level, feeling underdressed for the extravagantly expensive lunch in the formal dining room on the floor above them and not wanting the ambiance of the place to be subjected to their two enthusiastic boys.

"The Grand Hotel was the dream of Senator Frances Stockbridge, who bought this site in 1882." Evie said, " Stockbridge said he would hold the property for construction of "the world's finest and largest summer hotel." The boast found the ear of the leading resort hotel operator of the time, John Oliver Plant, who became interested in the project and decided to make Stockbridge' dream a reality. A corporation was formed with stockholders including railroad and Great Lakes cruise companies among others. The original hotel, about half the size of the present one, opened July 10 of 1897 and advertised as Plank's Grand Hotel until Plank sold his interest. Enlarged in 1897 and again in 1912, the hotel was completely remodeled in 1919, the hotel now boasted an eight hundred eighty foot porch exactly one hundred feet above the lake level. W. S. Woodfill, who now owns the Grand, bought the hotel   just two years ago and is dedicated to the growth and redevelopment of Mackinac Island as a destination, regardless of the Depression."

They returned home in the early afternoon to bed down their sons for naps and spend the balance of the day reading and writing postcards to friends.

Friday

Friday was Kaisa and Evie's last day to visit the island's attractions together, which they made casual, departing mid-morning. They decided to walk to Fort Mackinac to take Jordan and Mickey on a tour, which met with great approval by the boys. They looked in barracks, storerooms, arsenals and the commanders quarters. They peeked through rifle holes in the sentry stations at each corner of the fort, where the boys "pkew ... pkew"ed, firing imaginary rifles at invisible enemies. They climbed on the cannons and covered their ears when one fired a distance away.

Afterward they enjoyed a late lunch in the Tea Room at the fort.

"The British garrison at Fort Mackinac ...." Evie began, to be stopped by Kaisa's raised hand.

"I'm sure between the two of us we know all about it so let's just enjoy the sights and sounds of the island today.." Kaisa said.

"Oh come on, let me have one more. Not the Fort but another one I've been saving all week.

"All right. A quick one."

"You see the Mackinac Island School down there by the Father Marquette statue? That is the old Indian Dormitory, built by Indian Agent Henry Rowe Schoolcraft in 1838. The Treaty of 1836 transferred 15 million acres of Ojibway (Chippewa) and Odawa (Ottawa) land in Michigan Territory to the federal government. It also required improvements to the Mackinac Island Indian Agency, including a dormitory for Indians visiting the post. The Indian Dormitory was the agency's administrative headquarters for eight years and occasionally housed Indians who came to the island to receive their annual treaty payments.

"From 1846 to 1867 the building was used for a variety of purposes, including as a U.S. Customs House. In 1867, it became the Mackinac Island Public School.

"Now, see the huge cottage just to the left of the school? That's Anne Cottage, named for our famous Anne of Anne's Tablet. It was originally the site of the Agency House, where Indian Agent Henry Schoolcraft moved from the 'wild magnificence of nature' at Sault Ste. Marie 'back one step into the area of the noisy world' on Mackinac Island in 1833. From the Agency House, he continued his life's work documenting "the history, manners and customs, languages and general ethnology" of Michigan Indians. After Schoolcraft left Mackinac for his native New York in 1841, he continued to write and publish research on Michigan Indians .

"Constance Fenimore Woolson, who summered on Mackinac Island, once stayed in the building, which she describes in *Anne*. That structure burned to the ground in 1873. In 1899, Alvin and Sallie Hert of Brazil, Indiana built a mansion on the property that eventually grew to 32 rooms and 8,800 square feet, not including the caretaker's cottage, three-stall stable and carriage house. The Herts named their new home Anne Cottage after Woolson's then-famous novel. Later the Herts bought the country estate in-island called Stonecliffe. Anne Cottage remains a private home."

"Now can we let somebody else be tour guides?" Kiasa asked.

"Fine by me." Evie said. "But I really want to tell you how much this week has meant to me. By pushing me into studying the history here, you've opened a whole new world to me that I had lazily chosen to ignore. Besides that, your son tamed Jordan by example so that he is a pleasure to have around. I wish this could go on and on. Thank you."

"I didn't do much except woke up what you already had in you." Kaisa said. "It has been wonderful watching you come out of your shell. Even your voice is different, more confident. I hope you never retreat inside yourself again. You have a lot to give your family and the world. I've never enjoyed a week more in my life, nor made as good a friend as you. I hope we keep in touch."

After lunch they spent the afternoon haunting what tourist shops were still open, taking advantage of end of the season final weekend bargains on display. Of course much of the shopping involved Indian related gear for the boys and local history books for the women. They sampled fudge, tried on clothes, had tea at the Hotel Chippewa and watched ferries and yachts and freighters ply the Straits and harbor area of the island.

When Mark Maurice arrived on the late ferry, he expected them to meet him and was not disappointed. He was still slightly in awe of his wife, who had shed her perpetual soft voiced veil of tiredness to present a bright eyed, vivacious face to the world.

As with last week, they hired a taxi back to the East Bluff, where they parted company in front of their cottages, and Evie extended a dinner invitation for Saturday.

Saturday

Saturday morning, Kaisa took Mickey on the Manitou Trail off Huron road to a site she wanted to see before packing to return home. Robinson's Folly, an overlook a hundred and twenty-seven feet above the southeast curve of Lake Shore Road commanded a wonderful view of the

Straits. Kaisa felt kinship with Captain Daniel Robertson, who was Commander of Fort Mackinac from 1682 to 1697. Over the years his name was corrupted to Robinson as written word began recording mushy verbal pronunciation. Reading the stories about Robertson's misfortunes Kaisa realized that, like her, not even his name had survived his trials unscathed.

Robertson had been part of Fort Michilimackinac garrison in the massacre of 1763. He was saved by an Indian maiden who was attracted to him. When he became commander of the fort on the island, he brought the Indian girl and his white wife with him. Robertson had built a summer home on this spot at the cliff's edge to get away from the fort, and his wife. Here he brought fellow officers to drink, smoke and curse their isolation, until wind and the crumbling cliff edge sent the house crashing into the lake below. Robertson later died in a fall from this spot. Another story said he built the house for his Indian girlfriend and when his wife insisted he end the affair, the girl grabbed his hands as they stood at the crest of the hill, and jumped, pulling him to his death also.

Either way, Kaisa felt a bond with him. She shared what she called the Fecal Touch. For those with the Midas Touch, everything they touched turned to gold. For those with the Fecal Touch, ...well ....

She was feeling a little melancholy as the sojourn at the island ended. Alone, except for Mickey, she sort of envied Evie, who had a husband, a life of luxury and travel with the likelihood that she would see far more places to study history than Kaisa would during her workaday life at Mt. Pleasant. It seemed Kaisa's life was always taking right angle turns from her plans.

Initially, she wanted to escape the barebones life in

the wilderness of Michigan Upper Peninsula mining country for the luxury of living with her loving grandmother in Holland, Michigan. The harsh indifference of her grandfather thwarted that plan. The discovery of copper in the Delaware Last Chance Mine would have been a ticket to luxury but for the ironic cruelty of fate that the discovery also cost her father's life. Working with her mother in creating an enterprise, to augment their income from their half of a share in the mine and her mother's teaching salary, drew the two of them closer but it provided bare sustenance. Then her mother's tragic death sent her life careening in another direction, as if a fiendish genie had granted her wish to leave mining country but extracted a price paid in pain

Her move to Mt. Pleasant made the possibility of her getting a teaching certificate a distinct possibility following study after high school graduation, since Central Michigan Teachers College beckoned from less than a mile from her new home. Dreams of luxurious living gave way to the potentially fulfilling career of teaching, where she could share her love for learning. Then her maturing body and one night's mistake with Mickey Conroy in a grope of professed love, followed by his death in an oilfield accident threw her into the role of widow, then mother with the arrival of her son Mickey Eric, delaying her completion of high school on schedule. The deaths of her Uncle Jalo and Aunt Mina just over two years apart, plus Jim Dunnigan's offer of a good job, helping launch the *Michigan Oil & Gas News* magazine, brought her the dual roles of landowner and businesswoman, but again derailed another life ambition. While exciting and profitable, her position at the magazine kept her days full and provided a paycheck, in moments of reflection, she fostered a restless feeling of discontent. Maybe Mickey Eric's brush with disaster was a sign that an active business career at the cost of fulltime motherhood should not be her focus. The past few days, spent with her son with no distractions, had been glorious. Watching Evie develop a taste for reading and a talent for sharing her knowledge re-assured Kaisa of her own desire to teach.

Oh hell Kaisa, she chided herself, you're just touchy about leaving the life of leisure to go back to the daily grind. You'll snap out of it ten minutes after you get to work Monday morning. "But maybe I don't want to." an inner voice protested in retreat.

After finishing her packing, she walked next door to dine with the Mark Maurice family.

Mark and Evie were sitting on the front porch again and Mickey went to the back of the house to see Jordan.

"Sit down." Mark said seriously. "We want to talk to you. Evie and I have been talking. I would like to offer you a job. Governess, nanny, companion for Evie. Hell we don't know. She just wants you and Mickey around. I'm gone a lot on business and she gets lonely with nobody to talk with but Jordan and my ancient family. You are a good influence. Whatever you're making now, I'll double it and you will live with us as part of the family."

"I am not qualified to be a governess." Kaisa pro-tested.

"Not qualified. You speak three languages. You know more in five minutes than half the people I know will know all their lives. You are a great conversationalist, have poise and are attractive. Whatever you can't do, we will hire done. Join us please."

"May I answer you tomorrow?"

"Of course." The Maurices answered in unison.

"I know it is a big move." Mark continued. "You will want to give a couple weeks notice to your current employers and give yourself a couple weeks downtime. We are going home to Philadelphia now but will be leaving for the family's cottage at Jekyll Island, Georgia, after Thanksgiving. Then Evie and Jordan will spend the winter with the Maurice clan there while I commute from my law practice when time allows. So, if you and your son decide to become part of our family, we'll see you in Pennsylvania in a month."

"Darling," Evie said. "I've been thinking. Evie really isn't a name for an adult. I think I'd like to be called by my full name from now on."

"Evangeline it is then." Mark replied enthusiastically. "Now let's eat."

After a night of weighing pros and cons, Kaisa concluded, "If I don't take this opportunity, I'll spend the rest of my life wondering what would have happened if I had."

Another right angle turn, Kiasa thought, but this one seems more Midas than Fecal.

Next day at the ferry dock she told the Maurices "We will see you in Philadelphia."

Part V:
DEIDERICK

18

Aboard the German submarine Lone Wolf, Atlantic Ocean, near the Georgia Coast Pre-dawn Thursday, March 26, 1942

The Battle of the Atlantic was not about the most powerful navy; neither was it about glorious battles fought between battleships and submarines. But the Battle of the Atlantic was a commerce war waged by German U-Boats against Britain's merchant marine. For nearly six years, Germany launched over 1,000 U-Boats into combat, in an attempt to isolate and blockade the British Isles, thereby forcing the British out of the war. It was a fight which nearly choked the shipping lanes of Great Britain, cutting off vital supplies of food, fuel and raw materials needed to continue fighting.

By the end of the war, German U-Boats in the Battle of the Atlantic had sent over 2,900 ships and 14 million tons of Allied shipping to the bottom of the sea. In exchange, the Allies sank almost 800 U-Boats and over 30,000 of the 39,000 German sailors who put to sea, never returned – the highest casualty rate of any armed service in the history of modern war.

Website *http//www.uboataces.com*

Kapitanlieutnant Johannes Vogt, commanding officer of the <u>Lone</u> <u>Wolf</u>, a modified German Type IXD-2 submarine U-boat, settled into the chair in Captains' Quarters with his first of what he knew would be a day of many cups of coffee. Today would be the first time the boat was traveling alone during this voyage. During the night, the squadron of Nazi U-boats had separated for their respective missions along the United States east coast, while the <u>Lone</u> <u>Wolf</u>, largest of pack because of its *super-geheime,* super secret modifications, stayed the course for tiny Jekyll Island, Georgia. While the rest of the pack would be sinking shipping along the United States Atlantic coast, Vogt and his crew would be sinking U.S. economy and morale.

Range and speed of U-Boots suffered greatly when running submerged on batteries, so the <u>Lone</u> <u>Wolf</u> made most of the trans-Atlantic voyage on the surface using diesel engines, its ship-style bow slicing through the water. Vogt planned to submerge only briefly on the approach to their destination, to avoid detection and attack from the air. Submerging at all near the U.S.A. Atlantic coast was a new wrinkle in U-Boat warfare. Most *U-Boot* attacks during the early years of the war took place on the surface and at night. But the Americans were catching on to the danger of *U-Boot* attacks on their shipping near their home coast so the "happy days" of German submarine warfare success were coming to a close.

He smiled, thinking about how proud his deceased father would be of him; a boy from the Gröpelingen suburb of Bremen now commanding a submarine built by Aktien-Gesellschaft Weser shipbuilders on the Weser River near his boyhood home. A. G. Weser was not only in the neighborhood where Johannes grew up but was the shipbuilding factory where his father worked until his death from pneumonia four years ago. The old man had been proud of his role in producing submarines for the Third Reich.

Since its founding in 1843 as Eisengiesseri & Machinebau-Anstait Walten und Leonhard, as a foundry and machine factory, the company, now known as C. Waltjen & Company, converted to a ship building enterprise with the construction of the paddle-steamer Roland, a tug and passenger boat in 1847. The company produced: diesel and steam engines; exhaust steam turbines and steam turbines; ship gearboxes; passenger ships, merchant ships and war ships through its career, providing thirty years of employment for Gerhardt Vogt, Johannes' father.

Gerhardt joined the company in 1908, a year before Johannes was born. He loved his employer and filled Johannes' young head with stories of A. G. Weser company history, particularly its warship-building career. Johannes smiled into his coffee cup remembering his papa's recitations.

The A. G. Weser firm's first venture into warship construction in 1871, building three torpedo boats for Kaiserliche Marine, the Imperial German Navy. A year later, several Bremen bankers, merchants and politicians, recognizing the growing importance of shipbuilding, established a new, larger company, Actien-Gesellschaft Weser, dedicated to construction of ships of all kind and marine engineering, bought C. Waltjen & Company. Between 1871 and 1918, the company built 29 gunboats for the Imperial German Navy.

The new company started building smaller vessels, mainly for civilian use, Gerhardt told his son, until the Kaiserliche Marine ordered the gunboats. Originally located in the Stephanikichenweide area at the edge of the ancient city of Bremen. In 1901, Actien-Gesellschaft Weser leased property with bigger slipways at the entrance to the new Bremen ports several miles downstream on the Weser River at the Gröpelingen suburb of Bremen to accommodate the building of larger ships. The share of warships as a function of overall deliveries built at Bremen by the Weser firm was 50% in 1909 and almost 100% in 1916, midpoint in World War I. The firm would build 146 warships for the Imperial German Navy. The company built the first *U-Boots*, meaning "undersea boats", in 1917. The German *U-Boot* fleet was relentless in World War I, nearly bringing Britain to its knees with attacks on shipping stifling the delivery of virtal supplies.

When World War I ended in 1918, the Treaty of Versailles, as part of the 1919 Paris Peace Conference, restricted total tonnage of the German surface fleet and forbade the construction of German submarines. Article 191 of the Versailles treaty said: "The construction and acquisition of any kind of submarine, even for trade purposes, is forbidden to Germany."

Since Germans were the world's greatest experts on submarine technology, they revived *Reichsmarineamt,* growing Nazi party in Germany established *NV Ingenieurskantoor voor Scheepsbouw* in 1922. An engineering office for shipbuilding, the dummy company, known as the IvS, funded by the German Navy in the Netherlands, developed submarine knowledge, thwarting the Treaty of Versailles submarine building ban in Germany. The IvS developed designs for several submarine types for paying companies and actually built two submarines for Spain, later sold to Turkey. Five submarines were built for Finland. Restricted by the Armistice Treaty of 1918 and the 1919 Treaty of

Versailles which demanded all German *U-Boots* be destroyed or given to other nations, the Germans were also tightly restricted from using their own submarines. The IvS contracts required that IvS personnel would be involved with crew training and selection, and be allowed to take part in boat service trials - thus Germany gained first-hand knowledge of how their new prototypes worked in practice.

Meantime, the *Nationalsozialistische Deutsche Arbeiterpartei*, or National Socialist German Workers' Party, NSDAP commonly known in English as the Nazi Party, that grew out of the *German Workers' Party* (DAP), was growing rapidly in Germany. The party was created as a means to draw workers away from communism. Initially, Nazi political strategy focused on anti-big business, and anti-capitalist rhetoric, later downplayed in order to gain the support of industrial entities, and in 1930s, the party's focus shifted to anti-Semitic and anti-Marxist themes. Following his appointment as Chancellor of Germany by President Paul von Hindenburg in 1933, Nazi party leader Adolf Hitler rapidly established a totalitarian regime known as the Third Reich. When Hindenburg died August of 1934, Hitler became dictator of Germany when the powers and offices of the Chancellery and Presidency merged.

Germany became aggressive under the rule of Adolf Hitler in the late 1930s, seizing Austria and Czechoslovakia in 1938 and 1939. Hitler entered a pact with Joseph Stalin and Germany invaded Poland in September of 1939, launching World War II in Europe. Allying with Italy and other Axis powers, Hitler conquered most of Europe by 1940 and threatened Great Britain.

Johannes remembered Gerhard Vogt's account of German shipbuilding in the intermediate period between the two World Wars, The end of World War I and the cessation of submarine construction, brought tough times to the ship-building business in Germany, his father said. In 1926, A. G. Weser merged with seven other German shipbuilders to form a company named Deschimag A. G. Weser. Only A. G. Weser and Seebeckweft in Bremehaven (which was taken over by Weser) survived when most of Deschimag companies closed, sold or went bankrupt.

In 1929, the most famous passenger liner ever built, the Norddeutscher Lloyd *Bremen*, built by A. G. Weser., was brought into service. After the delivery of the *Bremen*, more than 5,000 saw lay-offs from Weser's 12,000 employees because of new order shortage. Johannes Vogt, 20 years old, was one for the 5,000 laid off.

It was a scary time for shipbuilders and for the Gerhardt Vogt family, poppa said, but Gerhardt was spared the layoff axe because of his versatility of skills in 21 years with the company. Not even Gerhard's seniority at the plant could save twenty-two year old Johannes Vogt's job there. Johannes, disenchanted with corporations, joined the Nazi party.

After 1931, when the last ship was delivered, no new shipbuilding took place at Weser for three years. The company survived on repair of ships, construction of engines and fabrication of other marine equipment.

The next new ship built was a freighter for the Norddeutscher Lloyd Company in 1933.

In 1933 Germany established a school for training *Unterseeboot* crews in Kiel, ironically under the title *Unterseebootsabwehrschule*, the "Anti-Submarine Defense School." This program involved provision for a small fleet of eight 500 ton submarines. This number was later doubled to 16.

Later, Germany developed plans for an actual navy.

The projected designs for the boats that were to be the composition of this navy, referred to as 'Experimental Motor Boats'. Deutsche Werke shipbuilder, in Kiel, was elected to build the new submarines, and a new U-Boat base was to be built at *Kiel-Dietrichsdorf.* Johannes Vogt immediately moved to Keil to join work on the new "Experimental Motor Boats"

When Nazi Germany dropped the ruse and Germany began in earnest to strengthen their armed forces, particularly their navy with heavy focus on rebuilding their U-Boot fleet, Johannes joined the German Navy.

Business improved for A. G. Weser shipbuilders after a 1933 freighter delivery. Several new ships were built, including a growing number of warships. By 1936, the ratio of warships built by A. G. Weser to the company's total ship output was 66%, a number that increased to 88% in 1938, the year Gerhardt Vogt died.

At Gerhardt's funeral, his son newly promoted *Oberleutnant zue See*, First Watch Officer Johannes Vogt, Executive Officer of a Type VII class submarine, eulogized his father, praising the man, his employer, his country and the Nazi Party.

Johannes grew up with submarines, accompanied his father on a number of shakedown cruises, worked in the A. G. Weser for two years and worked for a while for IvS in the Netherlands. As a result, he rose rapidly in U-Boot German Navy, achieving his own *U-Boot* command in 1940 and sinking six British freighters in the next year.

America stayed neutral for the first two years of the war, but sent military escorts for neutral and British merchants. German submarine warfare was hampered by American naval military support of British convoys and, while Germany and its Axis allies had no desire to go to war with the U.S.A. and Allies, tensions at sea accelerated. Hitler viewed American intervention as a hostile act .

In bad weather and at night, German submariners had problems distinguishing American from British or Canadian ships. In October 1941, a Nazi submarine mistakenly identified and sunk the *U.S.S. Reuben* James. The U. S. remained neutral.

On December 11, 1941, just four days after the Japanese took the world by surprise with their attack on Pearl Harbor, Germany and Italy declared war on the United States. Suddenly German *U-Boots* arena of warfare expanded to include the entire Atlantic Ocean.

Occupied in the Mediterranean and the Arctic, the majority of Germany's supply of larger long-range Type IX submarines, the only *U-Boats* capable of reaching the American shoreline could not be spared. The Nazis dispatched only five Type IX to the vulnerable American east coast. The Germans sent supply replenishment and refueling ships to the mid-Atlantic for use in supporting shorter-range Type VII Class U-Boats headed for American targets. Later a water tank was sacrificed to fuel to give Type VII submarines to extend their range.

Two years into the war in Europe and almost a month past Pearl Harbor, Americans in late 1941 were still acting like the war was "over there" and it was still peacetime. Fully lit unescorted ships plied the seas broadcasting their positions as crews chatted over the radios, ignoring orders to travel dark because it was more difficult to navigate by sight at night. Because it might discourage tourism, coastal towns ignored or only perfunctorily complied with blackout order. Air reconnaissance patrols were nominal and navigational beacons remained lit in the belief that an attack on the United States was unthinkable. In January

1942, Vogt and some of his English-speaking crew went ashore in southern Georgia and, after securing fresh vegetable, fruits and foodstuffs from cooperative swamp-dwelling Gullahs, went to the movies at the Olgethorpe Theater in Brunswick, Georgia. Johannes still owned the dated ticket stub kept as a souvenir of that little adventure.

One story about America's incompetence in sub-hunting broadcast in the U.S. quickly made the rounds of submariners worldwide. An anti-submarine operation in February of 1942 involved an aircraft carrier, navy destroyer and a Coast Guard Cutter. The vessels tracked and depth charged a signal they thought to be a U-Boat, only to discover they had destroyed a whale.

For the Nazi U-Boot fleet, the American Atlantic coast became a shooting gallery.

From January 14 to January 31, 1942, U-Boats sunk thirteen tankers and in the ensuing six months, protected by Americans lack of experience in hunting submarines, Nazi *U-Boots* flocked to United States coastal waters.

Among those U-Boat captains was Johannes Vogt, responsible for sinking three U.S. freighters within sight of the American shore, before recalled to Germany to take command of the <u>Lone</u> <u>Wolf</u> when commissioned. Commissioning of the modified Type IXD2 Class *U-Boot* took place at A. G. Weser Bremen shipyard within sight of Johannes Vogt's boyhood home, witnessed by a number of shipyard employees who had worked with either the senior or junior Vogt, or both.

The <u>Lone</u> <u>Wolf</u> was one of a kind, with the standard MAN-manufactured large bore nautical diesel augmented by two additional diesels for cruising on the surface. Additional fuel bunkers gave it a cruising range of 23,700 nautical miles. Weighing 1,616 tons at the surface and 1,804 tons submerged, the new submarine boasted a 252 ton freight capacity, 287 feet length, 24.5 feet wide, with a draught of 17.7 feet and was 19.2 knot surface speed. Those features were standard with the short-lived IXD1 and later the IXD2. The Lone Wolf, modification, however, saw expanded freight capacity with no torpedoes in the forward torpedo room and an oversize loading hatch to accommodate its unusual cargo.

Sipping his coffee, Vogt smiled again, thinking about his present mission. While others were sinking American shipping, something becoming so common as to be unremarkable, the Lone Wolf had the most important mission of the war, one that would make it and it's captain the most decorated in the Third Reich. As soon as the signal came letting them know the planned secret meeting of the American Federal Reserve hierarchy would indeed take place, his submarine would approach Jekyll Island to take some of America's most important financiers hostage and return to the Fatherland.

If they could kill the hated J. P. Morgan Junior, so much the better. Morgan was a well-known financier who had acted as a purchasing agent for Great Britain and as a financier for American allies in World War I and was repeating the actions in World War II. In 1915, German sympathizer Eric Muentner attempted to assassinate Morgan Jr. by entering Morgan's Long Island, New York home, shooting him twice in the chest. Morgan survived the attempt on his life, but Vogt swore to himself he would finish the job, given the chance.

Vogt's was a daring mission designed to demoralize America and destroy the country's economy. The experimental motorized landing craft *Schwimmwagen*, swimming car, would be used by the landing party, driven by a Dutchman conscripted by the Nazis to work in Germany at Volkswagen. Ironically, Johannes Vogt knew the conscriptee, Deiderick Ramecker, from both their days working at IvS shipbuilding engineering office in the Netherlands before the war. Working closely, they became friends until Vogt's devout Nazi-ism drove a wedge between them. Now Deiderick was polite, distant and terribly sad from the loss of his wife and son when Germany invaded the Netherlands.

A knock on his stateroom door announced the arrival of his *Funkmaat*, radioman, who handed him a brief message.

"Fox in lair, expecting pups tonight." Vogt read.

"Radio this message in reply," Vogt ordered, *"Caterer will be ready."* The radioman departed.

Johannes clapped his hands in glee and rose to unlock his desk drawer for a celebratory schnapps, already mentally writing his Iron Cross medal ceremony acceptance speech.

19

Glynn County Airport, Brunswick, Georgia, Bureau of Naval Intelligence Office, pre-dawn Thursday, March 26, 1942

"They took the bait," Naval Intelligence Officer Captain Aaron Rankling yelled excitedly. "Get Director Wilkinson on the phone. Get Captain Gould in here. Alert the detail. quick!."

"Yessir." His aide replied, knowing how nervous the captain became when an important mission was breaking and not anxious to be chewed out if he got the order mixed up. "In that order, sir?"

"Yes, in that order." Rankling replied, hardly believing that the ruse to lure Nazis ashore, a brainchild of his boss, Rear Admiral Theodore Stark Wilkinson, Director of the Office of Naval Intelligence, (ONI), was working out as planned.

In February, less than two months after Germany declared war on the United States in December 1941, following the arrest of two Nazi spies acting as waiters at the posh Jekyll Island Club, Admiral Wilkinson put the plan into motion.

Under intense interrogation, the waiters *cum* Nazi spies admitted to being part of a Nazi plot to kidnap some of the wealthiest members of the Jekyll Island Millionaires Club to hold for huge ransom, create economic havoc and undermine American morale.

Keeping the spies under wraps, the ONI began broadcasting coded misinformation about the happenings on the dogleg-shaped barrier Island that was the winter haven of America's ultra-wealthy, the Millionaires Club. The Jekyll Island Club staff co-operated admirably, passing on celebrity arrivals and departures, which in turn were transferred via messages from the "spies" to Germany.

ONI Captain Rankling, arresting officer of the Jekyll waiter/spies was assigned to the recently cleared site of the Naval Air Station Glynco, under construction adjacent to the Glynn County Airport. The Glynco base lay five miles north of the South Georgia coastal town of Brunswick, located seven miles west of Jekyll Island. Jekyll, the smallest of Georgia's so-called Golden Isles, named for the golden appearance of their swamp grass at sunrise. Brunswick was the closest mainland connection for the island. The seedling base hosted only one blimp and one fixed wing aircraft but plans called for two large wood construction hangers for aircraft to begin construction later in the year and ultimately serve as home base for eight blimps and a corresponding number of sub-chasing fixed wing aircraft.

One person intensely despised by the Nazis with long memories was Jekyll Island Club member 74 year-old James Pierpont Morgan, Junior, son of financier J. P. Morgan, one of the founders of the Club in 1886. Morgan Junior earned German malice during World War I when he played a prominent role in supporting British and French interests long before the United States got involved in that war. He acted as purchasing agent for and extended huge loans to, both countries. Morgan personally organized a 2,200-bank syndicate to float a loan of $500 million to the Allies. So profound was Germany's ire with Morgan Junior that they allegedly plotted the July 1915 assassination attempt that saw him survive two gunshots to the chest. Morgan had secured $100 million in loans to Benito Mussolini, Italian Fascist, just before World War II. Even though Italy became allied with Germany in declaring war on the United States in late 1941, the Third Reich had not forgotten Morgan Junior's role in helping bankroll their country's defeat thirty years before in the first world war.

Admiral Wilkinson kept Nazi interest in Jekyll Island alive by reporting that Morgan Junior was in constant attendance on the Island when he was not. Wilkinson wasn't sure what he was going to do with the hoax but he liked keeping the Third Reich circling the baited hook. Time was running out as the Jekyll Island Millionaires Club season was ending.

In March, two things happened to help crystallize a plan. One, Millionaires Club member 43 year-old Frank Miller Gould, grandson of legendary financier Jay Gould and an ROTC and National Guard member since his days at Yale, was commissioned as a Captain in the U.S. Army Air Corps. Two, a friend of Wilkinson in the Air Corps who knew of his "sting" in southern Georgia, passed along Gould's dossier, revealing that Gould was raised spending winters on Jekyll Island and in 1928 had built *Villa Mairianna*, the last cottage built in the Cottage Colony of the Jekyll Island. The Spanish Eclectic style "cottage", with fifteen rooms and six bathrooms, was located close to the back of the Gould property behind nine larger cottages facing the Jekyll River. Apart from the main body of cottages and closer to the wooded interior of the island, *Villa Marianna* seemed the perfect setting for Wilkinson's fabricated meeting of the Federal Reserve Board of Governors. Gould was promptly went on loan to the Office of Naval Intelligence and assigned to Ranking's detail at Glynco Naval Air Station. The detail was dubbed Operation "B. S." in recognition of all the bovine manure that would be spread in the sting operation designed to capture Nazis on U. S. soil, assuring residents of the east coast that their federal government was protecting them from the German *U-Boot* threat.

The ONI picked Thursday evening at the end of foreshortened Millionaire's Club season for the fictional secret meeting of the country's leading bankers. The two arrested waiters allegedly would be among several others from the Jekyll Island Clubhouse, serving the bogus meeting. It was normal for the Clubhouse to remain open after the end of the season while the staff covered furniture with sheets in preparation for nine months of disuse.

"Ah, Captain Gould," Rankling said as the tall, mustached, dark-haired Gould entered the room, "we're going to need to go over the map of Jekyll Island and your floor plan of your house again. It looks like your cottage is going to have visitors of the Nazi persuasion tonight. We are going to need your expertise about the island to plan our greeting reception."

Captains Rankling and Gould proceeded to decide on matters like the optimal hiding places for their troop of Naval Intelligence agents, police, and local island employees to lay in wait of intercepting and containing the Nazi landing party.

In the next room, ONI agents sent further coded details of the meeting place and easiest land route to the ersatz conference of America's leading bankers to the Nazi submarine <u>Lone</u> <u>Wolf</u> hovering fifty miles offshore.

The submarine was informed of the late night arrival of the seventh Chairman of the Federal Reserve Board of Governors, Marriner Stoddard Eccles of Salt Lake City, along with Board members: Ernest G. Draper of New York; Rudolph M. Evans of Richmond; John K. McKee of Cleveland; Ronald Ransome of Atlanta and M. S. Szymczak of Atlanta. Those gentlemen were indeed having a secret meeting to discuss the impact on the U. S. economy of dual wars in Europe and the Pacific. The meeting would be convened in Salt Lake City, Utah, where the Federal Reserve Governors had covertly flown in a curtain of secrecy. ONI agents traveled to Brunswick, Georgia, by train under their own names. The bogus Board would be housed and meet at the fifteen room *Villa Mariana*, 201 Plantation Road, Jekyll Island the faked spy messages said. ONI Captain Rankling and Army Air Corps Captain Gould, meanwhile, took a coffee break in Rankling's office.

"Personal question?" Rankling asked.

"Shoot." Captain Gould answered.

"What the hell's a member of the Jekyll Island Millionaire's Club and owner of a cottage there doing in the army?'

"Are you saying rich guys don't have a sense of duty to America?" Gould replied sternly.

"Oh, no. No." Rankling quickly answered. "I didn't mean to offend. I was just curious. I haven't run into many millionaires in the service is all and I sure as hell never met one from Jekyll Island.

Captain Frank Miller Gould leaned back his head and laughed. "My God, the look on your face gave me the best laugh I've had in years. I was kidding. The answer to your question is hard work, due diligence, sacrifice, luck ....

and being third generation of one of the wealthiest families in the country: I'm Jay Gould's grandson and Edwin Gould's son.

"My dad bought a cottage along with three lots in the Jekyll Island Cottage Colony in 1900. Dad named the cottage *Chichoata* after a Creek Indian Chief. The cottage was built in 1897 by the famous New York contractor David H. King, Junior. With his good friend Henry Hyde and member of the Club's Executive Board along with Frederic Baker, the Club's Treasurer, King worked on two projects. They remodeled and expanded the clubhouse and constructed the apartment building called *Sans Souci,* which is French for 'without care'.

"After his wife, Mary Lyon King died later in 1895, David King became more intensely interested in Jekyll Island and more involved with both the Island and his friend Henry Hyde. He bought two lots from Hyde and an adjacent lot from Rudolph Ellis. King proceeded to build an Italian Renaissance-style home on the property, next door to Frederick Baker's sprawling Victorian cottage *Sunterra*, meaning 'Sunland'.

"King's experience with Hyde and the Millionaires Club in 1897 was not the best. His life on the island seemed to go from the guy who had everything to the guy who, if he had no bad luck, would have no luck at all. First, his plan to construct a swimming pool surrounded by the house he was building met objections by his neighbor Frederic Baker, a very early member of the Millionaire's Club and self-appointed guardian of island of propriety, as defined by his strict Victorian principles. The Club Executive Board upheld King's right to build the pool but the seeds of animosity between King and Baker were sown.

"Undaunted, King jumped at the chance to work

with Hyde on a planned construction of a new stable, in which King planned to rent several stalls himself. Henry Hyde, an intense and impatient man devoted to the island, quickly lost his temper with King's more casual approach to the projects. The new stable would cause a rift between them. Appointed by Hyde as Chairman of the Stable building committee, King chose a site for the stable and ordered clearing of the land. Fellow committee members filed objections to the chosen site. In a snit, King had the work on the stable site suspended, then resigned from the Stable Building Committee, informing them he would not pay for his stalls, they should sell them since he would no longer need the stalls in the new stable.

"Next King proposed building a stable on the back lot he had purchased from Ellis, a plan turned down by the Executive Committee, mostly at the urging of Baker. By the end of 1897, King's house was completed and he remained in other island affairs for the rest of the season, leaving April 15, 1898.

Am I boring you with all of this?"

Rankling, who stood up to refill their empty coffee cups, said "Hell no! I like hearing about the squabbles of the rich and famous."

"My friends are wrong. You commoners do have a sense of humor." Gould jibed, continuing. "So anyway, in early October of 1898, the worst hurricane in Jekyll Island history struck and King's cottage was particularly hard hit. King was done with Jekyll Island. He did not return for the 1899 season and in November of 1899, just before the 1900 season opened, he came back only long enough to survey the damage to his house and to put it, furnished, along with all three lots on the market for $35,000.

"Nominated for membership in the Jekyll Island

Club on November 22, 1899, my father became a member December 13, 1899. Arriving first, before official opening of the 1900 season on December 14, 1899, Dad bought the whole King house and property package and within five days began modification, modernizing the hurricane-ravaged house. While he was busy supervising the house modifications, my mother headed for New Orleans to buy furnishings. Both my parents were initially enchanted by the island, so were we, my brother Eddie and me.

"My mother Sarah, everybody called her Sally, was a city girl. Even though she loved the seclusion and peaceful environment of the island, she was almost paranoid about the dangers of the rustic wild surroundings. Jekyll Island is bordered on one side by the Atlantic Ocean, with a hundred yards of hard-packed sand beach on the east side and a vast plain of swamp grass across the Jekyll River on most of the west side, punctuated by seven miles of open water between the north end and Brunswick. Jekyll was too remote and fraught with hidden dangers in Mom's eyes. Her apprehension remained from her first trip to Jekyll, when the Island's own steamboat *Nowland* ran aground on an sandbar and was then stranded them for almost an hour surrounded by open water.

When we returned north in April of 1901, an engineer on the folks' yacht *Nada* was seriously injured, catching his hand in the engine. We had to stop in Savannah to have his hand treated, which involved amputating a finger.

"Despite Mother's intense concern for our safety, we grew up loving lifeon the island, even though we were never allowed to roam without an adult watching out for us. It was kind of a pain. Jekyll Island life became made even more wonderful for us when in 1902 Dad built a bowling alley on the property and in 1913 added indoor tennis courts, a rifle range, locker room and rest rooms. It was known as the Gould "casino" and made us Gould kids the heroes of the rest of the Jekyll Island children.

"Dad acquired more adjacent property and built a cottage for our grandfather and grandmother on our mother's side, Dr, George Frederick Shrady and his wife Hester, in 1904. Grandpa Shardy died in 1907 and Grandma owned the cottage until 1925, when she sold to Walter and Helen James, who named the cottage *Cherokee*.

"We were raised escaping the frozen north in New York on the southern Jekyll Island semi-tropical paradise, laughing each time we saw a report of snowstorms and sub-zero temperatures at home. Millionaire's Club members are great at avoiding the bites; the frostbite and the bug bite so that pretty much defined our 'season.'

"My brother Eddie never much took to the books but I was a little more of a scholar. From 1912 to 1917, I was at New York's Browning School to prepare me to enter Yale.

"While I was at Yale, my father was in St Augustine, Florida and my mother at home in New York in February of 1917 when my brother was killed in a freak hunting accident on Latham Hammock, a 3,000 acre marshy island, just across the Jekyll River in the Marshes of Glynn within sight of the Jekyll Island Club. Apparently, Eddie had wounded a raccoon and tried to put the animal out of its misery by using the butt of his Scott double-barreled hammer rifle so as not to damage the hide. The gun discharged while Eddie was holding it by the barrel to use it as a club, blowing a large hole in his body.

Dad had bought the Latham Hammock to protect Jekyll Island privacy when he heard a speculator was interested in buying and developing the marshy outpost island in 1914. Since then, it has been used as a hunting preserve and is still in the family. In fact, it belongs to me now, and is open this season for hunting. Eddie had become a member of the Millionaire's Club in 1914 so Dad would at least know where he was during the winter months. During the rest of the time, he was mostly a free spirit. Eddie never got in any serious trouble but finally Edwin Gould had put his foot down and insisted his son Edwin Gould, Junior should be a part of the family railroad, real estate and banking business at a place of Eddie's choosing. Eddie acquiesced and was due to return to New York and transformed into an executive at the end of the 1916-17 season.

"My mother was devastated by Eddie's death and never returned to Jekyll Island. In fact the Gould's along with Grandma Shardy abandoned Jekyll Island and its sad memories of Eddie. Finally, in 1921, Grandma and I returned to Jekyll, she putting her grief aside and I, as a new Yale graduate, renewing the love for the place that had never left my heart.

"I joined the Reserve Officers Training Corps program while I was at Yale, then was commissioned in the U. S. Army as a Second Lieutenant and sent to Camp Zachary Taylor in 1918. I was with the 39th Training Battery for less than two months when the armistice was signed in November and I was discharged. I then joined the 212th Artillery of the New York National Guard.

"I graduated Yale in 1920 and was Secretary of the Southwestern Railroad. I married Florence Amelia Bacon, nicknamed 'Betty", in 1924 and we went together to visit Grandma Shardy the year before she sold her cottage. We stayed at my father's cottage, *Chichota,* during that visit. Mother was not happy we would stay in the cottage that brought her such painful memories. Our visit was the last time *Chichota* would be occupied. It sat empty for many years until mother had it demolished last year.

"During our first visit in 1924, Florence fell in love with Jekyll Island and we began making plans for a cottage of our own. In 1928, we built our own Jekyll Island hideaway, *Marianna*, naming the cottage after our daughter Marianna. It is the last cottage built in the Jekyll Island Cottage Colony.

"We've wintered there ever since until this season, when the threat of war made us nervous. My commission in the Army Air Corps became effective this month and here I am.

That's my story, now what's yours."

"Me? I'm just a small town boy from a little town named Warren, Indiana, located between Fort Wayne and Indianapolis, just a few miles from Marion. Not a place you would have run into but nice enough. ..." Rankling's aide appeared at the office door. "Captain Rankling, Director Wilkinson is on the telephone phone for you."

20

Forward cargo hold,
German submarine Lone Wolf,
Thursday afternoon, March 26, 1942

"*Onze Vader, die in de hemel* ....Our Father, who art in heaven" Thirty-two year-old Deiderick Ramecker subconsciously muttered the prayer to himself in Dutch as he reviewed a self-made checklist in preparation for invasion of Jekyll Island later in the evening. A wide shouldered Dutchman with sandy hair, light blue eyes and a slight psyche belying his shoulders, Deiderick carried himself in the deliberate manner of one accustomed to working with delicate precision instruments. He often thought and spoke to himself and others in the language of the Netherlands, a secret act of defiance toward his German captors. After nearly two years, he regularly feigned non-comprehension when ordered about in German, just to get under the skins of his captors.

Deiderick had long dreamed of coming to America, but never thought it would be as a prisoner of the Nazis, driving a vehicle such as the Volkswagen *Swimmerwagen* under his care.

Nor did he ever think he would be crossing the Atlantic in a submarine. A lot of things had happened he would never thought possible two years ago when he was tinkering in his garage behind his Amsterdam home happy with his wife, daughter and the prospect of a son on the way.

Born in January 1910 the Amstelveen district of Amsterdam, near the Trompenburg plant where his father worked on the assembly line of the Spyker automobile, Deiderick's childhood scheme for life was to become an engineer of design for Spyker. He loved the automobile made by the Netherlands only car manufacturer

He studied the history of Spyker and knew it began in Hilversum in 1880 when coach makers, Hendrik-Jan and Jacobus Spijker began to market their brand of passenger coaches. To reach a wider market, they moved to Thromburg, Amstelveen, Amsterdam in 1888, where they built the Golden Carriage, the official carriage of every Dutch Queen since manufactured. By 1899, the Spijkers were building automobiles, displaying their first models of two-cylinder, cars in 1900. In 1903, for ease of brand remembrance, they changed the name of the company to Spyker and came out with three horsepower and four cylinder six horsepower models. The same year, they introduced the Spyker 60 HP, a racer with the world's first six-cylinder automobile engine and first with four-wheel drive. In 1905, Spyker introduced the round radiator grille that soon became the hallmark of pre-World War I cars.

The Spijkers business talents did not match their automobile manufacturing talents and the company was frequently in narrow financial straits. After Hendrik-Jan Spijker died in 1907 on a ferryboat that sank as it returned from England, the original company went bankrupt. A group of investors bought the bankrupt firm and started manufacturing the Spyker automobile without Jacobus Spijker involved in the company. The new owners streamlined the model range and in 1907 introduced an eighteen horsepower model that nearly won the Peking to Paris Race. When the Spyker plant restarted, new hires included Jager Ramecker, who three years later would be Deiderick's father. Ironically, Ramecker's surname was a derivative of "Rademaker" meaning "maker of wheels."

By 1913, the company's financial woes returned and in 1915, when Deiderick was five years old, Spyker was taken over by new owners who renamed *it Nederlansche Automobiel en Vliegtuigfabriel Traomenburg*, the Dutch Car and Aircraft Company. During World War I, the Netherlands were neutral but manufactured airplanes and aircraft engines.

The company went bankrupt again in 1922 and was bought by Spyker's British distributor, who renamed it *Spyker Automobilefabreik*. Production continued but sales declined, despite attempts to stimulate them with new product lines. Money finally ran out as the last vehicles of the Spyker brand, C2 two ton trucks and C4 automobiles, rolled off the line. Popular opinion said Spyker did itself in by their attempt to make an automobile model to suit everybody and ending up with more models than the buying public could keep straight. Like so many before them, Spyker learned the hard way that when you try to be all things to all people, you end up being nothing to anybody. All told, Spyker is said to have made an estimated 2,000 cars, in a 30 model range, not all at the same time.

Undaunted, Jager Ramecker recognized that those people who owned Spyker cars were fiercely loyal to the stylish exquisitely handcrafted vehicles and would need parts, repair and restoration in the coming years. Jager mortgaged everything he owned to buy quantities of Spyker parts before the junk man hauled them away, setting up shop in his garage with his sixteen-year-old son as an eager inventory clerk, repairman and apprentice restorer. The business thrived enough so that, bolstered by a scholarship, Deiderick was sent to the *Technische Hogeschool Delft*, the Technical College Delft, for a degree in engineering. Delft's location, only fifty kilometers from Amsterdam, meant the younger Ramecker could help in the shop on weekends.

When Deiderick Ramecker graduated from Delft after only three years, Jager retired and moved to the Friesland province of the Netherlands to fulfill his lifelong dream of raising Friesian horses. Distinguished by its deep black coat color, often wavy, thick mane and tail and "feathers", (long silk-like hair on their lower legs), the Friesian horse looks like a light draft horse but is more surefooted and graceful. The Friesian breed is believed to descend from the Middle Ages war horses, much in demand because of their ability to carry a knight in armor yet be agile enough to maneuver in battle.

Deiderick hired someone to run the business during the day and worked at night restoring Spyker cars. He was able to find an engineering design job in one of the few places hiring during the Depression years, a German-owned business called *NV Ingenieurskantoor voor Scheepsbouw*, IvS or short. At IvS he worked with a number of engineers and submarine designers, including a young German named Johannes Vogt.

Deiderick and Vogt developed a friendship, stemmed from their mutual interest in the Spyker automobile. The friendship grew when Deiderick was able to find a rare part for Vogt's Spyker 1907 six- cylinder model 60/80 roadster. Johannes found the car rusting in a German farmer's field and did an admirable job restoring it on a young man's meager budget. The two became friends and even double-dated a couple of times. It was on a double-date where Deiderick's was a blind date that Ramecker met Aldia Koningh of the Netherlands town of Gouda, not far from where Deiderick had gone to college. In a few weeks Ramecker was seeing more of Aldia and not so much of Vogt, who had already dropped Aldia's friend and moved on to other female conquests.

As the *Nationalsozialistische Deutsche Arbeiterpartei*, or National Socialist German Workers' Party (NSDA), gained momentum in Germany, Johannes Vogt became increasingly fanatic on the subject. Deiderick limited his association with his former friend to strictly business-related conversations in the office. Besides his zealous tirades about the wonders of the Nazi party and enthusiastic adoration of Adolph Hitler, Vogt seemed to grow touchier over the subject of Aldia and jibed often when Deiderick refused to accompany him on double dates any more.

"You are too easy." Johannes said ruefully. "One smile and a bat of eyelashes from a farm girl from town known for nothing but cheese and you are like a moonstruck teenager."

After that remark, even at-work conversations ended between the two. Communication was strictly by formal memo.

By the time Deiderick and Aldia got married in late 1933, Nazi Germany was a reality, the IvS office in Amsterdam closed and Johannes Vogt had returned to Germany to join their navy. The Rameckers never heard from him again.

Over the next few years, tensions grew in the Netherlands that their traditional neutral independence would soon cease and their unthreatened relationship with Germany would end in the midst of Nazi Germany's economic difficulties. Deiderick Ramecker's Spyker car restoration business seemed immune to economic stress and politics since love for the automobile was universal. In 1934, their daughter Klaarte, meaning "bright", was born after an eight hour period of labor that allowed Alida to justify the meaning of her own name, "noble maiden."

The Netherlands declared its neutrality at the beginning of the Second World War in Europe in 1939, a status the country had declared in World War I. A Netherlands general mobilization nonetheless was declared in late August, 1939. Nazi accusations that the Netherlands violated neutrality were launched regularly by the Third Reich. By aiding British spies and creating a camp for Jews fleeing Germany and Poland, Holland was committing a de facto act of war, Nazi Germany claimed.

Politics and hysteria over German aggression seemed remote to the busy, happy, and financially stable Ramecker couple of Thromberg Avenue, Amstelveen, Amsterdam, Holland.

21

The Netherlands, May 1940

In early May 1940, Aldia grew homesick for the annual tulip-strewn countryside of her home area and decided to visit her parents in Gouda with daughter Klaarte.

"Do you think there will be any danger?" she asked.

"Because of the nuts in Germany and their fanatic saber rattling?" Deiderick replied. "I don't think they will ever do anything but stomp and shout like that lunatic leader of theirs, what's-his-name Hitler."

"No, I didn't mean that." Aldia said. "I meant any danger to the baby."

"I don't think so." Her husband replied. "You're only four months along. Just don't hit any big potholes in the road and you should be all right."

Aldia and Kaarte left for Gouda on Monday, May 6, 1940, intending to stay with her parents for two weeks. Business at Ramecker Spyker Restoration enjoyed a burst of activity as car owners became anxious to tour the spring countryside. Deiderick talked to Aldia on the phone midweek and told her he might not be able to join her and the Koninghs on the weekend because of his backlog of work.

"I'll call you Friday afternoon to let you know if I'm coming." Deiderick said.

"All right" Aldia replied . "I love you."

"Love you more."

Friday morning, May 10, 1940, Deiderick rose early but without optimism that he could catch up enough by evening to head for Gouda that evening. He decided not to turn on the radio in the kitchen since he didn't feel like starting such a beautiful day listening to politicians blame one another for the nation's woes. He lingered over coffee watching the birds quibble over seed in the backyard feeder before walking to the garage to begin his work day.

Turning on the lights in his triple garage, he headed for the 1904 four-cylinder Spyker 20/24 to begin cleaning its engine, turning on the radio resting on his front counter along the way.

"Damage and death toll reports are still coming in from Rotterdam in the wake of the early morning attack of Waalhaven airport by Germany. Nazi paratroopers are reportedly on the ground engaged in gun battles with Dutch troops at Waalhaven airfield just south of Rotterdam. The attack took place at 3:55 a.m. as Nazi bombers filled the sky in a vicious act of undeclared war on the Netherlands. We will be on the air live all day with updates."

Deiderick stopped in mid-step, reaching for the telephone to call Aletta and Dirk Koningh's home in Gouda, a scant twenty kilometers northeast of Rotterdam. He dialed the Koningh's telephone number quickly, was greeted with a busy signal, hung up, dialed again repeating the process more than a hundred times. Then, during one of his hang-up periods, the phone rang in his hands.

He raised the receiver to his ear but froze in icy terror as, before he could answer, the hysterical voice of Dirk Koningh ended his happiness in life forever.

"Deiderick, I have been trying to reach you for

hours. Aletta, Alida and Klaate left yesterday morning to go see my mother in Rotterdam for two days so a trip down there wouldn't interrupt your weekend with us. My God, Deiderick, the reports are awful. I'm afraid they're gone. God, Deiderick, what are we to do?"

Waalhaven, the harbor in Rotterdam, opened the Netherlands first civilian airport in 1920. Because of the airport's location close to his home, Dirk Koningh's father, Cort and auto mechanic quickly retooled for aircraft, applied for a job at the airport as soon as it opened and worked there sixteen years until his 1936 death of a heart attack. Located less than two miles from the airport's runways in an old Rotterdam neighborhood, the Cort and Lamberta Koningh home laid in the danger zone for bombing.

Throughout May 10th, Waalhaven airport was attacked four times by Dutch Air Force, trying to wrest control from Nazi troops. The Nazi fighter aircraft and paratroopers mounted heavy defense of the airport, acting as cover for more than two hundred Junkers 52, *Ju 52*, transport planes bringing in troops. At day's end, Waalhaven airport and the bridge at Dord, called Dorrdrecht in English, were in German hands. The Third Reich, controlling one of Holland's important commercial centers, was in position to launch full-scale invasion of the Netherlands.

For the next few days, travel in and out of Rotterdam was forbidden to all but military personnel. Deiderick kept in contact with Dirk Koningh and threw himself into his work to keep from fretting. The Nazis landed at the Hague, hoping to capture the Dutch Royal family and found the family had fled to England. The Nazis advance in the invasion of Holland, slowed by Dutch Army resistance at Afsluitdiijk, Dordredht, Grebbeberg and Rotterdam, lost over 520 airplanes, including 280 *Ju 52* troop transports at airfields in Ockenberge, Valkenberg and Ypenberg. The Third Reich invasion of the Netherlands was originally meant to distract attention from Nazi Germany's plan to invade France and then attack Great Britain. The heavy loss of German aircraft to Dutch military resistance delayed the planned invasion of Britain.

On May 14, frustrated Germans threatened to bomb Rotterdam if the Dutch did not surrender the city. Trying to protect its own citizens, the Dutch forces agreed to surrender Rotterdam but Germany bombed the city anyway, killing 950 civilians and devastating the town center. Using the excuse that British troops had landed by the Maas River, endangering German military personnel, the Nazis attacked Rotterdam, resulting in 30,000 civilian casualties. There had been no such British landing. Germany next threatened such an attack in the city of Urtecht, forcing Holland's surrender on May 15, 1940.

Lamberta and Aletta Koenig, Aldia and Klaate Ramecker were never heard from again. After Gouda fell to Germany, Deiderick heard no more from Dirk Koningh.

Now occupying all of the Netherlands, the Germans formulated a *Glichschlatung*, forced conformity, policy, eliminating all non-Nazi organization. The Germans appointed Austrian former *Reichsstattlater,* Reich Governor, Arthur Seyss-Inquart Reich Commissioner for the occupied Netherlands. Seyss-Inquarts duties included the deportation of Jews, shooting of hostages, suppression of all political groups except the Dutch National Socialist Movement, Dutch economy exploitation, and the abduction of alien workers.

Almost immediately upon Nazi entry into Amsterdam, Deiderick Ramecker came before Seyss-Inquart

"Ah, the Spyker car restorer." The slight, dark-haired, high fore-headed Reich Governor said with precise indifference as he looked at Deiderick through perfectly round spectacles. "My countrymen have spoken to me of your work. In fact, the Fuhrer himself once mentioned the magnificently restored 1911 Spyker 25/30 a friend and former customer of yours owned. The Fuhrer has also expressed to me his belief that you are an ideal candidate to work with Herr Porsche designing improved military vehicles at the plant opened in 1938 at the new town known as *KdF-Stadt*. You may not have heard of the plant, or the town, both named *Kraft durch Freude*, "strength through joy," a program Hitler and Porsche have been working on for almost a decade to bring the people affordable automotive transportation. They produced the Volkswagen, people's car, until last year but now are working on military vehicles to travel on land and water. You will depart immediately.

"Dismissed!"

Deiderick thought he had been singled out to work in a German automobile factory but he quickly found out how the notion was delusional as he was loaded with thousands of others on trains headed for German factory towns. Wanting to protect its own citizen's from potential bombing by enemies, Nazi Germany imported people from vanquished countries to work in German factories. Thousands of Dutch men and women were shipped to factories in the Fatherland to live in conditions only slightly better than the internment camps for Jews. The "alien workers" were worked long hours, were fed only enough to sustain their productivity and were allowed to die unceremoniously when they were no longer useful to the Third Reich. The alien labor workforce increased substantially when the Nazi invasion of Russia brought many thousands more into the ranks of captive labor.

Deiderick Ramecker, attached to Ferdinand Porsche's design group, was treated slightly better than most of the imported forced labor at *Kraft durch Freude*. He shared a sparse apartment with two, later three, other forced labor members of the Volkswagen military design department. While the accommodations were Spartan, the apartment at least had its own bathroom and the cafeteria on the ground floor of the guarded meeting served serviceable, if not gourmet, fare. Others fared much worse.

Grudgingly, he began to gain a guarded respect for the automotive genius and friend of Adolph Hitler, Ferinand Porsche. Both Porsche and Hitler had read Henry Ford's autobiography and were great admirers of Ford, along with Frederick Winslow Taylor, whose scientific management principles were applied by Ford. Between wars, Porsche visited Detroit several times, where he learned that monitoring labor and systematically spying on workers from one end of the chain to the other was of great importance.

Porsche was obsessed with increasing production in his plants and since labor was comprised mostly of imported prisoners, labor relations regarding hours and wages were not a factor. Porsche was also a brilliant designer, capable of meeting any challenge the Fuhrer put forth. He had met Hitler's desire for the "People's Car" capable of carrying two adult and three children passengers in 1933. Porsche now leapt gleefully into designing lightweight military vehicles, first for land use in the *Kubelwagen*, the "bucket car", then the amphibious *Schwimmwag*en, swimming car. Translating concepts to workable reality often fell to Deiderick's design team.

22

Forward cargo hold, German submarine Lone Wolf, Thursday evening, March 26, 1942

Nearly twenty-three months later, in the torpedo room turned cargo hold of the <u>Lone</u> <u>Wolf</u> that also served as his quarters and those of the *Uber Schwimmwagen,* Deiderick Ramecker shivered at the memories. The stab of grief that felt like an icicle plunged into his heart when he first heard of the Waalhaven airport attack and the Rotterdam bombing still felt fresh.. Shrugging off the memory, he continued inspecting the engine of the *Uber Schwimmwag*en, symbol of his professional pride, testing the vehicle's battery charge while he thought about what happened last year.

He felt a little bit guilty for his pride in this vehicle. But he could not suppress his engineer's love of mechanical perfection and sense of accomplishment that accompanied the successful completion of a task that started out as a sketch on a napkin adorned with a swastika. Ferdinand Porsche had returned from a dinner with Adolph Hitler during one of the Fuhrer's inspection visits in September 1941 to rush to Deiderick's quarters, handing him a napkin on which was drawn what looked like a bigger, longer *Schwimmwag*en.

"Here," Porsche said "make it happen. The Fuehrer has this idea of a water car capable of carrying as many as ten prisoners and their guards across seven miles of water."

"But sir," Ramecker replied, "It will be difficult to elongate the vehicle this much yet give it the body strength it needs to support that many passengers. Then there is the weight factor and ....."

"Enough!" Porsche shouted with the same stridency Deiderick has seen Hitler use in newsreel speeches. "The Fuehrer wants it to happen so it will happen. If you could build the *Schwimmwagen,* you can build a bigger, better one. You will drop everything and make this your priority until this project is completed. Oh yes, and it must be done by spring and must operate as quietly as possible."

Porsche turned and stalked out of Ramecker's apartment as if he were on parade, a stiffness the prisoners often noted when Germans were in Hitler's presence. Deiderick stared at the drawing on the napkin well into the night and in his mind until the early morning.

Next morning, Hitler came personally to discuss with the entire design department his concept of an *Uber Schwimmwagen,* an amphibious vehicle capable of carrying a dozen passengers besides the driver and front seat passenger, likely a guard.

Through weeks of failed tests, re-designs, sleepless nights and days fraught with pressure from Porsche's regular terse demands "Progress?" the *Uber Schwimmwagen* was finished. When Nazi Germany declared war on the United States and began bombarding American east coast shipping with *U-Boots*, the design group had an inkling of the purpose for their super water car.

In spite of captivity, Deiderick found himself fascinated with the engineering and manufacturing challenge. He
often thought about a quote by American inventor Thomas
Alva Edison when someone asked him if he had ever been
discouraged when his laboratories were testing material of
the filament of the electric light bulb, failing over 10,000
times before finding the answer: tungsten. "Each time a material failed," Edison said, "We went to our list, happy to
check off one more thing that wouldn't work."

Last month, on the first successful test of the *Uber
Schwimmwagen*, he had almost cheered.

The new water car did not stay idle for long, nor did
Deiderick. A week ago he was summoned to Porsche's office and told he and the *Uber Schwimmwagen* would leave
for a mission of the utmost importance and secrecy.

"You will be leaving from here in a few minutes."
Porsche said formally as if the Fuhrer stood beside him.
"You will not speak to anyone or identify yourself to anyone. Someone is gathering your personal effects from your
apartment as we speak. You have been a good worker and I
will miss your talents. The Fuhrer is most pleased. Farewell
and good luck."

Deiderick had heard stories of people suddenly disappearing, never to be heard from again throughout the
Third Reich. Most of those who disappeared were Jews, political activists and religious zealots. He was none of these,
but he feared his knowledge of a secret project and its im-
plementation might be his undoing and his anxiety must
have shown on his face.

Porsche noticed and began to laugh,

"Oh no, no Deiderick. You have been chosen to
drive the *Uber Schwimmwagen* on its maiden mission.
There is no time to train anyone on the vehicle and you

know it better than anyone. You will board a *U-Boot* tomorrow on a super secret undertaking. You were chosen by the Fuhrer himself for this honor. Afterward, you will be allowed to return to your home in Amsterdam in reward for your splendid performance here. I have come to admire your professionalism and dedication even as a prisoner. I wanted to tell you that, after this is all over, if you ever need a job, contact me."

Fat chance, Ramecker thought. After this is all over, I hope never in my life to see another German. I may even become a vigilante and murder every one of them I see to avenge my family. But he only smiled and replied. "Thank you, and goodbye."

Now he was readying the vehicle, dubbed by the design department at *Kraft durch Freude* as Jumbo, for its first combat mission. He didn't know his present location for sure, or where he was headed. Since boarding the Lone Wolf he had talked only to his guard who brought his food. Helmut, the guard, had passed along the scuttlebutt that America was their desitination. The cargo hold where he and Jumbo were housed had a bunk and bucket for sleeping and body functions. Without human interaction, he developed the habit of talking to Jumbo as if the silent vehicle understood.

"Well, Jumbo, old friend, looks like you and I will soon be going on the adventure of our lives. Since I think we have been traveling for a week or more I am pretty sure we are not in Europe."

The hatch to the main body of the submarine suddenly opened and he turned to see his former friend Johannes Vogt, in full German Navy officer uniform, looking at him curiously.

"Who are you talking to?" Vogt demanded.

"Just myself," Deiderick replied. "What the hell are you doing here?"

"I am *Kapitanlieutnant*, commanding officer, of this submarine <u>Lone</u> <u>Wolf</u> and I have been your host the last few days. Have you been treated well?'

"As well as could be expected. The slop jar could have been emptied more often, I smell like a goat and could use some fresh air. Other than that, I'm just fine. Have you brought the wine list for my next meal?"

"Good old Deiderick, always the smart ass." Vogt said, smiling as he thought of the vacant cabin in officer's country that could have been, but had not been ordered to be, Rameckers. Johannes had exercised his own authority to place Deiderick in these primitive living conditions, "I just thought I would come down and say hello. We are nearing our destination and in a few hours you will bring the *Uber Schwimmwagen* ashore with a guard and a small raiding party of the Third Reich's first raid on American soil. I am very proud I was chosen for command of this new vessel to transport this new machine, which I understand you helped design and build. I did not need to come down here. But I wanted to see this revolutionary *Uber Schwimmwagen and* to congratulate you. I'm glad I recommended you for the job at Volkswagen when we occupied Holland. My instincts were correct. You have served the Fatherland admirably. I will think of you when I receive the Iron Cross for this mission. Too bad forced labor cannot receive Third Reich commendation. You'd probably love another medal for your famous trophy shelf."

"Save it, Johannes. You and your goddamned Father land have cost me a wife, daughter and mother-in-law that I know of and maybe a father-in-law in the bargain. Everything I have done, I have done because my fine Catholic upbringing taught me to do the best job I know how. So don't misconstrue that as anything other than living through this war to try and find peace in peacetime."

"I could have you shot for that. I come to see an old friend and you insult me."

"Don't stand there in the uniform of mass butchers and call me your friend, you pipsqueak son of a bitch. The only reason you are such a fanatic Nazi is it makes you seem like a bigger man than you are and now you can screw the world the same way you used to screw every woman that would give you the time of day. Go ahead and shoot me. Then you can drive this thing, to do that transplanted house painter's bidding. If you are successful in this mission, whatever it is, maybe you'll get to go to Berlin and compare with your precious Fuhrer how far you both have come on ego to mask your inadequacies."

"Fine. I will wait to shoot you when you return from the mission. You have always acted superior to me, you smug bastard. You were the football star. You had the talent, a business, and beautiful wife and family and a cocky smug attitude that begged to be spoiled. Now you have nothing. It will be a pleasure to put a bullet through your superior acting brain."

"I had no idea you had such jealous feelings for me, Johannes. You're a perfect Nazi. Anxious to destroy good while you pat yourself on the back for being a super race."

Vogt turned and knocked on the hatch, waited for the armed soldier on the other side to open it, then turned to Deiderick.

"Until your return."

He stomped out of the room while Ramecker turned back to prepare his surprise for the Nazi landing party.

It was well after dark when the <u>Lone Wolf</u> broke the surface of the glass smooth Atlantic Ocean seven miles east of Jekyll Island. In the distance, the lights of Brunswick, Georgia, cast a glow of light in the sky and an occasional light blinked on the darker band of darkness that was the shoreline as shaded car head lamps seemed to signal the presence of an active city, like semaphore, saying "Here we are. Come attack us."

"Stupid Americans." *Kapitanlieutnant* Johannes Vogt, <u>Lone Wolf</u>'s commanding officer, sneered to himself as he and his entourage reached the platform atop the conning tower to observe the historic event. "American shipping has been sunk by us twice within a few kilometers of here and they conduct themselves like it happened in a movie somewhere far away. They have not yet learned the ways of war and blackout protection. We have much to teach the arrogant swine."

The sub shuddered as part of the deck slid aside. Hydraulics hissed as an elevator brought months of secret engineering topside, bringing the Fuhrer's pride, the *Uber Schwimmwag*en. The amphibious troop-carrying land/water vehicle looked ominous in the *U-Boot's* minimal deck lights. Even more ominous were the four German storm troopers in full night battle gear sitting on the bench seats of the water car's open passenger area. Up front, another German guard sat alongside Deiderick in the passenger's seat

The mission: kidnap six members of the U. S. Federal Reserve Board of Governors from their secret meeting on Jekyll Island, Georgia and, if possible, kill J. P. Morgan Jr., symbol of American support for the enemies of Germany. Besides the shock of being attacked on their home shores, the kidnappings would demoralize America's financial structure.

Under armed guard, Deiderick Ramecker drove Jumbo down the hastily laid ramp and into the water, retracted the wheels, lowered the screw propeller from the rear engine cover and engaged the coupling providing an extension of the engine's crankshaft to drive the props. The front wheels would double as rudders so steering could be done with the steering wheel at the driver's seat whether at sea or on land. The vehicle moved away from the submarine toward the sparse lights showing through the trees of Jekyll Island.

Johannes ordered the cargo hatch closed. As the panels began swinging slowly toward sealing on the submarine's deck, he noticed an odd thing about the sky. A ponderous shadow like a dark cloud bore down on the Lone Wolf from the northwest, blocking view of the stars as it came.

"Dive, Dive. DIVE" Johannes screamed, recognizing the ill-defined shape of a blimp.

The submarine exploded in a huge pyrotechnic display as the first bomb ignited the fuel tank while the second hurled through the closing gap of the hatch plates and eviscerated the interior of the submarine. The submarine's oversize fuel tanks flamed with ferocity to rival midday. Burning pieces of the vessel rose skyward like parts of a broken toy flung by a giant.

"Guess that's it" the pilot of the U. S. defense blimp from Naval Air Station Glynco at nearby Brunswick said to his bombardier, as they looked down on the few pools of flame signaling the remains of their handiwork "Those jerry spies weren't just flingin' wiener schnitzel. We might have been a little late, but we got 'er. That U-Boat's saluting Hitler from the bottom o' the briny so let's go home. Tell 'em mission accomplished"

In the darkness beyond the explosions, the *Uber Scwimmwagen* made fast toward the island.

****

Back at Naval Air Station Glynco, ONI Captain Aaron Rankling was handed a message telling him the German submarine had been sunk successfully just as the cargo hatch doors were moving.

"Wait a minute." He said. "Were they opening or closing?'

"A moment sir." The radioman said as he sent a message to the returning airship. "They say the light from the hatch was getting narrower as they approached the target sir."

"Damn! It was closing. Have them make a sweep toward Jekyll Island and be alert for movement. Also, notify the island detail and the folks at *Villa Mariana* to be on the alert. The German landing party is loose on the water."

Turning to Army Captain Frank Gould, Rankling said. "We had hoped to sink the sub before the landing party launched but it looks like we missed the chance. Now the landing party will know they are trapped on the island. That could make them desperate so there may be some shooting because all of our fake Federal Reserve directors are armed. Of course the U. S. government will compensate you for any damage to your home.

"Don't worry about it" Captain Gould said. "Just get them. I just don't want them harming any of the club members and staff who may be on the island. The Millionaire's Club is slowly dying anyway, with the improvement of transportation and the development of Florida, not to mention the impact of the Depression. You have to remember that when the Millionaire's Club was formed, Florida was jungle. The new breed prefer the luxury of Palm Beach to the hoary old stuffy Victorian traditions of Jekyll Island. This war will probably do the Club in completely, so what happens to *Villa Marianna* tonight doesn't make much difference."

****

Aboard the *Uber Schwimmwagen*, the Germans looked back on the burning oil slick that marked where their submarine was just moments ago.

"*Mein Gott*." One muttered.

"It is of no consequence." The leader of the landing detail said. "My secret orders say that another submarine cruising nearby will pick us up when we are finished." He picked up his radiophone to notify the other submarine of the fate of the <u>Lone</u> <u>Wolf</u> and giving coordinates for the new pick-up location near the south end of the island. He did not mention that his secret orders also instructed him to kill the driver and scuttle the *Uber Schwimmwagen* at the completion of the mission if the <u>Lone</u> <u>Wolf</u> was not available to them. "Make for the beach about mid-island and look for a light." he told Deiderick.

They approached the widening low dark mass of Jekyll's live-oak lined barrier island beach. The landing party commander used binoculars to scan the shore, looking for the lantern marking the road to the cottage colony on the other side of the island. True to captured spies' word, ONI agents had placed a lantern where Shell Road met the hundred-yard beach lining Jekyll Island's east shore.

"There" the detail leaders said loudly, pointing to the

pinpoint of light.

"I see it." Deiderick responded, adjusting course to steer toward the light. As soon as he felt Jumbo's tires touch the sand of the beach, Ramecker paused to disengage the propeller, then came ashore, making for the gap in the woods marked by the lantern.

"Slowly." The detail leader ordered "About a hundred meters in we should find a small maintenance road that will take us to our destination. Use the headlights only sparingly and stop just at the edge of the forest."

A few minutes later, after following the maintenance road across what seemed to be a golf course and entering a large, thick copse, the vehicle stopped about twenty meters inside the woods at the edge of a large lawn. Across the yard lay the bulk of a large white Spanish-style villa, lit dimly by a few small lights.

"Halt. We will go the rest of the way afoot. The driver and his guard will stay here to turn the vehicle around for a fast escape. Come quietly now."

Secretly, Deiderick flipped the toggle switch under the dashboard, killing the battery, effectively disabling the *Schwimmwagen*. Unaware, the German storm troopers silently dismounted the vehicle, stealthily advancing on the quiet villa ahead.

Just inside the woods line, a contingent of armed ONI agents lay silently in wait for the German landing party to pass into the open yard so they could attack from the rear. Another group hid in the sheds and outbuildings to challenge the landing party. The plan was to capture the Nazi's in a vice-like surrounding maneuver, hopefully without bloodshed. Most of the Germans had passed the American's hiding place, when one of the ONI group stumbled over a gnarled root hidden by the low fern forest floor, pulling the trigger of his machine gun as he fell.

No one knew who fired but everybody seemed to fire at once in a torrent of gunfire strobing the woods with muzzle flashes. The Nazis, out gunned, mostly in the open and in the middle of a crossfire, died to a man where they stood.

Beachward in the woods on the maintenance road, Deiderick used the distraction of the gunfight to pull his guard's Luger sidearm from its holster and shoot the man, who fell to the ground. Deiderick started to run diagonally through the woods in the opposite direction from the gunfire. He took only a few steps before the guard on the ground fired his rifle at him, the bullet tracing a shallow trench across the Dutchman's forehead as he turned. Deiderick, resorting to his firing range training, turned and leveled a kill shot at the guard, then rushed through the trees, ignoring the pain beginning to radiate from his forehead.

He came to another clearing of the trees behind a large building where lights were beginning to click on and people were rushing outside. He concealed the gun as a black man in dark pants and a white shirt approached him in the dark.

"What is happening?" The man asked in English.

Deiderick shrugged.

"You're right behind the colored servant's quarters. Next building beyond ours is the white servant's building." The man pointed.

Deiderick shrugged

"Must be one of them furriners from the maintenance crew." The other man said, disappearing into the night toward the sound of shouting around the curve of the woodland.

Eyes following to be sure the man was gone, Deiderick stood in awe at the sight a short distance away. In the night, a faintly lit stained glass scene met his gaze from a darkened building to his right,

Sanctuary, he thought, heading for the small chapel, just making out a steeple as he approached. As he drew closer, details of the stained glass scene became more distinct. To the right, the Virgin Mary held the Christ Child on her lap while three variously dressed figures knelt in adoration, one with head bent in supplication. Yes, he thought, I can find help there.

He rounded the building and entered, looking toward the cluster of light and sounds of excited movement from a growing group of people next door across a wide yard. The chapel was empty except for a few candles burning as he looked for a hiding place. He did not want to be in the open for fear someone would notice his wound and associate him with the Nazi invaders.

He ventured around the inside to the building looking for a place of concealment. Finding nothing but a too small open room just off the altar where vestments were stored, he re-entered the main chapel. A wave of dizziness caused him to steady himself against a cabinet beside the altar just in front of the railing separating the altar area from the pews.

The cabinet moved slightly. Curious, he pushed a bit more. The hollow decorative cabinet-like table moved away from the wall. Just as he gauged the hollow space, thinking it might be too small for him, someone rattled the handle of the front door. Ducking quickly into the tight cavity of the mock cabinet, he eased it to the wall from the inside and listened.

Footsteps echoed in the small building and then a

voice said "Guess this place is clear" as the two men left.

Deterick remained motionless, listening, and some-time in the night fell asleep.

****

On the mainland, Aaron Rankling was talking by telephone to his shore detail leader at *Villa Marianna*. Rather than getting all military, the leader of the Jekyll Island party figured it was just easier to telephone from the villa.

"Are you telling me every damn German is dead?" He asked. "What the hell happened? We were supposed to just capture them quietly and go on about our business. Now half the damn east coast has admired our fireworks display when the submarine went up so gloriously and every light sleeper on Jekyll Island is calling local law enforcement to find out what all the gunfire was about."

"I don't know what happened," His island contact replied. "Somebody fired and all hell broke loose. Our guys din't stop shooting 'til every German was down because the Nazis were blazing away like they thought they were going to shoot their way through to Kansas. Brave sonsabitches, I'll say that for 'em. We don't know how many there were supposed to be but we're pretty sure we got 'em all, Somebody said they thought they heard shooting behind us and we did find a dead Nazi by their vehicle but I don't think any of them got away. We've done a search of the area and didn't find anything suspicious. We did find a pistol at the edge of the woods, but we figure somebody must have lost it at another time.

"Anyway, the big thing I wanted to tell you was that we found the thing they came ashore in. We thought they were just gonna come by boat but this thing is like a staff car had an orgy with a school bus, a pick-up truck and a motorboat. I'm tellin' you Captain, you never seen anything like it."

"Any of our men injured?"

"Three gunshot wounds, no deaths. We made out pretty good but for the other guys it was a slaughter."

"Well, clean up over there and bring that vehicle back over here. Report to me when you're get here."

Hanging up the phone, he said to Frank Gould "No real estate damage except some scuffed up lawn. No German prisoners either, but we didn't lose anybody so I guess the evening wasn't a total loss."

"Maybe there is propaganda value in letting the Germans know we have their water wagon."

Part VI: KAISA

23

Hollybourne Cottage, Jekyll Island, Georgia, pre-dawn, Friday, March 27, 1942

"*Uw koninkrijk kome, Uw wil geschiede* .... Thy kingdom come, thy will be done." Kaisa Conroy put water on to boil for a cup of tea in the kitchen of the spacious kitchen of the seventeen–room *Hollybourne* Cottage on Jekyll Island's Riverview Road. The post-season quiet on the island unnerved her a bit as she looked across the Old Plantation Road behind the *Hollybourne* to see *Villa Mariana* through a curtain of pre-dawn mist. At least the noisy bunch had quieted down over there. What a party they must have had at that cottage the previous evening, setting off explosives and shooting their guns around midnight. The group of men looked so serious and staid when they moved into Frank Gould's cottage yesterday evening. She thought their performance later that night was completely out of character. She heard the ruckus from her bed as she lay thinking about her past and future. She thought about complaining to the Jekyll Island Club Director, but dismissed the idea since technically she no longer had status on the nearly deserted island.

In a few minutes, she would make her way just across Old Plantation Road kitty-cornered one lot to Faith Chapel for an early morning prayer before waking her son, eleven year-old Mickey. He would be all right alone, sleeping, for the few minutes it would take her to say a quick prayer. She had adjusted to the lack of a Catholic priest or regular Masses on Jekyll Island by making it a point to go to the nondenominational Faith Chapel for prayer and reflection once a day, generally in the early morning. She needed a lot of prayer this particular April morning. She was glad she had asked for and received permission from the Maurice family to remain on the island for an additional week after they left, to contemplate the next step in her life.

How she would miss this island. In her nearly seven years employment with Mark and Evangeline, splitting time between Philadelphia, Pennsylvania, Newport, Rhode Island and Jekyll Island, Georgia, Jekyll was far and away her favorite.

When she first went to work for the Mark Maurice family, joining them in early November 1935 at their stately Philadelphia home, she quick acclimated to the flow of their family life. During the week, she home taught her son Mickey and their son Jared in the morning. After lunch, while the children succumbed to quiet time, she and Evie, (as Kaisa still thought of her), continued their intellectual gymnastics game of "did you know", matching wits over facts of local history. It was a game begun on Mackinac Island and grew with Evie's blooming intellectual curiosity. Evie, now Evangeline to the world, began voraciously reading the works of author Constance Fenimore Woolson, whose works had captivated her back on Mackinac. Determined to read the tragic Miss Woolson's lifetime body of work, which included seven novels, 65 poems and 30 nonfiction and travel articles, Evie began to take notes. Then the determined Mrs. Mark Maurice began looking for articles about Miss Woolson and writing anyone who might have known her. Later, she would enthusiastically undertake writing Woolson's biography.

After Thanksgiving, the Maurices set about packing to winter at Jekyll Island, Georgia, a place mysterious to Kaisa's Michigan experience, where they would stay at the family's ancestral cottage *Hollybourne.*

"You will love the island," Evie said. "some of Mark's relatives are a bit stuffy but there will be separate quarters for you and Mickey to share if you don't mind staying in the servant's wing at the upstairs back. The service wing is not used any more since the help now either has their own homes on the island, live in the Servant's Quarters buildings or commute by ferry from Brunswick, Georgia, seven miles across St. Simon Sound. Some of the family now uses bedrooms in the service wing when the family rooms are all taken and they don't want to miss all the action by staying at the Club House.

"Mark is worried you will be offended to house in servant's quarters but wanted me to assure you that at Jekyll, like here, you are a part of our family. "

"It's not a problem." Kaisa replied. "Just how big is this 'cottage'?"

"About seventeen or eighteen rooms, I think. Let's see, there are six big bedrooms upstairs for the family, three bedrooms in the service wing, and a bathroom each in the family part and the service wing upstairs. Downstairs there's the dining room and parlor flanking the main entrance hallway in the front, along with a kitchen pot closet, butler pantry, gun room servant's dining room and service porch in the back. So how many is that? Anyway, *Hollybourne* was the first cottage built in the Cottage Colony by a founding member of the Jekyl Island Millionaires' Club. It is also one of the few that has its own kitchen, unusual because in the early days of the Club, all the members took their meals at the Club House."

"That's quite an inventory for a gal who said she didn't pay much attention to what went on around her."

"That was the old Evie. The new Evangeline notices everything. Besides, I cheated. I knew you were going to ask about the cottage so I looked at the floor plan in a history one of the family wrote about *Hollybourne*. It was built in 1890 by Mark's grandfather, Charles Stewart Maurice, a prominent bridge builder from Athens, Pennsylvania, a little town on the Susquehanna River up near the Pennsylvania-New York border. Charles Stewart Maurice and his wife Charlotte Marshall had nine children, five girls and four boys, the oldest of which, Archibald, is Mark's father."

"You are reciting again."

"You're right." Evie/Evangeline smiled. "Here, it's all in this *Hollybourne* history. and here's another book on the history of Jekyll Island and the Millionaires' Club."

"Will there be a test?" Kaisa mimicked the first question their sons asked when told something new.

"Maybe."

They bundled up the boys and went off on another field trip to one of Philadelphia's treasure trove of historic sites.

****

In her room that November night in 1935, Kaisa began earnest study of the cottage and island that apparently would be her home for much of the winter. She started with the simple booklet entitled *Hollybourne.*

Charles Stewart Maurice, a Civil War veteran, was a pioneer in steel bridge building who had merged his business with several others in 1884 to form the Union Bridge Company. The new firm built some of the most important bridges of the time, including; the Cairo Bridge over the Ohio River; Cantilever Bridge over the Niagara; Memphis Bridge astride the Mississippi River; and the Poughkeepsie over the Hudson, making Maurice and his partners wealthy. Maurice joined the Jekyll Island Club in 1886, before it had been chartered, bringing along three of his business partners and a good friend. From the beginning and for the balance of their lives, Charles and Charlotte Maurice were avid boosters for the Island and the Club. They collected legends and history tales of Jekyll Island, which they published privately as *Jekyl Island: Some Historic Notes and Some Legends Collected by Charlotte Marshall Maurice , and a Brief Of the Early Days of the Jekyl Island Club by Charles Stewart Maurice.*

Kaisa laid the booklet aside and looked at the other book Evie gave her. Sure enough, it was the same undated book published by Charlotte and Charles.

"Don't worry if you see Jekyll spelled sometimes with one 'l' and other times with two." Evie had warned her. "James Oglethorpe named the island after his friend Sir Joseph Jekyll, The second 'l' was for some reason dropped when the Club was formed in 1886 and for more than four decades it was known as Jekyl Island, one 'l'. Then in 1929, a historian discovered the mistake and in July of that year the Georgia legislature voted to return the second 'l' to the name. Some say this action brought about a curse on the Club because three months later the Great Depression started a decline in the Jekyll Island Club members' fortunes and those of the Millionaire's' Club and bringing about the end of the golden era. Membership is declining and each year fewer people come to Jekyll Island. The younger crowd seems to favor the action of Florida to the more staid Victorian era feel of Jekyll Island. There are exceptions. Mark is a third generation of those raised wintering there and Frank Miller Gould, who is closer to our age, built his *Villa Mariana* almost across the road behind *Hollybourne* a few years ago."

When Charles Stewart Maurice built eclectic Tudor style *Hollybourne*, he combined design features of his shipbuilding experience as well as the historic traditions of U. S. southeastern coastal building materials. Using shipbuilding methods, he outfitted Hollybourne with steel trusses in the attic to eliminate beams or pillars in the large dining room and parlor, then installed nineteen brick support piers in the basement. He clad the exterior of the cottage with tabby, a mix of oyster shell, lime and sand. *Hollybourne* remained the only winter home in the Cottage Colony built of tabby.

Members of the Maurice family had been wintering at Hollybourne since 1890, with the exception of 1894 and 1895, when the scourge of yellow fever made coming to the island dangerous to their health. Some years they arrived before the "season" began. First it was Charles Stewart and Charlotte Maurics with their eight surviving children (a ninth, Charlotte Marshall, died in infancy) and later with their extended families.

Over the years, typhoid occasionally caused the deaths of Jekyll Island employees and Club members. The typhoid problem came sharply into focus when Charlotte Maurice, the mother, died in September 1909 of typhoid she caught at Jekyll Island in April of that year. Club doctor William H. Merrill in April, 1909, thought the chronic typhoid problem stemmed from the method of the island's sewage disposal methods, which he thought was placed too close to the oyster beds that supplied the Club one of their most popular menu items. The belief that a typhoid carrier must be among the island guests overshadowed Merrill's theory about the source of the typhoid situation. Six Jekyll Island Club members died of typhoid one year later. This time, Dr. William Ford blamed the problem on sewage disposal too near the oyster beds. The Club updated their sewage disposal system and the typhoid problem disappeared.

When Charles Stewart Maurice died in 1924, he had already disinherited youngest son Albert so five of the Maurice children, including Mark's father Archibald Maurice, united to keep *Hollybourne*. Margaret Maurice, selected by a draw of lots by the Maurice heir's consortium, took possession of the Maurice Jekyll share, which could only be held in a single name.

"Margaret, unwed, and her single sister Marian have continued to come to Jekyll Island every year for the entire season," Evie told Kaisa the next morning. "while the rest of the family go sporadically. Mark and I probably go the most often. Mark likes to be sure his aunts are getting along all right as they take on the years and, also, he loves Jekyll Island more than anyone else in the family except the two sisters."

From the first moment she stepped from the Club launch *Sydney*, Kaisa fell in love with Jekyll Island. The exquisitely groomed grounds of the turreted Victorian style Clubhouse, the manicured lawns of the ten magnificent winter homes in the Cottage Colony, all surrounded by lush fern-carpeted sub-tropical forests of live oak, palmetto, pine and magnolia conspired to win her awe and affection immediately. She had read the history of the island extensively, but nothing prepared her for the beauty of the place.

She knew the ten-mile long by two-and-a-half mile wide dogleg New York Strip Steak-shaped barrier island was once inhabited by Timucuan of Guale Indians and had been a favorite hangout of coastal pirates. It is believed Robert Lewis Stevenson was inspired by Jekyll Island to write his famous adventure book *Treasure Island*. The island was the smallest and southernmost of the Georgia's four "golden Isles", which also include Little St. Simons Island, St. Simons Island and Sea Island across St. Simons Sound to the north of Jekyll. Cumberland Island, south across St. Andrews Sound is a National Seashore famous as a protected loggerhead turtle nesting ground.

Jekyll Island's first European settler was Major William Horton, assigned to establish an outpost on Jekyll Island by General James Oglethorpe, founder of the colony of Georgia. Purpose of the outpost was protection of Fort Federica on St. Simons Island northward across St. Simons Sound from the Spanish troops from Florida in the south.

Horton built a prosperous plantation on the island before his 1749 death. The remains of Horton's two-story Colonial home, made of native tabby, were restored by Jekyll Island Club members in 1898, but fell again to ruin. The walls of the Horton House stand to modern times, a tribute to the durability of tabby.

A parade of island owners followed until Jekyll Island was sold to Christophe Poulkan DuBignon in 1792, who raised cotton there, passing the property to his son Henry who continued raising cotton until the Civil War. In 1863, Henry deeded the island to sons Henry Junior, Charles and John, along with his daughter Eliza. Later, John DuBignon bought the southern part of the island from his relatives and, with brother-in-law Newton Finney, started a hunting club. In 1884, John DuBignon built a house on the island.

In 1886, a group of wealthy northerners, primarily members of the Union Club of New York City and others from Chicago, seeking a haven from winters, formed the Jekyl Island Club and bought the island from DuBignon. Initial members of what would be known as the Jekyll Island Millionaire's Club included the cream of the nation's leading moneyed: J. P. Morgan; Joseph Pulitzer; Cornelius Newton Bliss; Marshall Field and his brother Henry; Charles Stewart Maurice; William Rockefeller; William Kissam Vanderbilt and John Wyeth among them. A hundred shares of the Jekyll Island Club shares were to be sold to fifty members for $600 each as start-up funds for the club.

The Jekyl Island Clubhouse opened in 1888 and in the beginning members stayed at the clubhouse, taking their meals there. Later members built their own "cottages", elaborate structure replicating what some were accustomed to at their summer quarters in Newport, Rhode Island. Most of these cottages did not have kitchens, their owners preferring the social intercourse of dining at the clubhouse. Some wanted to live apart from the clubhouse but did not want the expense of building and maintaining a structure as a winter home. Among those members, in 1896 William P. Anderson, James J. Hill, Henry B. Hyde, J. P. Morgan, James A. Scrymser and Joseph Pulitzer formed a syndicate and built a building of six separately owned apartments called *Sans Souci*, meaning "without cares." The three-story Colonial Revival building, considered one of the first condominium apartment houses, had two apartments per floor, each with three bedrooms and a drawing room. There were no kitchens or dining rooms because, like many cottage owners, apartment owners took their meals at the clubhouse.

Other non-Clubhouse accommodations included the Club Cottage, the refurbished DuBignon Cottage, where members and guests could rent rooms by the day of periods up to two months.

Jekyll Island and actions of its Club members influenced a number of aspects of American life.

During the 1899 season, United States President William McKinley vacationed at *Solterra*, Frederic and Elizabeth Baker's cottage. McKinley held a reception at *Solterra* to meet Jekyll Island Club members and declared the island "simply delightful," McKinley's assassination took place just over two years later. *Solterra* burned to the ground March 9, 1914, and was replaced by William Tyler Crane's *Crane Cottage* in 1917. The *Crane Cottage*'s seventeen bathrooms, not surprisingly, were outfitted with Crane Company plumbing fixtures.

In the fall of 1910, United States financial leaders met on Jekyll Island, ostensibly for a duck hunt. The meeting was so secret that the participants used only their first names throughout their stay, earning the moniker "The First Name Club." Here J. P. Morgan and others discussed the idea of another attempt at central banking in America (two previous central banks had failed to have their twenty-year charters renewed). Rhode Island Republican Senator Nelson Aldrich, Chairman of a bipartisan commission studying banking reforms following the Panic of 1907, met with Morgan and several representatives of large banks. During the Jekyll Island "hunt" they drafted what would become the Federal Reserve Act, enacted by President Woodrow Wilson's signature December 23, 1913.

While a guest at the Club Cottage January 25, 1915, Theo N. Vail, President of American Telephone and Telegraph (AT & T) was suffering from a leg injury and could not travel, so he had 1,000 miles of cable run to Jekyll Island so that he could participate in the first transcontinental telephone call. The call included Vail, Alexander Graham Bell in New York, Bell's assistant Tom Watson in San Francisco and President Woodrow Wilson in the White House.

Local oral history has it that if all Jekyll Island Club members were present on the island at the same time, its peak, one-sixth of the nation's wealth would be represented.

■■

Life on Jekyll Island during "the season" was idyllic for Kaisa. She quickly shucked the northern mindset that after August, it was farewell warm weather and hello a parade of progressively thicker coats until May (if you were lucky). The seemingly eternal summer of the Georgia Atlantic barrier masked the barely noticeable winter presence.

On the Jekyll Island social scene, the influence of the stiff-necked formality of the Victorian-era rulebook the original Millionaire's Club members brought from northern climes was beginning to be less obvious. Now into the fourth generation of membership, the modern Millionaire's Club took greater interest in enjoyment than in stilted appearances of "propriety." Older members, for instance, avoided dining room seats in the Clubhouse that overlooked the swimming pool, as post-Victorian-era mores abbreviated swimwear. Many younger members of Millionaire's Club families were not picking up their elders' memberships, preferring instead the more carefree aura of Florida's Palm Beach and Fort Lauderdale.

The early-season socials on Jekyll were a study in the fluid sociology of changing upper-crust attitudes, played against a background of tongue-clucking for the old guard and spontaneity from the new breed. Kaisa loved her new life. At one such party at one of the Cottage Colony winter homes in 1940, she came face-to-face with her pre-Maurice employment days.

"Kaisa," her hostess gushed, "There is a charming gentlemen here visiting from Sea Island across the Sound that you should meet. He is from Tennessee but spent some time in the Michigan oil business. Kaisa Conroy, this is Walter McClanahan. Walter, Kaisa"

"Hello, little lady," The soft voice of the big man whose wealth-defining oil well explosion cost her an uncle and the father of her child said. "We've come a long way from that little Michigan oil town, haven't we? I now have two places on Sea Island; one for my family of teetotalers and one to entertain my business associates who like a toddy or two. You must come and visit. How do you come to be here?"

"Mr. McClanahan," Kaisa said frostily, "Just as I was not then, I am not your 'little lady'. My job in those days required I tolerate you then but I am under no such restraint now. You will address me as Kaisa or Mrs. Conroy or this conversation is over."

Taken aback, McClanahan recovered quickly. "Certainly, Mrs. Conroy, I did not mean to offend you. I understand you now are the employ of the Maurice family. I wonder of you would introduce me. I have a oil prospect in Michigan that may interest them ..."

Kaisa walked away. Kaisa thought she might have to apologize to the party's hostess but the opposite happened. McClanahan's heavy-handed investment solicitations apparently did not fit well in the rarified atmosphere of Jekyll Island because she never saw him on Jekyll Island again.

24

Hollybourne Cottage,
Jekyll Island, Georgia,
early morning,
Friday, March 27, 1942

Sitting in *Hollybourne's* kitchen in 1942, Kaisa thought about the seven wonderful winters she'd spent with the Maurice family here. Once they realized Kaisa was not just another in a parade of short-lived nannies who had been run off by Jared Maurice's rowdy ways, the Maurice sisters followed Mark and Evie's ways and treated her and Mickey like part of the family.

Wednesday she had waved farewell to the two un-married surviving daughters of *Hollybourne's* builder Charles Stewart Maurice, seventy year old Marian and fifty-nine year old Margaret Maurice. Both were infuriated with the 1942 foreshortening of the Jekyll Island Club's normal January through April "season" because of fear for mem-ber's safety in the face of German submarine raids on ship-ping along the American east coast. She was glad Margaret and Marian had left for the north before last night's ruckus across the road at *Villa Mariana*. The previous Monday, she'd tearfully said goodbye to her employers for the past six-and-a-half years, Mark and Evangeline Maurice and their twelve year-old son Jared, her former charge as governess.

She agreed with the Maurices that this should be last year as Jared's governess anyway, since he would soon leave for an upscale military boarding school in preparation ultimately for West Point. She and the family were beginning to drift apart. Mark was perpetually busy with his Philadelphia law practice; Evangeline with her research and writing of her soon-to-be-published biography of Constance Fenimore Woolson; and Jared was on the early path to the military.

She was still adjusting to the fact that her position with the Maurice family was no longer viable and had only begun to consider her future when this new bombshell arrived by mail last week. Even before hearing from the attorney in Holland, Michigan, her personal financials were extremely comforting. Payments for her father's share of the Delaware Last Chance Mining Company had finally shrunk to nothing. However, her salary and severance pay from the Maurices was ample, her expenses nearly nonexistent since 1935. Additionally, in the late 1930s she sold her Mt. Pleasant, Michigan, house to Spang Oilfield Machine Shop Office Manager Charles McCament and his wife Gertrude, where they were now raising daughters Wilma and Martha. She planned to return to Michigan's Upper Peninsula to visit her parents graves at Delaware and perhaps find any remaining members of her father's family while raising Mickey in a small town atmosphere.

That plan accelerated and changed again by the combination of the Nazi threat and the certified mail she received last week. It came so close to April Fool's Day she immediately called Holland, Michigan.

"Yes Mrs. Conroy," the dusty-sounding voice of attorney Agular Van Slooten, Esquire, said on the telephone. "I sent you those letters. It certainly took some time to find you. When my investigator finally persuaded Mr. John Murphy of the *Michigan Oil & Gas News* to give him your address, Murphy said your job is still waiting if you decide to return to Mt. Pleasant. I suspect after we meet, you'll not have to worry about a job anywhere. When may we expect you here to discuss the matter of your grandparent's estate?"

"I will get back to you later." she replied.

"We will look forward to meeting you, Mrs. Conroy."

"And now this." she thought, removing two envelopes from her letter file to read the two letters for the hundredth time since receiving them.

The cover letter was succinct:

Dear Mrs. Conroy,

We regret to inform you of the recent deaths of both your grandparents, Hermann and Marta Golder, each of whom named you as their sole heir.

At your grandfather's request, we delayed contacting you when your grandmother passed on because he knew he would soon follow. A sealed letter from him is enclosed.

Your inheritance of their assets and your grandfather's business is considerable. We would appreciate your contacting us at a suitable time.

Sincerely,

Agular Van Slooten, Esquire

Van Slooten, Dykema & Ramulin

Attorneys at Law

She unfolded the second letter and laid it on the table

in front to read as she drank her Earl Grey tea. Even though she knew the contents by heart, the flourish of the old time script made for slow going.

My dearest Kaisa,

By the time you read this, I will be gone along with your grandmother, who passed on a few weeks ago. The doctors tell me my time is severely limited and I am at a loss for a way to address you properly after all of these years of regret. My beloved Marta, your grandmother, once told me I would die a lonely old man and now her prophecy has come true.

As I sit alone in the house she and I shared loveless for nearly three decades, I do not know how to begin expressing my regret for the ill treatment I have subjected you to, and your mother before you. My stubborn contempt for her for not following the life-plan I envisioned for her is, I know now, unforgivable. Then you came along, a near mirror image of the daughter my foolish ego believed had betrayed me. My treatment of you with cold indifference was reprehensible.

Many times over the years, I wanted to take it all back. But business always seemed to get in the way, For a while I was able to follow your life through friends in the Upper Peninsula, but after your mother's tragic death, I lost track of you in the demands on me to keep my business afloat during the Depression.

All of it rings hollow now. My soul is as empty as my life and I hope death brings blessed relief.

I will not ask for forgiveness, for I will never know if it is granted. I will only say I am sorry, with the hope my legacy will bring you more happiness than it has brought me and you will wear your wealth better than I have worn mine.

With love and eternal regret,
Hermann Golder
Your Grandfather

As with each previous reading, Kaisa felt tears well in her eyes for the lost opportunity to love and be loved by both her grandparents. She was happy with her life to date, but mourned that her mother did not live to see this plea for forgiveness by her father. Kaisa had never known love from Hermann Golder and so did not particularly miss it, but she knew the contempt for him borne by Kristina, her mother, was rooted in hurt over his rejection. Kaisa thought about the slim times she and her mother had endured after her father's death and about how Hermann Golder must have known about their plight. Yet he had done nothing.

"Oh well," she concluded, "none of us can get that time back so there is no sense brooding over it. Back to the life I have."

The current season on Jekyll Island began as normal for the Maurice family, who often arrived in December rather than waiting for the "season", since *Hollybourne* was self reliant and not dependent on the Clubhouse kitchen. Kaisa and Mickey, along with Mark, Evangeline and Jared Maurice had arrived December 3, 1941 to find Margaret "Peg" and Marian "Mamie" Maurice in residence since December first. The Japanese attack on United States Navy Sixth Fleet at Pearl Harbor Hawaii Sunday, December 7, 1941, followed immediately by the United States' declaration of war on Japan made little impression on Jekyll Island. When Nazi Germany declared war on the U. S. and began dispatching their submarines, called *U-Boots* (U-Boats in English) along the U. S. Atlantic coast, sinking shipping,

Jekyll Island Club members began to take serious notice.

The Jekyll Island January to April season opened normally in 1942. A number of members cancelled their arrival because of the war, further depleting the dwindling number of regular season club attendees. Mark's cousin Thomas F. Maurice and his wife visited *Hollybourne* briefly in late February and his aunt Emily Dall came from her Cedarhurst, Long Island New York home for a brief visit in early March. Those visits were brief and the 1942 season was a shadow of the glory of earlier Jekyll Island seasons; no elaborate adult or children's parties; no group journeys to haunt the shops of nearby Brunswick for the latest fashions; no raucous hunting expeditions (except the one last night); no world famous visitors; and no real island social life.

Evie and Kaisa (and Mark when he was there) filled their days with activities designed around the boys; fishing trips; picnics on the beach; wildlife hikes; bicycle rides,and attending the occasional movie showing at the old Tea House at the ocean side of the island. Evenings consisted largely of listening to the Maurice sisters mourn the deteriorating Island life and reliving the glories of Jekyll Island Club seasons past until time to study for the next day's history expedition. Twice, Kaisa and Evie took the Maurice sisters to Brunswick to visit longtime Jekyll Island Club Superintendent Ernest Gilbert Grob, a good friend who retired in 1930 after more than forty years with the Club to travel before he suffered a stroke in 1940. The sisters often visited Charlie Hill, who lived year-round on the island, employed by the Club from the beginning, employed by the Maurice family as coachman and caretaker for much of his working career.

Soon after they arrived on Jekyll Island in December 1935, Kaisa and Evie resumed their "study and recite" routine they established on Mackinac Island. Often they would visit a Jekyll Island site with their sons, with whichever woman had selected the site telling the others what she has learned in researching that place. The "information game" became a standard of each season, serving as an education tool for Mickey and Jared while allowing Kaisa to fulfill both her roles as governess and companion.

The illustrious Jekyll Island Club membership represented the upper echelon of American culture from finance to journalism to government to industry manufacturing. Therefore, in studying and speaking of the people and events of the Club, they were an education for the boys and themselves about the highlights of United States history. Though they often complained about the education expeditions, over the years Mickey and Jared began absorbing the lessons and soon were chorusing bits of previous lessons. "That's Mr. Pulitzer's cottage, isn't it Mom." from Mickey. "He was a great newspaperman, wasn't he, Mother? He published the *St. Louis Dispatch and* the *New York World*, didn't he?" from Jared.

The day after Mark, Evie and Jared Maurice left the island, notification came from the federal government mandating evacuation of Jekyll Island by April 5, 1942. An announcement that the U. S. Army 104th Infantry Division would be guarding the Georgia coast accompanied the evacuation notice. The Jekyll Island Pier Road boarding house and dining room as well as one of the employee houses would be used by the 104th, with soldiers stationed at a watchtower at the north end of the island to communicate with the "main base" on the island. Most of the Club guests departed immediately and those staff living on the island hastily arranged for accommodations ashore in Brunswick and beyond.

Knowing the following week would be full of packing away furniture, shuttering windows and generally shutting down the Club and the island, a going away party was hastily organized for Friday. The party organizer was the island schoolteacher, Anna Hill, daughter of Maurice longtime family retainer Charlie Hill. Anna, teacher at the school for Club staff children, always included Mickey Conley and Jared Maurice in the school's special activities, recognizing the two boys had no one else on the island even near their age. Anna taught at the colored school from its 1930 beginning. An earlier school for Jekyll Island Club members' children had closed for lack of students.

Leaving the island for the last time would be sad.

Today the children of the island, offspring of both staff and the few remaining members would be attending the going away party. Enthusiastically enjoined by members and staff alike, the all day party would be a farewell to Island culture.

The Maurice sisters decided "all the real people have already left so this party is a lot of foolishness" and departed on Wednesday.

The party would provide swimming, pony rides, games, cake and, most of all, with Mickey gone for the day, give Kaisa time to organize the last of the packing for their Saturday early morning departure. They would attend an early Mass in Brunswick before catching the train for the journey to Holland, Michigan, to meet with her grandfather's attorney.

Yesterday Kaisa and Mickey took almost the whole day for a farewell bicycle ride around the almost deserted island. They took a picnic lunch, leaving midmorning to take River Road north, primarily to see what was happening with erecting the watchtower on the dunes overlooking the entrance to St. Simon Sound.

The famous *Brown Cottage*, on their left, was the first major landmark they encountered riding north just beyond Wylly Road. The *Brown Cottage* was the first cottage built, but never occupied by a Jekyll Island Club member, Edie had related once when it was "her day." McEvers Bayard Brown hired an architect, approved plans for the cottage, and left the United States forever in 1888, living on his yacht in England in solitude until his 1926 death. The millionaire banker was elected to membership of the Club at its first meeting September 15, 1886, so was not a founding member. Brown, who loved the isolation of the island, bought Lot 71 on the Island, a remote half-mile from the Clubhouse location. The elaborate three-bedroom cottage with a sweeping semicircular porch overlooked the tidal marsh, Jekyll River and Latham Hammock to the west of the island. Brown maintained the cottage, kept up the taxes on it, paying his dues to the Jekyll Island Club regularly, but never occupied the home.

The *Brown Cottage* sat empty for a long time before the Club decided it needed a live-in caretaker and island's boat Captain James Clark moved in. Clark later moved out when he married the Club housekeeper Minnie Schuppan, who thought the cottage too remote from the club happenings. For a time *Brown Cottage* was the only empty house on the island. Although there were inquires about it, ultimately potential occupants would decide it was just too far from everything. No one wanted to rent the place, ever. So it sat, forlorn and empty, it's owner shrouded in mystery.

Next they pedaled past the abandoned island dairy, on their right, created by the Jekyll islanders because delivery of milk, butter and eggs to the island was too erratic for their sensibilities. The barn where cows were once milked by a small staff was overshadowed by a silo. Apparently dairy product delivery schedules by local merchants improved because the island dairy was closed in 1930, Kaisa had learned.

Farther along on their right, they stopped at the abandoned *Horton House* to stand in the doorless doorway one last time. They admired the thickness of the tabby walls. They played their little game, imagining the windowless interior crowded three hundred years before with gentlemen and lady friends of General Horton.

Directly across River Road from *Horton House* lay the du Bignon Cemetery. Here a bronze plaque stood out among the crumbling headstones, memorializing the March 21, 1912 drowning of George Harvey and Hector Deliyannis. Kaisa knew from Evie's research that Harvey and Deliyannis were waiters at the Jekyll Island Club who perished in a freak accident while on an off-duty swimming outing on the island's Atlantic-side beach thirty years before. Since there were no known home addresses or next of kin for the two unfortunates, the Club had them buried and immortalized in this historic cemetery.

They continued around the northern tip and down the east side of Jekyll Island, drinking in the splendor of the birds singing in the woods and the sun ruffled dance of the azure Atlantic Ocean, banded by the 100 yard beach. After lunch on the beach, they napped in the sunlight for a while. They rode past the 1909 built golf course, waving to island golf professional Karl Keffler, a renowned Canadian champion hired by the Club in 1910. Reaching Shell Road, they cut across the island past the Jekyll Island Clubhouse and home to *Hollybourne*.

Shaking herself from her revelry, Kaisa cleared the table and walked out *Hollybourne's* back door toward Faith

Chapel.

Along the way, she startled herself with her reflection in one of the cottage windows. She nearly didn't recognize her own image because she was wearing her blonde hair down to her shoulder after years of wearing it up in what she views as a more dignified "governessly" formal bun. The girl in the glass was pretty. Not bad for an almost twenty-seven year-old mother, she thought to herself. What's up with you, kid. What's next.?

Part VII: KAISA & DEIDERICK

25

Faith Chapel,
Jekyll Island, Georgia,
early morning,
Friday, March 27, 1942 (continued)

She approached Faith Chapel, remembering that Charlotte Maurice had been a strong booster of the interdenominational aspects of the worshiping place. Charlotte was Episcopalian but saw that all faiths and races were welcome to exercise their religions in the shingled building. Charlotte had hosted six Catholic nuns and Father Dunn, a Catholic priest at *Hollybourne* and Faith Chapel in 1908, a year before she died.

What a great lady, Kaisa thought as she placed a kerchief on her head and crossed herself entering the chapel.

"*Eer aan de Vader, de zoon en de Heilige Geest....* Glory be to the Father, the Son and the Holy Spirit..." Kaisa began the Lord's Prayer in Dutch to begin her morning meditation in the front row of pews of Faith Chapel.

"*Zoals het was in het begin en nu en altijd zal wereld, zonder einde. ....* As it was in the beginning, is now and ever shall be, world without end." A muffled male voice echoed through the silence of the room, completing the prayer's first stanza.

Startled, Kaisa challenged. *"Wie is daar? ...* who is there?" She thought the voice came from the cabinet at the right of the altar and moved in that direction. She started to pull one of the handles on the cabinet, only to realize the handles were false. The mock cabinet pulled away from the wall to reveal a stranger crouched there.

Still in a semi-sleep stupor, causing him to respond to the opening of the Lord's Prayer a moment ago, Deiderick Ramecker half opened his eyes. With the background of the exquisite stained glass window glowing brightly in the morning sun, the face of a beautiful blonde woman appeared in the soft light of the chapel, her hair cascading to her shoulders, framing her face

"Mijn God, ben ik in de hemel? ..... My God, am I in heaven?" he asked.

"Hemel? Wat een onzin, je bent in Jekyll Island, Georgia in de Verenigde Staten. Wie ben je en wat doe je hier? ..... Heaven ? What nonsense, you are in Jekyll Island, Georgia in the United States. Who are you and what are you doing here?" Kaisa replied, noticing for the first time that the blonde, broadshouldered man was dressed in rough workman's clothing and had a wound on his forehead.

Fully awake now, Deiderick said quickly *"Niet schieten! Ik geef me over. Mijn naam is Deiderick Ramecker. Ik ben geen nazi. Ik ben Nederlands.* ..... Do not shoot! I surrender. My name is Deiderick Ramecker. I am not a Nazi. I am Dutch."

"Ik weet dat je Nederlands van uw toespraak zijn, maar wat is dit allemaal over nazi's en waarom zou ik schiet? Wat doe je hier? Was u schipbreukelingen? Spreek je Engels?. .... I know you are Dutch from your speech,

but what is all this about Nazis and why should I shoot? What are you doing here? Were you shipwrecked? Do you speak English?"

"*Nee, alleen Nederlands. Sommige Duitse* ..... No. Dutch only. Some German." Deterick replied.

"*Heel goed, zullen we in het Nederlands spreken vanaf nu*...... Very well, we will speak in Dutch from now on."

Deiderick quickly explained why he was on the island, telling Kaisa the story of the loss of his family in the Rotterdam invasion by the Nazi's, their takover of the Netherlands, his conscription by the Germans to work at forced labor in the Volkswagen factory where he was instrumental in development of the *Uber Schimmwagen* and his escape from his captors during the gun battle the previous evening.

Kaisa listened to the words but was more impressed with the incredible sadness of this stranger's demeanor. She had no idea what was happening but it was clear to her that she should protect this man, a fellow countryman of her ancestors, from further grief.

When she asked where he came from and he mentioned a part of Amsterdam where Kiasa's grandmother said was where her ancestors lived, Kaisa made up her mind.

She motioned the man to come with her and led him across the road to *Hollybourne* Cottage.

"*Is dit uw huis?* ..... Is this your home?" Deiderick asked.

Kaisa quickly explained that this was the home of her former employers, who had already returned to their home up north. She took him to the covered sunken laundry drying enclosure adjacent to the laundry, a nod to the modesty of the Victorican era when the cottage was built. She gave him some food and explained he should keep quiet and get some rest, until her son left for the day. She woke Mickey, fed him breakfast and when his friend fourteen-year-old Nancy Hurd stopped by, waved goodbye to both when they left for the all-day party at the Clubhouse.

Kaisa let the handsome young Dutchman sleep for a while as she did some packing for the trip back to Michigan the next day. A strange engine noise outside caught her attention and she looked outside to an odd dull dun-colored unmarked vehicle coming down the lane in front of *Villa Mariana* to turn toward the wharf area, evidence of the veracity of Deiderick's story. In an upstairs closet she found some of Mark Maurice's old work clothes he wore when helping Evie garden. She brought them downstairs for her guest to wear while she washed the grimy outfit he was wearing when she found him.

While Kaisa was back in the kitchen preparing lunch, a U. S. Navy officer in uniform knocked at Hollybourne's back door. "Excuse me ma'am" he said, "I don't know if you have heard but late last night we were able to stop a German kidnap attempt across the road at Mr. Gould's cottage. You may have heard the gunfight. If so, I'm sorry if we disturbed you folks. Anyway, we think all of the Nazi invaders were killed. But one of the residents of the colored servant's barracks says he ran into somebody at the edge of the woods behind the barracks who seemed to be a stranger to the island,. We are canvassing all the occupied cottages and searching the vacant ones to be sure we got 'em all. Have you seen anyone around this morning who looked out of place?"

"No I haven't" Kaisa answered quickly, instinctively realizing that Deiderick's lack of English and speaking in

Dutch could be construed as German and cause him a lot of trouble. She needed more time to think what to do with the Dutch stranger and knew she could always turn him in later if he acted suspicious."

"Thank you. If you see anyone who doesn't look right please let us know. We'll be headquartered in the parlor at the Clubhouse for the rest of the day."

"I will, thank you. Does this have anything to do with that huge explosion I heard last night?"

"Yes ma'am. After they unloaded their landing party, the German submarine was sunk by people from the air base at Brunswick. We are certain there were no survivors from the submarine."

"Do you really think there's a Nazi loose on Jekyll Island?"

"Probably not, but we're just making sure. If nothing turns up, we will be leaving tonight.''

"Well, thank you for stopping by. I must get back to my packing. My son and I are leaving tomorrow for Michigan."

The naval officer left and Kaisa steadied herself with another cup of Earl Grey Tea while she hatched a plan to explain Deiderick **Ramecker's presence to Mickey. Next she plotted how to get Deiderick off the Island.**

Late in the morning, she woke Deiderick with the clothes she had found for him and as he entered the kitchen he said morosely. *"Dank u. Deze kleding je me in gevonden werden door de Duitsers naar mij afgegeven. Zij zouden de dwangarbeid mensen te voorzien van periodiek kleding. We dachten dat ze kwamen uit de Joden, die regelmatig verdwenen uit onze landen. Dat werd bevestigd op een dag wanneer iemand kreeg een pak jas met een gele ster of Da-vid nog steeds genaaid aan de mouw......* Thank you. These clothes you found me in were issued to me by the Germans. They would furnish the forced labor people with clothing periodically. We figured they came from the Jews who regularly disappeared from our countries. That was confirmed one day when somebody got a suit coat with a yellow Star of David still sewn to the sleeve."

"Dear God in Heaven." Kaisa exclaimed in English in shock that needed no translation. Deiderick gave a "what can I say" shrug. They discussed Kaisa's plans for him in Dutch with him nodding all the way.

"When my ten-year old son gets home, I will introduce you as the Dutch cousin of an old friend from Holland, Michigan, who stayed for a time as a boarder in my boarding house in Michigan. When the friend, who knew I was here, found out you worked on the island, he directed you to me. Since we are going to Holland, Michigan, and you are going to visit your cousin there also, we will be traveling on the same trains to Michigan. I will tell Mickey my friend asked me to keep watch over you because you do not yet have your English. Since you have been living at the lumber camp, you will be staying with us tonight to catch the early ferry. I will give you a note in English and some money for the train so you can give them to the ticket clerk at the train station in town. Once we leave the ferry at Brunswick, we will separate and act as strangers until we are on the train. I don't want to be drawn into a diplomatic incident if you are captured. I don't think it is likely, but I must protect Mickey and I"

Deiderick nodded in approval. *"Ik begrijp het. Je bent een heel slimme dame. Ik denk niet dat ik zou willen schaken met je spleen....* I understand. You are a very clever lady. I do not think I would like to play chess with you." He said, smiling for the first time since she met him.

God he's beautiful, Kaisa thought as she smiled back, then mentally shook herself. Come on girl, she mentally scolded, this is serious business, not time to get girly.

As if reading her thoughts, he asked about her husband. She answered about being widowed almost eleven years before by a Michigan oilfield accident, so her son never knew his father.

In the afternoon, the final issue of her subscription to the *Brunswick News* newspaper was delivered. She read with interest the front page story,

NAZI KIDNAP ATTEMPT THWARTED ON JEKYLL the headline screamed. She read with interest the story that followed, punctuated by photographs, obviously taken at night, of the strange vehicle she had seen this morning and a row of covered bodies:

JEKYLL ISLAND – The midnight sky was alive with flame last night as an armed blimp from Glynco Airbase sunk a Nazi U-Boat. Minutes before, the submarine offloaded a revolutionary landing craft (see photo) bearing a German raiding party intent on kidnapping members of the Federal Reserve Board of Governors at false meeting fabricated by the U. S. Office of Naval Intelligence (ONI).

The story went on to describe the trap laid for the boarding party and the gunfight leaving seven of the Nazi stromtroopers dead. At the end of the account, Kaisa's eyes fell on the last paragraph, which she translated for Deiderick.

Though authorities say there is no danger of any of the Germans surviving the submarine bombing and the gunfight, they urge Citizen's to be extra cautious and on the lookout for suspicious strangers. Even before this incident, there have been scattered reports of Germans mingling with our coastal citizens, mostly for pleasure, at dances and in movie theaters. Remember, there is a war on, with our shipping being sunk almost daily within sight of our shores. TRUST NO ONE!

The breathless piece was drenched in hysterical hyperbole. but it served as warning to them.

"Since you have no identification, you must carry yourself confidently and not attract attention to yourself." Kaisa told him.

"Are you not frightened?" he asked.

"Scared to death." She replied.

Mickey was so excited about the party when he came home, he never questioned the story of Deiderick's presence. Adding to the thrill of the party was the chaos caused by the captured Nazi water vehicle and the German corpses that were inadvertently paraded across the yard a few yards from the party goers. " .... an' they had helmets and holsters and blacked out faces and everything." Mickey squealed. Kiasa concluded that Tom Mix could be staying at *Hollybourne* and Mickey would never have noticed.

Next morning they were at the Jekyll Island Club wharf when the Club's sixty-five foot cruiser, the yacht *Sydney*, arrived bringing the first load of island workers who lived ashore. When they boarded, Mickey immediately ran to the bow of the twin engine cruiser, where he would stay until they docked in Brunswick. He loved to stand at the bow and have the sea breeze rush over him as the boat sped across St. Simons Sound. Like a dog hanging out a car window to let his ears flap in the wind, Kaisa thought.

"Captain, I'd like you to meet my friend Deiderick." Kaisa said to the *Syney's* skipper, A. J. Spaulding. "He's been working on the timber crew at the north end of the island and is traveling with us back to Michigan."

"Can't say as I've ever seen him before so he must

281

'o come over when I wasn't on duty." Spaulding replied. "Not a surprise though. They been shiftin' me back and forth from runnin' the *Sidney* to runnin' the *Sylvia* and back again that I wouldn't know if Hitler himself had come over some morning. Folks have sure been in a hurry to get outta here this past few days. Them Navy fellas said I'm sp'ose to check out anybody I don't know but if you're vouching for him Miz Conroy I'm sure not gonna cross ya. Welcome aboard, fella."

"Thank you. Nice to meet you." Deiderick said in flawless English. Just the way Kaisa drilled into me last night in countless rehearsals, he thought. I wonder what I said.

They took their seats and watched silently as the lowslung outline of Brunswick, Georgia's meager skyline grew as they approached, wavehopping across the water.

****

"What a goldam comedown this is." Glynn County Georgia Sherrif's Deputy Judy Glenhaven muttered to herself as she made the twentieth circuit of the morning around the lobby of the Brunswick train depot. Three years ago she was living in New York City working for a topnotch private security firm protecting international millionaires and business big shots. A local Brunswick girl, she had left this seaside town a decade ago and done everything from waitressing to ticket taking at a movie theater. She was a big girl, tall, beefy and sort of pretty from the neck up but the rest of her body seemed to have been designed by someone wearing a blindfold. She was small where she should have been big and big where she should have been small, her broad hips narrowing to a thin chest before broadening to shoulders that would have done a football fullback proud. But she couldn't really complain she thought, it was her size and formidable strength that caught the attenion of one of the agents from Algonquin Security Company in New York City.

Her unusual strength lying beneath what appeared to be a layer of flab made her an ideal covert escort for their well-heeled clients. Best of all, her appearance precluded any love or lust interest from co-workers and clients alike. She knew she didn't get the security job on her good looks, but what the hell. The money was good and she'd gotten to travel all over the world with all kinds of people to many an exotic place.

Then the bottom fell out. The Great Depression didn't end quite quick enough. Financial giants became peasants in rapid order right until the end, before the war machine in Europe got things humming again. But Judy Glenhaven lost her job with Depression-related cutbacks. She still remembered leaving the Algonquin office building for the last time with a box containing five years accumulation of personal effects topped by an envelope containing a glowing reference and a piddling severance check. As she left the building she saw a headline on the Wall Street Journal. Proclaiming *Rate of economic recovery gradually increasing.* Balls, she thought, don't do a damn bit of good to know the death rate from the Black Plague is decreasing if you are that last one to catch it.

She returned home because even in bad times, New York was one expensive place to live. Her uncle knew the Glynn County Sherrif so the next time a deputy slot opened, she got it. It was good to go to work again even if her fellow deputies thought that since she was the only woman deputy she was just a secretary with a uniform.

For the last month she'd been stationed in the Brunswick Depot watching for suspicious characters. The Nazi's declaring war on the United States and bombarding American shipping had military and law enforcement in a tizzy, seeing German spies under every park bench. In the month she'd been here Judy had had run ins with everything but spies. She'd been asked to carry luggage for high hats fleeing Jekyll Island. She'd been swung on by lunatics shouting news of the world's end. She'd been vomited on a dozen times and been called just about everything derogatory that could be uttered by a human when she checked identification of a few people, including a man she had just watched lift a wallet from another unsuspecting traveler.

The Brunswick Depot was once a gem of elegance. The dropping off place for Jekyll Island, the depot sometimes had hosted half a dozen private train cars belonging to millionaires headed for the Jekyll Island Club. Unduly ornate for a town the size of Brunswick, the depot presented the facade of gentility for the arriving and departing ultra-rich and their servants. Age and declining use eroded the fancy fittings of the depot, like a broke heiress in a once stunning, now outdated party frock.

Rather than watch people, Judy began entertaining herself by watching clothing. She loved clothes and in every country she'd traveled for work she was a shopaholic during her off-duty time. That may have partially explained why she got broke so fast when her job ended. Her closets were full of expensive clothing from all over the world. She kept seeking the perfect fit but everything she tried on, or even had tailored, ended up looking like it belonged to somebody else.

But she did know clothes. She could spot quality: an

Italian suit; a French skirt; a British hat or a Japanese blouse a mile away. She could equally spot fashion disasters. People should not try to do things they are not good at, Judy believed. Icelanders should not try to make swinsuits. Fat Africans should not try to design clothes for skinny white women. The Swiss should stick to clocks and chocolates, not try make high fashion suits. Most of all, those engineering geniuses, the Germans, should buy their shoes from somebody else. To her practiced eyes, German shoes were by far the greatest sins against fashion. Judy loved beautiful shoes because her feet were the easiest to fit and when clad in nice shoes were the most beautiful part of her. Thus she was sensitive to bad shoes and in her opinion German shoes were the worst.

Idly she watched the parade of humanity headed for the ticket windows, then the waiting rooms, anticipating the arrival of the northbound train that would take them to the land of icky mud and slush as winter turned to the spring Georgia had been enjoying for weeks.

God, how she envied them. To be going someplace to see something different while she sat here on her observation stool making sure drunks didn't relieve themselves in the ash trays. She was as fascinated by the privileged as she would be with some exotic bird new to her experience.

Take this group coming in. The woman's blond hair cascaded to her shoulders, clad in an exquisitely tailored light gray suit with matching boots. The boy with her had her features and was dressed expensively but in the tosseled way of boys. The man right behind them was a little less fancily dressed and she couldn't tell if he was with the boy and woman although he was watching them closely. A purse grabber? Judy wondered. A pickpocket? Or maybe just a workingman in a hurry. She looked at him more critically. Expensive but old shirt, slightly short legged but fashionable pants, also older. and clunky .... my God ... German shoes.

She went on point. These were not older shoes pre-dating the European war but were fairly new, if slightly scuffed. She looked at his face, northern European, maybe German. The woman and boy bought their tickets just as the arrival of the train was announced and hurried toward the boarding gate. The man approached the ticket window and nervously handed a note and some money to the clerk.

Deputy Judy Glenhaven approached him. "Excuse me sir. Could I see some identification."

Deiderick Ramecker turned and innocently said the only thing he knew in English, "Thank you. Nice to meet you."

From the train, Kaisa watched as Sherrif's department cars converged on the depot, sirens wailing. As the train pulled away, she caught a glimpse of a blonde man, surrounded by armed deputies, being led to one of the sherrif's cars.

"Mr. Rameker has been delayed and won't be joining us." she told Mickey.

26

Near north of Moline, Michigan
NW NW NW Section 07 T4N-R11W
Leighton Township,
Allegan County, Michigan
Tuesday, May 4, 1943, 1:55 p.m.

Kaisa Conroy sat alone in the idling non-descript ancient pickup truck she purchased recently through a third party. She was parked facing south on rural Division Street just off 146th Avenue a half mile north of Moline, Michigan, hoping she would not have to outrun any law enforcement cars in this junk heap.

It was now nearly fourteen months since Deiderick Ramecker's mistaken arrest as a German spy in Brunswick, Georgia. Now, there he was, just across the road in a field twenty-four miles from her home. He and the rest of the small crew of prisoners of war were bent to the task of hand-snapping asparagus. The crew of a dozen German POWs from Fort Custer were a work party housed with a guard at the Mooren Asparagus Farm while bringing in the crop. The long green stalks are one of Michigan's first crops to appear in the spring, she had recently learned.

Michigan asparagus, unlike asparagus from other states, is hand-snapped above the ground, yielding a more tender and flavorful product. Not that she gave a rip but it was mentioned in the investigator's report on Ramecker's current location.

She glanced anxiously at her watch hoping the train was on schedule. She wasn't sure just how many Federal laws she was about to break but she knew the Geneva Convention required that all prisoners of war had to be returned to their country of origin and she knew the crew of P.O.W. she watched in the nearby field was no exception. Deiderick Ramecker was not a prisoner of war since he was not a combatant but a Dutch conscriptee forced by the Nazis to work in their Volkswagen plant. But government red tape and bureaucratic complexity dictated that since he was a foreigner with no identification captured on United States soil at a time of war, he was to be interred until the war ended.

Wartime hysteria is so strange, she thought. On one hand, German prisoner of war interment camps in America were praised in the worldwide press for their humane treatment of prisoners. On the other hand, in Michigan, a Detroit restauranteer named Max Stephan had been sentenced August 6, 1942, to hang for helping a Nazi airman who had escaped a Canadian prisoner of war camp and crossed the Detroit River in a rowboat

Stephan had sheltered and fed the man for two days before buying him a bus ticket to Chicago. Stephan, a naturalized American citizen, had been a sergeant in the German Imperial Army before emigrating to the United States. The Stephan case was the first conviction for treason since two traitors were sentenced to hang in 1794. Both Stephan's hanging sentence and the hanging sentence of the

1794 pair of convicted traitors were commuted by Presidents Franklin D. Roosevelt and George Washington, respectively.

The treason conviction story had agitated Kaisa greatly, since she was in the middle of formulating a plan to rescue Deiderick Ramecker from the German prisoner of war camp at Fort Custer, just north of Battle Creek, Michigan and the legal quagmire in which the Dutchman found himself. The journey for both of them from March of last year to this point had been long and frustrating.

Meeting with her grandfather's attorney, Agular Van Slooten, in late March a year ago at Holland, Michigan, and taking possession of her grandparent's house at 18 East Twelfth Street, Kaisa spent a few days familiarizing herself with it, the automobile she now owned, her newly inherited wholesale grocery business and other aspects of Hermann Golder's substantial estate. She was astonished to find that 320 acres her grandfather owned just southeast of town bounded by Mason, and Ottogan roads and 104th and 117th avenues had several producing oil wells as part of the Fillmore oilfield encompassing parts of southern Ottawa and northern Allegan counties. The Traverse geological strata field discovered at 1,516 feet in 1940 was generating a considerable royalty income. Since she was now a royalty owner, she resolved to contact her former employers at the *Michigan Oil & Gas News* magazine for a subscription and join the Michigan Oil and Gas Association.

Once oriented to her new lofty financial status, she asked Mr. Van Slooten for the name of the investigator he used to track her down earlier. She contacted the private detective and hired him to determine Deiderick Ramecker's status and whereabouts within the prisoner of war system. She was amazed how quickly problems were solved by throwing money at them.

The American experience with German prisoners of war (POWs) was not new, she learned. During World War I, the American involvement in actual combat had been very brief, only six months. German prisoners reaching the United States were relatively few, most of them sailors captured far away from the battlefront. Three locations, Forts McPherson and Oglethorpe in Georgia and Fort Douglas in Utah, became POW camps designated during the war by the United States Department of War.

The Glynn County Sheriff's department had a situation with Frederick Ramecker akin to the dog that spends years chasing cars and finally catches one..... they flat didn't know what to do with him. They held him for weeks, at first basking in the publicity spotlight of being one of the first local government law enforcement agencies of World War II to capture a "Not Zee". The novelty soon faded and the press had a new darling *du jour* in a couple of days so the Sheriff began inquiring about what to do with the strange "furriner".

The United States began housing German POWs for the Government of the United Kingdom after entering the European Theater of World War II in 1941, because of a housing shortage in England, where prisoner of war facilities were few early in the war. The U. S. Office of the Provost Marshall General finally took custody of the hapless Dutchman. Ramecker's lack of English language and the confusion of the Dutch language he spoke with German by his captors did not help him to plead his case. By the time the U.S. was in the big war a year, as many as 30,000 German prisoners a month were being brought to America a month by Liberty Ships returning from transporting troops to the European Theater.

KAISA

Through the investigator Kaisa hired, Deiderick Ramecker's dilemma was explained to all who would listen. While his story met sympathetic ears at lower levels of the bureaucracy, Ramecker's case was so unusual that it was bounced through a hopeless morass of "passing it on to the next fella." Meanwhile Deiderick stoically waited, hoping to find someone who spoke Dutch.

When Fort Custer at Augusta, north of Battle Creek, Michigan, had opened a section of its facilities to German prisoner of war interment earlier in the year, Kiasa's agents pleas got Deiderick transferred there. Basis of the plea had been that he, being Dutch, would be more comfortable close to one of the nation's foremost Dutch communities until his problem was resolved and he could be released. The Provost Marshall General's office generously approved the transfer. When the Moorens, a family of Dutch asparagus farmers south of Grand Rapids, filed a request for help under the POW work program, a clerk at Fort Custer familiar with Deiderick assigned him to the crew. The Geneva Convention equal treatment for prisoners mandate of equal treatment entitled the POWs to be paid American military wages for their work. The American shortage of labor caused by millions of U. S. soldiers sent overseas made the German POW work program popular, particularly in agricultural areas.

Many of the German soldiers captured were not, and in fact hated, Nazis. Members of the regular German Army often resented the fanaticism of the National Socialist Party. Nazis permeated the armed forces and decimated the German economy to feed the war machine's "invade and dominate" approach to the rest of the world.

Life as a German prisoner of war was often better than their life at home. Prisoners often enjoyed more food and better living conditions than those of their families in Nazi Germany. Interaction between prisoners and local citizens was often friendly. Prisoners were sometimes allowed out of camp without guards. In remote areas, prisoners grasped the vastness of the American interior and knew that flight or escape would likely be fruitless. Several camps allowed social receptions with locals and some prisoner-local woman liaisons led to marriage. It seemed the further from national borders, the more relaxed the discipline for German POWs.

When Deiderick arrived at the Mooren farm, it did not take long for Kaisa to establish communication with him. She did not visit him because she wanted to avoid being recognized during the investigation that was sure to follow after she helped him escape. They exchanged notes through her hired agent and talked on the telephone sometimes. She would call as his cousin Katrina and they would speak in circumscribed brevity because it was a party line. The site of his crew's work was surveyed and a plan took shape.

In the warm sunlit May afternoon, the flatlands of southwestern middle Michigan basked under dazzling blue skies laden with cottony clouds. Under a photographer's sky, high humidity produced a slight humid haze.

Behind her in the distance, the mournful brittle sound of the southbound freight train whistle sent its penetrating warning it was about to cross 146th Avenue. Kaisa looked in her rearview mirror to see the serpentine cloud of thick black smoke pour from the train's smokestack and fall to blanket the road. Division Street alongside the tracks was covered with a thick layer of impenetrable black. She gently opened the passenger side door of the pickup and looked up to see Deiderick look her way while edging closer to the road edge of the field. They nodded to each other solemnly.

At the last possible moment, Ramecker charged across the train track and jumped into the pickup beside her as the locomotive passed, spewing its noxious smelling ribbon of thick black smoke to engulf the road. Kaisa hit the gas and popped the clutch. The pickup roared and lurched to life, passing the locomotive to emerge into unlimited vision while the length of the freight cars shielded their flight and a band of black filled in behind them to obscure escape route. A few minutes later they skirted the village of Moline before turning west on 142nd Avenue to head toward Holland. In a wooded area near the small hamlet of Burnips, Kaisa stopped so Deiderick could change into the undistinguished clothing she purchased for him ..... including <u>American shoes</u>.

Before they pulled away from the roadside, he said *"Een ogenblik ..... one moment."* When she turned, he kissed her, giving wordless acknowledgement to the love that had grown mutually during their separation. *"Dank u ..... Thank you. "*

In half an hour, they were pulling into the drive of the imposing brick house at 18 East Twelfth Street, Holland, Michigan.

"Deze keer, dit is mijn behuizing. she said, then gave him his first English lesson by repeating the phrase in that language aloud. "This time, darling, this is my house."

*"Ik hou van je en wil met je trouwen ..... I love you and want to marry you." Deiderick declared.

"Onzin! Je bent gewoon het gevoel dankbaarheid. Je hoeft niet eens willen weten wat er gebeurt als ik een relatie met iemand. Zij, of iemand anders dicht bij mij, sterft. De enige persoon die ik nog heb is Mickey en ik zal niet de kans op verlies zijn voor u nemen ..... maar ik zal je vertellen, ik

kon je liefde ook......" Kaisa replied. " Nonsense! You are just feeling gratitude. You do not even want to know what happens when I get romantically involved with someone. They, or someone else close to me, dies. The only person I have left is Mickey and I will not take the chance of losing his for you ..... but I will tell you, I could love you too."

"Ik waag het erop .... en Ik zal u ook overtuigen, ook...... I'll take my chances .... and I will persuade you too, also." Deiderick said.

■ ■

Back in the asparagus field at the end of the day, the guard did a headcount of his team before returning to their quarters at the Mooren farm. He counted twice, then looked around.

"Where's the Dutchman?" he asked.

Some of the Germans shrugged while another who understood English said "Gone."

"What the hell." The guard said. "He never belonged here anyway according to the scuttlebutt at camp and from what the Moorens tell me. I'll square the count with the clerk. Hope somebody teaches him English.

When told he was short one member of the asparagus field and which one, Emil Mooren said "Good. I hope he finds happiness. Such a sad, sad man."

EPILOGUE

Faith Chapel
Jekyll Island, Georgia – April, 2002

Kiasa smiled through tears, remembering the moment she realized Deiderick shared the love she had developed for him during their fourteen-month ordeal nearly six decades ago. It did not take long for him to fulfill his promise to persuade her to marry him, despite her reservations.

He stayed with her at the big house in Holland. She introduced him as the fiancée she met at Jekyll Island, Georgia. They were able to secure bogus identification documents for Deiderick passable enough that he was able to petition for and receive American citizenship, after learning English and passing all the required tests.

"Het is een nieuwe wereld voor ons beiden. Het is beter om samen de onbekende delen dan toe eenzaamheid aan onze beproevingen." He repeated until he won her over. "It is a new world for both of us. It is better to share the unknown together than add loneliness to our trials."

Kaisa and Deiderick were married in late August, 1943.

Deiderick's command of both Dutch and English worked well for his position as Logistics Director at Golder Wholesale Grocers. In 1954, they read that Volkswagen was contemplating launching an American marketing campaign and the Rameckers promptly secured western Michigan's first and later Michigan's largest Volkswagen dealership as the foreign import Volkswagen "Beetle" grew in popularity. The "Love Bug" craze swept the nation as its charm and

JACK R. WESTBROOK

economy overshadowed memories of its Third Reich origins.

Kaisa kept in touch with Mark, Evangeline and Jared Maurice, who in the late 1940s, purchased the *Crow's Nest* Cottage on Mackinac Island, originally built by the Mathers, who had erected Anne's Tablet on the island. Evie's book about the life and works of Constance Fenimore Woolson was an instant bestseller and was still popular in the Mackinac Island area. Evie was a much in demand speaker when in summer residence. Mark Maurice died in the 1960s and Evangeline followed in the early 1980s. Now Jared Maurice and his family lived full time on Mackinac Island where he held the position of official Island historian, having achieved a Master's degree in Michigan History.

After the 1942 season, Jekyll Island was taken over by the military for the duration of World War II. Cottage owners were not allowed back on the island until the war was over. The Jekyll Island Club disbanded in 1947, when the State of Georgia bought the island and paid off the cottage owners to establish a State Park and designate the Cottage Colony as a Historical District. The most vehement enemies of the idea of the state takeover of the cottages were the Maurice sisters, Margaret and Marion, who were so angry that after the forced buyout of *Hollybourne* Cottage, where they had wintered most of their lives, they avoided the state of Georgia en-route to Florida for the rest of their days. All the cottages in the Cottage Colony were restored except *Hollybourne.*

Winter vacation and year-round homes on a less grand scale than the Millionaire's cottages began to populate Jekyll Island in later years. Deiderick and Kaisa built a winter home on North Riverview Drive at Bond Street, where they wintered on Jekyll for years before selling last year when failing health made the trip from Michigan too burdensome. Besides Kaisa's son Mickey, Deiderick raised the two daughters they had together, Katrina and Aldia. All were married and the girls were building their own lives in other states while serving on the board of directors of the family corporation. Mickey ascended to the presidency of K and D Corporation, the blanket organization for the Volkswagen dealerships and grocery operations, remained in Holland, Michigan. After law school, it was Mickey's suggestion that in the face of the major chain self-branded grocery giants, Golder Wholesale Grocers should phase out wholesale grocering except for their chain of ethnic, primarily Dutch, food mini-markets. The mini-market franchising catapulted the family fortune.

****

Just after Christmas of 1949, as she and Deiderick were preparing to depart Holland for "the season" on Jekyll Island, she received a package from her old friend Norman X. Lyon in Mt. Pleasant. Lyon was apparently back at work for the *Isabella County Times-News.* (Lyon would ultimately switch between the *Michigan Oil & Gas News* to the local Mt. Pleasant newspaper several times before his 1972 retirement, at the end of the John Murphy ownership of the oil and gas reporting magazine, depending on his and the magazine owners respective temperaments) Inside the package was a note from Lyon saying "Thought you would like to see the send off I gave your old buddy-bud." Along with pages from the December 27, 1949 *Times-News.*

"*Heart Attack Fatal to W. L. McClanahan: Rites held Monday for Leader in State's Oil Industry*" the two column headline screamed from the paper's front page. McClanahan had returned to his Sea Island, Georgia, winter home from a pre-holiday business trip to Michigan arriving the day before Christmas. He played six holes of golf as part of a foursome of friends, the collapsed on the seventh tee and died without regaining consciousness, the paper said. The article went on to recount the peaks and valleys of McClanahan's rollercoaster oil career, beginning with his lean years in Michigan prior to his Struble 1 well discovery in 1931, which catapulted him to prominence. The article continued *"He parlayed the well income into one or two fortunes and organized a company which was to wildcat and develop valuable oil properties in most of the major oil fields in Michigan."* McClanahan was "King of the Wildcatters", according to the piece, who went from "Hard Luck Mac" to "MR. Mac" several times.

"McClanahan was spectacular." The front page obituary said. *"He made friends easily and money, whether to entertain or for a new deal, was quick to come. He was known in Detroit as well as Mt. Pleasant. Newspapermen found him the same whether riding the wave of a new field or in the dumps of a dud or battle with creditors."*

Kaisa read the rest of McClanahan's obituary, chronicling: his love of flying, his private plane and pilot; his lush suite in a Detroit hotel; his habit of buying a new suit for drilling crew members when a well came in; his love of golf; and other accolades. "Mr Mac" moved from Mt. Pleasant in the early 1940s but maintained a summer home on the Au Sable River near Graying.

"His passing will leave a void not to be easily filled." The newspaper concluded.

"Sorry Mr. Mac." Kaisa said, tossing the newspaper pages aside. "You may have been a prince, but you always made me feel like I had my dress on backwards and you expected me to genuflect. I made it on my own too, no thanks to you, without needing my own brass band to sing my praises."

Then she went to church and lit a candle for him.

****

Kaisa stayed in touch with and subscribed to the *Michigan Oil & Gas News* magazine and periodically dabbled in oil and gas lease speculation. Never drilling wells but investing in leases of small tracts likely to be included in drilling units and thus yield royalties she avoided the headaches and expense of being a working interest holder. In the mid 1950s, she was intrigued by a drilling location in Hillsdale County being drilled by a woman named Ferne Houseknecht that seemed to be taking forever to drill.

When she located Houseknecht, the woman told her a fortune teller had told her there was "a black river of oil" under her property and she was drilling, as well as financing the well on her own. She drilled further only when she could earn enough money to afford it. Kaisa offered investment money but Houseknecht was adamant about finishing the well herself, using the services of her uncle, part time driller/farmer Clifford Perry. While Ferne drilled the well, with no money to lease the mineral rights under the surrounding lands, Kaisa hired a petroleum landman to lease small tracts of land in the area surrounding the rank wildcat Houseknecht venue, which began drilling in May of 1954. More than three-and-a-half years later the Houseknecht well came in, followed rapidly by an offset well drilled by Alma, Michigan's Harold Mc Clure Junior, on a drilling unit that included some of Kaisa's leased acreage.

The Houseknecht Number 1 well turned out to be the discovery well of the Albion-Scipio trend, a subterranean "Golden Gulch" that would see 774 producing wells drilled, producing more than 150 million barrels of crude oil and 225 billion cubic feet of natural gas over the ensuing four-plus decades. Many of those drilling units included acreage where Kaisa's agent leased mineral rights. Every time she opened a royalty cheek, she smiled at the so-called experts who laughed at the crazy lady who drilled to the Black River geological zone and discovered Michigan's only giant oilfield by worldwide definition, having produced over 100 million barrels of oil from a single contiguous reservoir twenty-nine miles long by a mile and a half wide.

Kaisa's status as the Golder's grand daughter and her new fortune cemented her firmly near the top of Holland's social tower. She was readily accepted in the Women's Literary Society and, when the annual Holland Tulip Festival's resumed after World War II, she was active on the Tulip Time Committee for many years.

" .... *als het nu is en altijd zal wereld, met eind* ..... as it is now and ever shall be, world without end. " She finished her rosary as Mickey and the girls came up the aisle of the chapel. "Mother, they are ready."

"I'm coming", she said taking a final look at the false cabinet beside the altar that had sheltered the love of her life when he had to hide on Jekyll Island. "Come, Deiderick."

She followed her children outside, handing over the urn containing Deiderick Ramecker's ashes to the waiting gardener. She watched the gardener her husband's remains in the neat little hole he'd dug among the flowers flanking the front door to Faith Chapel while her family bowed their heads in prayer.

"*Zo lang, mijn liefde.* So long, my love." She whispered. "*Ik zal je snel zien.* I'll see you soon."

Author's Note

You usually think of a historical novel as a fictional tale with a dab of history thrown in for good measure. This book has striven to be the opposite.

Is this story history? Yes. All of the events and places, except: the fictional 1927 reopening of the Delaware Mine; the Nazi landing on the island; the sinking of the submarine off Jekyll Island and the Mooren's Asparagus Farm actually happened or existed.

All of the people herein were real, except: the Koistinens; the Golder family; both Mickey Conroys; Sarah Boransky; Evangeline, Mark and Jared Maurice; Jager, Deiderick, both Aldias and Kaarte Ramecker, Johannes; Aletta and Dirk Koningh; Johannes and Gerhardt Vogt; Aaron Rankling; Agular Van Slooten; Judy Glenhaven and (maybe) the guy who yelled "fired" in Italian Hall.

Since there were no Koistinens, there obviously was no boarding house or boarders at the Fancher Avenue house, though George Lindberg and Jim Dunnigan were real figures in Michigan oilpatch history. The house on Fancher Street in Mt. Pleasant and those on the flanking lot-and-a-half, are real to this day.

Conversations between the real folks and my made up people, of course, took place only in my head.

There was never a Nazi Type IXD3 Long Range Attack U-Boat named <u>Lone</u> <u>Wolf,</u> the mission described in this story. The Volkswagen Company in Nazi Germany was, however, developing the *Schwimmwagen* in early 1942.

During World War II, A. G. Weser built 196 warship units for the *Kreigsmarine* in the Third Reich. Descriptions of U-boat threats to America's east coast during World War II are authentic.

The German town of *KdF-Stadt,* where Volkswagen opened a plant in 1938, was renamed Wolfsburg in 1945 and is now the fifth largest city in the Lower Saxony state of Germany.

In the Author's Note of her marvelous book about Jekyll Island, *Splendid Isolation: The Jekyll Island Millionaire's Club 1888-1942,* Pamela Bauer Mueller says that book is of the genre "non-fiction novel", crediting Truman Capote with coining the phrase. I hope this is not the only part of this volume to invoke memories of those two literary giants.

The seed of this book began with my first trip to Jekyll Island, Georgia, with my partner in this effort and in life, wife Mary Lou, in April 2002, to celebrate my first retirement. We compared favorably Jekyll Island with our beloved Mackinac Island, Michigan. We were charmed, biking the trails and streets of this barrier island, mercifully flat compared with our hilly northern Michigan terrain. We drank in the beauty of the sun-dappled Caribbean-like beach at the south end, the more developed center and the wilder north end of the island. Only one year out of the demanding grind of cranking out a weekly magazine, the *Michigan Oil & Gas News* (still alive and well in Mt. Pleasant, Michigan, thank you) the temperate island's historical charm was a tonic.

We took the tram tour of the historic Millionaire's Club district and as the tour ended, the guide mentioned the Clubs abandonment after the 1942 "season" in the face of the threat of German submarine traffic sinking shipping off the United States' south Atlantic coast. I asked if there had ever been a novel written about that situation. She said no. Click!

Near the end of the tour, we visited the chapel the

members of the Club had built and I looked at the cabinet near the altar, wondering if a man could fit inside. Click!

So began an eleven-year incubation period as I gathered bits and factual pieces about a number of places we visited in our travels, filling a file drawer with things I thought might fit someday into the yet-unnamed, yet-forming tale you hold in your hands.

Seven years ago my second career sneaked up on me and has led to my writing eight photo-history books. Additionally, I have produced: one commissioned memoir; one publication preparation of a Canadian fishing reminiscence for a friend; and an "as told to" autobiography of a friend named one of the 100 most influential persons in the petroleum industry of the Twentieth Century.

Early in 2013, having mined the vein of Mt. Pleasant area photo history book possibilities to near depletion, I realized this is the hundredth anniversary year of the Keweenaw Peninsula Copper Country miners' strike and there would never be a better time to release the story of a child of that strike.

So you've met Kaisa. I have known her for years and I hope you enjoyed her as much as I enjoyed bringing her to life. She is crusty and conflicted, tender and tough, intelligent while prone to doing dumb things, and I hope you'll be friends for a long time.

A couple of notes, before somebody as picky as me rises up and says *"Hey .... you screwed up that part."*

Michigan is still a viable oil and natural gas producer, ranking 16th among the 34 petroleum producing United states and annually producing 129 billion cubic feet of natural gas and 7.8 million barrels of crude oil. Crude oil and/or natural gas is produced from 64 of Michigan's 68 Lower Peninsula counties. Owing to the nature of the Michigan

Geological Basin, no commercial production of oil or natural gas has been found in Michigan's Upper Peninsula, nor is there likely to be, as George Lindberg explains to Kaisa on pages 116-117.

The *Michigan Oil & Gas News* did not have a 500-gallon tank as a kiosk until the 1937 Michigan Oil and Gas Exposition, which by that time had become the Michigan International Oil and Gas Exhibition. The Expositions took place until 1938 and were done in as an annual event by the beginning of World War II in 1939, when rationing, along with a shortage of men and materials ended such shows. The first Exposition drew more than 25,000 attendees, in 1935, a number that grew to over 50,000 with the 1938 event, all when the population of the city was under 10,000. The Oil and Gas Expositions remain, to my knowledge, the largest single event attractions in the history of Mt. Pleasant.

No one knows what caused either the Italian Hall Disaster or the McClanahan Struble #1 well fire, though the woods are full of theories. I hope my alternative explanations will please you.

Walter J. McClanahan, "Mr. Mac", was indeed the only person in history to have two Sea Island, Georgia "cottages"; one for his mother and other teetotaler relatives and the other for partying with business associates and golfing/drinking buddies. By the late-1940s, McClanahan was in narrow straits, again with dry holes, debt and high flying (literally, since he was much into having and promoting private aircraft) eroding his money supply. Still maintaining appearances, he kept both Sea Island places and died of a heart attack on he a Sea Island, Georgia, golf course two days before Christmas, 1949.

James Patrick Dunnigan would sell his share of the Oil News to John Murphy and be involved in oil exploration, refining and asphalt until his 1996 death in Naples Florida. He would serve on the Mackinac Island State Park Commission, as three-time Mayor of West Branch Michigan, as a delegate to the 1961 Michigan Constitutional Convention, as an extra in the Movie "Somewhere in Time" filmed on Mackinac Island, and as a candidate for the U. S. House of Representatives. He purchased _Yononte_, the East Bluff Mackinac Island cottage he arranges for Kaisa to use in this book from two Ann Arbor, Michigan, families named Fletcher and Lewright, who co-owned it until 1950. Dunnigan renamed it _"Donnybrook"_. Jim Dunnigan served on the Mackinac Island State Park Commission from 1949 until 1981, was Vice-Chairman of that commission. _Donnybrook_ cottage remains in the Dunnigan family.

For the record, in 1972, Mary Lou and I witnessed a scenario with a family of loons as described in Chapter 14.

The descriptions of the attractions Kaisa and Evie view in Chapters 14 through 16 are in keeping with what they would have seen in 1935. These are in no way a complete menu of Mackinac Island attractions so theses chapters are a little like watching a three dimensional movie blockbuster on a smart phone screen. The Island has so much more to offer. As a word of warning, there is no way you can "do" either Mackinac or Jekyll Island in a day.

Readers looking for real life thrilling stories should investigate the German U-Boat raids on America shipping along our east coast. Riveting reading.

In the entirety of the World War I and World War II years, 425,000 German military prisoners of war were interred in 700 camps located in 46 of the then 48 United States

Michigan ranks third in the nation for asparagus production, producing up to 25 million pounds annually. In fact, in 2011 the Michigan asparagus production was valued at over $1.7 million. Michigan growers harvest approximately 11,000 acres annually. Another thing I learned on the way to finding out about something else. That's what makes research fun.

The train smoke-over-the-road method of Kaisa's rescue of Deiderick is based on an incident near where I described it here. During World War II, my parents along with my brother Jim and I, went to Gobles, Michigan, to visit our grandparents. This was an era of two lane roads in the wonderful world pre-freeway. We traveled a road paralleled closely by a railroad track and as a train passed us, it's smoke settled across the road blinding us. Dad stopped the car and said "I hope the truck behind us stopped too.". When the smoke cleared, the semi behind us was about ten feet from our back bumper. I was about four years old, but I have never forgotten the event.

From the beginning of this project, I discovered nuggets of facts and actual incidents, that fit in the environments of my imaginary friends. The last such authentic fact was discovered at Sunday breakfast August 4, 2013, when the "This week in Michigan History" article in the *Detroit Free Press* told about Michigan's last hanging conviction for treason was handed down in 1942, caught my eye. In each such "eureka moment", I have commented to my wife that they were another evidence this story was "meant to be."

Jack R. Westbrook,
Mt. Pleasant Michigan, September 2013

KAISA
Acknowledgments

First, as always, thanks to my proofreader, critic, researcher, wife and mother of our five great citizens of the world Mary Lou, who steered me away from the horribly contrived and very punny title of "To Hide on Jekyll Island" for this book.

Besides *Wikipedia*, I am beholden to a legion of authors of websites and newspaper articles sifted through to build this story. Translations of Dutch and German exclamations to English were accomplished using the Google search engine's Translation software.

Special thanks to Traverse City author A. A. Wasek for his permission to use Henrik Rytilanhti's speech about the upcoming miner's strike from his outstanding book *The Cost of Copper*, the book that humanized the strike for me.

Other useful tools for researching the strike were: the Michigan Tech Library website *Tumult and Tragedy*; the U. S. Department of the Interior National Park Service Keweenaw National Park publication *Downtown Calumet-Guide to the Historic Mining Community*; Steve Lehto's *Death's Door – The Truth Behind Michigan's Largest Mass Murder*; Larry Lankton's *Cradle to Grave – Life, Work and Death at the Lake Superior Copper Mines*; Arthur W. Thurner's *Rebels of the Range – The Michigan Copper Strike of 1913-1914* and the Michigan Department of Natural Resources Geological Survey Division 1992 publication *Contributions to Michigan Geology – 9201, Michigan's Copper Country by Ellis W. Courter*.

Thanks posthumously to petroleum geologist and hobby hard rock geologist, Charles Moskowitz, a former Trustee of Michigan Technological University, who guided me through some mining procedures.

Holland, Michigan and Tulip Festival information was gleaned from the Holland Historical Society; *The Interurban Era in Holland, Michigan* by David L. von Reken; the Tulip Time Committee; the *Hope College Living History Project 1980 Interview with Ruth Kappel*; and *A Short History of the Holland Michigan Post Office* by Peninsula State Philatelic Society Member #14296, published in 1987.

The Michigan oil and natural gas Mt. Pleasant parts of the book were the easiest. Forty years of writing about the industry made me my own source. References for the industry parts of this book came from: *A History of Michigan Oil and Gas*, an exhibit catalogue from a 2005 exhibit at the Clarke Historical Library on the Mt. Pleasant campus of Central Michigan University; *Michigan Oil and Gas*, published by Arcadia Publishing in 2006 and my columns from the <u>View from the Monkeyboard</u> series of the *Michigan Oil & Has News* magazine. Back issues of Mt. Pleasant's *Isabella County Times-News* (now morphed into the *Morning Sun*, one of the few small city daily newspapers left in the state) and *Michigan Oil & Gas News* magazine were valuable research territory.

Many, Many Thanks to Brian Leigh Dunnigan, Associate Director and Curator of Maps at William L. Clemens Library, A Library of Early Americana at University of Michigan, Ann Arbor, Michigan. Brian sent me a copy of the unpublished and limitedly circulated booklet *AROUND MY WORLD IN EIGHTY YEARS*, a privately circulated 1980 autobiography by his father, James Patrick Dunnigan. Jim was the personification of Horatio Alger "rags to riches" tales, who came from nowhere and prospered everywhere.

Thanks to the Michigan Oil and Gas Association and

President Frank L. Mortl for hiring me to bring the publication back in print after a three month hiatus of printing on April, 1973. The Association acquired the magazine that year when John Murphy retired so the vital weekly industry information flow could continue. We took a chance on one another, each unknown to the other, to begin a forty-year association. Thanks for the opportunity to have the experience, Frank.

Eyewitness account of the Struble #1 fire came from a notebook called *Schoolbook Memories bring back Pleasant Thoughts of Happy Hours spent in Work and Play* by Walter McClanahan's daughter Marion, as quoted in an unpublished narrative called *Mister Mac* by Marion's husband, Walter's son-in-law, Robert Wernick.

Mackinac Island and its "cottages" are described through information from historian Phil Porter's *View From the Veranda – The History and Architecture of the Summer Cottages of Mackinac Island, Reports on Mackinac History and Archaeology Number 8*, published by the Mackinac Island State Park Commission publication. Also valuable for Summer Cottage information was *Historic Cottages of Mackinac Island* by Susan Sites and Lea Ann Sterling, along with *100 Years at Mackinac: A Centennial History of the Mackinac Island State Park Commission 1895-1985* by David A. Armour. Overall useful Mackinac Island history and attractions information was found in *Mackinac Island * Historic Frontier * Vacation Resort *Timeless Wonderland* by Pamela A. Piljac and Thomas M. Piljac, as well as 1974 vacation guide named *Mackinac Island: The Story of the Straits Country, Three Hundred Years of History* By Robert E. Benjamin.

Thanks also to Samantha of the *Town Crier*, Mackinac Island's weekly newspaper, who late on a June Friday afternoon called me back twice to help answer my question about what newspaper Kaisa would have read on the island in 1935.

Background on the Nazi invasion of the Netherlands came from *The Encyclopedia of the Third Reich*, a two-volume set by Christian Zentner and Friedemann Bedurftig, English translation edited by Amy Hackett, a fascinating reference..

The original Spyker automobile company history described in this book is related to modern Spyker automobile company in name only. The reborn company, founded by Victor Muller and Maarten de Bruijn in 1999, according to the new company's website, and is building exclusive sports cars.

Jekyll Island's *Chichota, Cherokee, Hollybourne and Villa Marianna,* cottages background was found in: *Jekyll Island Club*, a publication of the Jekyll Island Authority Museum and Preservation Division; *The Jekyll Island Club – Southern Haven for America's Millionaires* by William Barton McCash and June Hall McCash; *The Jekyll Island Cottage Colony* by June Hall McCash; *The Jekyll Island Club – A Novel* by Brent Monahan: and two Arcadia Publishing Images of America series books by Tyler E. Bagwell, *The Jekyll Island Club* (1998) and *Jekyll Island Club – A State Park* (2001).

Nazi U-Boat data was found on two outstanding: websites: *uboats.net* and *uboataces.com* and an e-book entitled The *Jekyll Island Enigma,* by Jack Owen.

The item about the 1942 hanging sentence for treason of Max Stephan came from an article by Ziati Meyer in the Sunday, August 4, 2013 (page 12A) edition of the *Detroit Free Press*.

Any errors in interpretation of these works lie solely

with this author

As always, thanks to Director Frank Boles, John Fierst and Reference Specialist Bryan Whitledge, of Clarke Historical Library on the Mt. Pleasant campus of Central Michigan University for another fine job in helping locate microfilms and files.

I started these acknowledgments thanking my wife for her technical aid in producing this book. Now I thank her again for her patience when I have annoyed her with unexpected updates on things in my characters' lives when she thought I was talking about something that happened to real people we know.

Finally, thanks to the loyal reading audience of my previous writings. I know you are used to looking at pictures but this time I have used the thousand words instead to draw pictures of our past.

JACK R. WESTBROOK

ABOUT THE AUTHOR

JACK R. WESTBROOK is a Mt. Pleasant, Michigan, resident, retired Managing Editor of the Michigan Oil & Gas News magazine and author of four previous historical photo review books for Arcadia Publishing Company: *MICHIGAN OIL & GAS* (2006); *MT. PLEASANT THEN and NOW* (2006); *CENTRAL MICHIGAN UNIVERSITY* (2007); and *ISABELLA COUNTY (Michigan) 1859-2009* (2008). He has self-published: *YESTERDAY'S SCHOOL KIDS OF ISABELLA COUNTY,* with co-author historian/genealogist Sherry Sponseller (2009); *ANOINTED WITH OIL: MY JOURNEY WITH FAITH FROM THE OIL-FIELDS OF MICHIGAN TO THE LEGISLATIVE HALLS OF WASHINGTON DC and BACK AGAIN*, by C. John Miller as told to Jack R. Westbrook (2010); *THE BIG PICTURE BOOK OF MT. PLEASANT, MICHIGAN: Yesteryears to 2010* (2010); *MICHIGAN NATURAL RESOURCES TRUST FUND* (2011) and AT HOME IN EARLIER MT. PLEASANT, MICHIGAN (2012).

KAISA is Westbrook's first work of fiction.